Cynewulf

Cynewulf's Christ

An Eighth Century English Epic

Cynewulf

Cynewulf's Christ
An Eighth Century English Epic

ISBN/EAN: 9783337163693

Printed in Europe, USA, Canada, Australia, Japan

Cover: Foto ©Andreas Hilbeck / pixelio.de

More available books at **www.hansebooks.com**

CYNEWULF'S CHRIST

An Eighth Century English Epic

EDITED, WITH A MODERN RENDERING, BY

ISRAEL GOLLANCZ, M.A.,

of Christ's College, Cambridge.

London
PUBLISHED BY DAVID NUTT

IN THE STRAND

1892

PREFACE

'Ræd sceal mon secgan,
Rune writan,
Leoð gesingan,
Lofes gearnian,
Dom areccan,
Dæges onettan.'

' It is but the cloudes gathered about our owne judgement that makes us thinke all other ages wrapt up in mistes, and the great distance betwixt us that causes us to imagine men so farre off to be so little in respect of ourselves.'

§ 1.

N the year 1071 died Leofric, first Bishop of Exeter, sometime Chancellor of England, the friend and favourite of Edward the Confessor, a distinguished disciple of the Lotharingian schools. Contemporary accounts have come down to us describing the pomp which attended the bishop's installation; how, in the presence of the chieftains of the realm, supported by the king on his right and by the noble Eadgitha on his left, he ascended his episcopal throne in the ancient minster of St. Mary and St. Peter the Apostle. The minster, when it came into his possession, had been despoiled of its lands and of nigh all its ecclesiastical appurtenances; 'of twenty-six estates which the pious king Athelstane had conferred upon it scarce one remained.' During the twenty years

of his rule, Leofric's energies and wealth were devoted to the restoration of its former fortunes, and when he died he left it more richly endowed than it had ever been before. But he bequeathed to his cathedral-church something besides a magnificent rent-roll,— something even more precious. When he took office, the library at Exeter was in a pitiable condition; he found there nothing but five worthless service-books; at his death it numbered no less than sixty volumes,—Bibles, service-books, homiletic literature, theological commentaries, and the chief classics of those days, to wit, the works of Statius, Prudentius, Prosper, and Boethius. Leofric's library at Exeter did not, it is true, number as many volumes as some of the rich Anglo-Saxon libraries of which we have record; it certainly did not rival Archdeacon Egbert's famous collection at York, that called forth Alcuin's enthusiastic praise :—

> ' Illic invenies veterum vestigia patrum,
> Quidquid habet pro se Latio Romanus in orbe,
> Græcia vel quidquid transmisit clara Latinis ;
> Hebraicus vel quod populus bibit imbre superno ;'

nevertheless, one item in the catalogue of Leofric's books places him in the first rank of our early bibliophiles, and has earned for him, or should earn for him, the undying gratitude of his countrymen. In the catalogue, which is extant, writ in choicest Anglo-Saxon, there is an entry which runs as follows :—

' I. mycel Englisc boc be gehwilcum þingum on leoðwisan geworht ';

i.e. 'A great English book on all sorts of subjects wrought in verse.' Happily, we have not to bewail the loss of the volume thus described. Exeter Cathedral still cherishes the possession of this most glorious relic of pre-Conquest literature. The 'Exeter Book,' the name by which it should be known to Englishmen all over the world, may well claim to be the noblest product of early Teutonic genius. True, it cannot boast of great beauty of workmanship,—it is not, like the 'Codex Argenteus,' written on purple vellum in letters of silver and gold ; no wondrous miniatures adorn its pages, like the 'Book of Kells,' —'Angles,' not 'Angels,' wrought it,—but its contents claim for it a higher consideration than even the supreme philological interest of the former and the artistic glories of the latter. It has preserved for us a whole library of national literature, that would otherwise have been irrevocably lost ; it is in itself a 'bibliotheca' rather than a 'book.'

§ 2.

It is not my purpose on this occasion to dwell on the contents of the volume ; a study of the 'Exeter Book' would practically amount to a survey of old English poetry through all its varied vicissitudes, harking back to the songs that glee-men sang before the legions of imperial Rome surrendered Britain to its fatal conflict with barbaric Teuton. Fierce and brutal as were these pirate-hordes towards their foes, yet their harps were

attuned to tender strains as they sang their sailor-songs
of the dear ones left behind :—

> ' To the Frisian wife
> comes a dear welcome-guest ;
> the keel is at rest ;
> his vessel is come ;
> her husband is home ;
> her own cherished lord
> she leads to the board ;
> his wet weeds she wrings ;
> dry garments she brings.
> Ah ! happy is he,
> whom safe from the sea
> his true love awaits ! ' [1]

But, for the most part, the Anglo-Saxons took to their
poetry very sadly. The prevailing note of the old
English lyric is elegiac ; intense melancholy, harmonis-
ing with the gloom of Northern sea and sky, with
the fatalism of their Pagan faith, is the one mood
reflected in the subjective poems of the ' Exeter
Book ' :—

> ' Ah ! thou bright cup ! Ah, thou mailed warrior !
> Ah ! the glory of my lord ! Now has the time passed,
> darkened 'neath the veil of night, as if it ne'er had been.
> Where once loved warriors trod, now stands
> a wall of wondrous height, worm-eaten, grim ;
> the might of the spears, slaughter-loving weapons,
> has swept away the chiefs,—theirs was a glorious fate,—
> but storms lash the rocky slopes,
> and falling snowdrift binds the earth,
> and all the winter's terror, when the dark night falls

[1] From the *Gnomic Verses* of the Exeter Book ; the rime is a mere accident
of the translation.

xvi

with its black shadow, and summons from the north
fierce storms, to the grievance of mankind.
All the realm of earth is full of hardship,
the world 'neath heaven is turned by fate's decree.' [1]

This turn for melancholy is an abiding element in English poetry throughout its history; there can be little question that it is essentially an English characteristic, despite Matthew Arnold's oft-quoted dictum that it is altogether derived from Celtic source. But while the note of the old English lyric is elegiac, as far as its form is concerned it belongs to the epic,—the all-absorbing art-form of our oldest poetry. Epic dignity and distinction, not lyrical rapidity of movement, mark even the shortest of Anglo-Saxon songs.

And what better instrument for the grand epic style than the wondrous blank verse—the old alliterative line —of these ancient poets. Critics of Elizabethan literature delight to dwell on ' the mighty line ' created by the greatest of Shakespeare's predecessors ; but, ten centuries before Marlowe's genius impressed itself on the English drama, English poetry had already ' unlocked the secret of blank verse,' and had played upon ' its hundred stops.' The secret of Marlowe's great discovery lies in this, that he Teutonised the ' versi sciolti ' imported from Italy, and unconsciously imparted thereto the flexibility and vigour that characterised the national metre used by the oldest of English poets, whose work has come down to

[1] From *The Wanderer*, ' Exeter Book.'

us. The high seriousness and earnestness of old English poetry; its epic style, absorbing lyrical and even dramatic elements; its subjectivity and melancholy; its subtle power of thoroughly nationalising foreign materials; its rich vocabulary and phraseology; the wonder of its varying verse, expressive of every shade of human emotion; its artistic consciousness; its avoidance of anything approaching mediæval grotesqueness,—all these qualities distinguish the remarkable poem which holds the first place in the *Codex Exoniensis*. This poem, which is probably the oldest Christiad of modern Europe, is herewith introduced to English readers, its text carefully studied and interpreted.

§ 3.

The text is based on the editor's unpublished edition of the Exeter MS., in preparation for the Early English Text Society. The variations from the MS. will be found in 'Critical Notes' at the end of the volume.[1] The MS. has been followed minutely, not merely in the matter of spelling, but also as regards the divisions of the poem,—a matter of special importance hitherto neglected. Though there are no titles to the various passus, the scribe has clearly indicated the beginning of each by means of a

[1] The system of punctuation employed has no MS. authority, neither have the capital letters at the beginning of the lines; there is no break between the lines in the MS., where the poem is written throughout as if prose. I have not marked the letters expanded; the accents are reproduced from the MS.

long flourish of capital letters, distinguishing carefully the smaller sections from the main divisions. Thus, the MS. makes it certain that Passus III. begins with words '*Donne mid fere*,' and does not include the previous section. External evidence corroborates this view. Appendix II. gives the source of Passus II.; it is obvious that the final section of the passus is directly due to the final section of the homily. It is strange that Dietrich, who first called attention to the unity of the poem, and to the chief source of its second division, should have missed this point.

In Appendix I. I have printed fifty-eight lines hitherto regarded as part of the present poem, but most assuredly, if the original scribe may be credited, the opening lines of the 'Legend of St. Guthlac'; there is absolutely no break in the MS. between these lines and the passage usually printed as the first section of the latter poem. I make bold to suggest that the whole section is a prelude to 'St. Guthlac,' with motives derived from the concluding portion of the 'Christ.' Thorpe, the first editor of the Exeter MS., is no doubt answerable for this error, which even the ingenuity of Dietrich and Grein did not detect.[1]

---

[1] Thorpe's *Codex Exoniensis* appeared just fifty years ago. Unfortunately, he failed to see the value of ' the first 106 pages ' of his book (*i.e.* the portion containing the present poem); his comment ran as follows :—' Though interesting to the philologist, they possess little attraction for any other class of readers. The pieces they contain are, no doubt, translations from the Latin ; but their subject is not of a nature to stimulate many to search after the originals, which, if discovered, would prove of little use in elucidating the

Appendix III. is a valuable contribution made by Professor Cook to the sources of the poem, and may be regarded as affording external evidence in favour of the theory propounded above concerning the limit of the third passus. It remains but to point out that unfortunately the first part of Passus I. is lost; to give to the epic the appearance of completeness a single word has been omitted; the capital letter at the beginning of the text has no MS. authority.[1] The frontispiece has been added to the volume as a specimen of Anglo-Saxon art, illustrative of the subject of the second part of the poem; it belongs to the famous series of miniatures that adorn the 'Benedictional of St. Æthelwold.'[2]

obscurities, or correcting the errors of a version, in this and all similar cases yet known, too paraphrastic to admit of comparison.'

In 1853 Dietrich called attention to the unity of the poems, but as he had no opportunity of examining the MS., he did not perceive the real state of affairs, though he and others might have inferred it from Wanley's description of the MS. (v. page 280), where 'Passus' I., II., III., are styled 'Liber' I., II., III., though the connection of the 'Libri' was not noted. In 1857 Grein's *Bibliothek* included the 'Christ,' which was based on Thorpe's text. Grein accepted Dietrich's views on the subject of the poem, but printed it unnecessarily as one long poem, with twenty-two sections. In 1857 appeared the same scholar's 'Dichtungen der Angelsachsen stabreimend uebersebzt.' Little has been done for the interpretation of the poem since Grein's monumental work, though the need of a new edition has been long felt. It is a strange fact that after 1100 years and more the 'Christ' now appears for the first time as a separate volume. The translation which accompanies the text is the first attempt that has been made to interpret the poem as a piece of English literature.

[1] Cf. note l. i. The initials at the commencement of Passus I., II., III., are taken from the Anglo-Saxon *Codex Psalterii Vossianus* (Bodleian Library), as reproduced in Professor Westwood's *Facsimiles of Anglo-Saxon and Celtic Miniatures*.

[2] Reproduced in reduced facsimile by Mr. Griggs, with kind permission, from the last-named book, (v. page 132.)

Long and patient search has failed to discover the source of Passus I. ; this failure is especially to be deplored as one would much wish to know from what original the poet evolved the earliest dramatic scene in English litera- ture, (*v.* page 18.)   What a contrast an Anglo-Saxon religious drama would have presented to the homely miracles and mysteries of later centuries!   The original of the greater part of Passus I. must, I think, have been a Latin hymn-cycle, the 'Joseph and Mary' section being derived from an undiscovered hymn arranged for recital by half-choirs.   The crude materials used for Passus II. and III., printed at the end of the volume, attest in a remarkable way the transforming power of the poet ; the well-sustained simile that closes Passus II. owes its exist- ence to the words in the last section of St. Gregory's Homily, 'Quamvis adhuc rerum perturbationibus animus fluctuet.'   The passages in the Appendix form a valuable commentary to the greater part of the text.

§ 4.

The Exeter MS. was written some time in the tenth century, or early in the eleventh ; the bulk of its contents is, however, at least two centuries older.   Its dialect is West-Saxon, or 'Anglo-Saxon,' as it is generally called, but one is able to detect in a number of the poems the fossil remains of another and an older dialect.   Minute philological criteria lead to the conclusion, supported strongly by other evidence, that the first of the poems pre-

served in the codex, and many more besides, are Saxon
(*i.e.* Southern) transcriptions of Anglian (*i.e.* Northern)
originals. Wessex merely preserved the poems, Northumbria produced them. Indeed at no time in its
history has Wessex been productive of poetical work ;
from the days of Alfred onward its special strength lay
in prose literature. Did not Chaucer recognise the fact
when he made his parson exclaim :—

> ' Trusteth wel, *I am a Sotherne man*,
> I cannot geste, rom, ram, ruf, by my letter,
> And God wote, rime hold I but litel better,
> And therefore if you list I wol not glose,
> I wol you tell a litel tale in *prose.*'

It seems almost certain then that the 'Christ' is an
Anglian poem, written before Northumbria ceased to be
the great centre of poetical activity, *i.e.* before the beginning of the ninth century, and critics are at one in placing
the 'floruit' of its poet during the second half of the
eighth century. The poet in question has bequeathed to
us his name by a strange device ; by means of mystic
runes Cynewulf worked a subtle spell whereby his authorship of this and of three other poems is incontestably
established. In an 'Excursus on Cynewulf Runes,' at the
end of the volume, I have considered the many questions
at issue concerning this important point. It remains but
to add that I am sceptical on the subject of the supposed
charade-character of the so-called 'First Riddle.' Interesting attempts have been made to write the biography of

xxii

the poet ;[1] it is not my purpose in this place to attempt a similar task, which would involve a discussion of the whole problem of Cynewulf's relation to the extant remains of Anglo-Saxon poetry. In conclusion, I would apply to our poet the commendation bestowed by an old historian on one of Cynewulf's masters and predecessors, whose fame rests solely on his Latin verse, though he too composed in the vernacular :—

'Omnium poetarum sui temporis facilé primus, tantæ eloquentiæ majestatis et eruditionis homo fuit, ut nunquam satis admirari possim unde illi in tam barbara ac rudi ætate facundia accreverit, usque adeo omnibus numeris tersa, elegans, et rotunda, versus edidit cum antiquitate de palma contendentes.'[2]

---

[1] Cf. *Ten Brink, Early English Literature*, pp. 51-59, and Appendix.

[2] Quoted by Samuel Daniel in his *Defence of Ryme*, concerning 'Aldelmus Durotelmus, of whom we find this commendation registered'; the lines occur in an interesting passage on the learning of Saxon England, whence, too, the quotation that heads this Introduction. If only the old Elizabethans had known of Cynewulf.

CYNEWULF'S CHRIST

A

I.

Þ U eart se weall-stan þe ða wyrhtan íu
    Wið-wurpon to weorce·   Wel þe
      ger, iseð
    Þæt þu heafod síe healle mærre
    And gesomnige side weallas
    Fæste gefoge flint unbræcne
Þæt geond eorð-b[yri]g eall eagna gesihþe
Wundrien to worlde wuldres ealdor·
Gesweotula nu þurh searo-cræft þin sylfes weorc
Soð-fæst sigor-beorht and sona forlæt
Weall wið wealle·   Nu is þam weorce þearf   10
Þæt se cræftga cume and se cyning sylfa
And þonne gebete nu gebrosnad is
Hús under hrofe·   He þæt hra gescop
Leomo læmena nu sceal lif-frea
Þone wergan heap wraþum ahreddan
Earme from egsan swa he oft dyde·
Eala þu reccend and þu riht cyning
Se þe locan healdeð lif ontyneð
Eadga us siges oþrum forwyrned
Wlitigan wil-siþes gif his weorc ne deag·   20

Part first. The Nativity.

I.

'THOU art the wall-stone that the workers once
      rejected from the work.   It well beseemeth thee,
that thou shouldst be the head of this great hall,
and shouldst unite, with fastening secure,
the spacious walls of adamantine rock,
that throughout earth all things with sight endowed
may wonder evermore, O Prince of glory !
Show now thy skill ! reveal thy handiwork
firm-set in sovran splendour ! yea, leave anon
the opposing walls erect !   The work hath need now
that the Craftsman and the King Himself should come,
and should restore the house, which lieth waste
beneath the roof.   He formed the body erst,
and the limbs of clay ; now shall He, Lord of life,
deliver from their foes this abject throng,
these wretched ones from terror, as He oft did.
O thou Ruler, and thou righteous King !
Thou Keeper of the keys that open life !
bless us with victory, with a bright career,
denied unto another, if his work be worthless !'

Huru we for þearfe þas word sprecað
[Nu gemærsi] giað þone þe mon gescop
Þæt he ne hete . . . ceose sprecan
Cearfulra þing þe we in carcerne
Sittað sorgende sunnan wil-sið·
Hwonne us lif-frea leoht ontyne
Weorðe ussum mode to mund-boran
And þæt tydre gewitt tire bewinde·
Gedo usic þæs wyrðe þe he to wuldre forlet
Þa we hean-lice hweorfan sceoldan   30
To þis enge lond eðle bescyrede·
Forþon secgan mæg se ðe soð spriceð
Þæt he ahredde þa for-hwyrfed wæs
Frum-cyn fira·   Wæs seo fæmne geong
Mægð manes leas þe he him to meder geceas·
Þæt wæs geworden butan weres frigum
Þæt þurh bearnes gebyrd bryd eacen wearð·
Nænig efenlic þam ær ne siþþan
In worlde gewearð wifes gearnung·
Þæt degol wæs dryhtnes geryne·   40
Eal giofu gæst-lic grund-sceat geond-spreot
Þær wisna fela wearð inlihted
Lare long-sume þurh lifes fruman
Þe ær under hoðman biholen lægon
Witgena woð-song þa se waldend cwom

4

Forsooth in very need we speak these words;
Him who created man we supplicate,
that He elect not to declare in hate
the doom of us who sad in prison here
sit yearning for the sun's propitious course.
When the Lord of life revealeth light to us,
be He the guardian-angel of our souls,
and wreathe the feeble mind with radiant grace.
May He glorify us thus, His favoured ones,
when we must needs depart in abject plight
unto this narrow land, bereft of home.

Verily he may say it, who speaketh truth,
that when the race of man was all depraved,
He came and rescued it.   Young was the maiden,
a damsel sinless, whom He chose as mother.
It came to pass without the love of man,
that the bride was great by child-conception.
Never before or after in the world
was any meed of woman like to that;
it was a secret mystery of the Lord.
All ghostly grace o'erspread the realm of earth,
and many a thing became illumined then
through life's Creator, teachings of ancient day,
which lay concealed beneath the veil of night,
the sages' songs prophetic, ere the Ruler came,

5

Seþe reorda gehwæs ryne gemiclað
Ðara þe geneahhe noman scyppendes
Þurh ho[r]scne had hergan willað·
Eala sibbe gesihð Sancta hierusalem
Cyne-stola cyst cristes burg-lond
Engla eþel-stol and þa ane in þe
Saule soð-fæstra simle gerestað
Wuldrum hremge·   Næfre wommes tacn
In þam eard-gearde eawed weorþeð
Ac þe firina gehwylc feor abugeð
Wærgðo and gewinnes·   Bist to wuldre full
Halgan hyhtes swa þu gehaten eart·
Sioh nu sylfa þe geond þas sidan gesceaft
Swylce rodores hrof rume geond-wlitan
Ymb healfa gehwone hu þec heofones cyning
Siðe geseceð and sylf cymeð
Nimeð eard in þe swa hit ær gefyrn
Witgan wis-fæste wordum sægdon
Cyðdon cristes gebyrd cwædon þe to frofre
Burga bet-licast·   Nu is þæt bearn cymen
Awæcned to wyrpe weorcum ebrea·
Bringeð blisse þe benda onlyseð
Niþum geneðde nearo-þearfe conn
Hu se earma sceal are gebidan·

50

60

who speedeth on its course their every prayer,
if mortals will but praise full earnestly
their Maker's name, as wisdom biddeth them.

O sight of peace! holy Jerusalem!
choicest of royal thrones! citadel of Christ!
the native seat of angels and of the just,
the souls of whom alone rest in thee ever,
exulting in glory. No sign of aught unclean
shall ever be beheld in that abode,
but every sin shall flee afar from thee,
all curse and conflict; thou art gloriously full
of holy promise, e'en as thou art named.
See now thyself how all the wide creation
and heaven's roof surveyeth thee about,
on every side, and how the King of heaven
seeketh thee in His course, and cometh Himself,
and taketh His dwelling in thee, as in days of yore
soothsayers so wise declared in words;
they made known Christ's birth; they told it for thy comfort,
thou best of cities! Now the Child is come,
awakened to destroy the Hebrews' works;
He bringeth thee joy; He looseneth thy bonds;
He hath adventured Him for men; He knoweth their need,—
yea, how the wretched must await compassion.

ALA wifa wynn geond wuldres þrym·   70
 Fæmne freo-licast ofer ealne foldan sceat
Þæs þe æfre sund-buend secgan hyrdon·
Arece us þæt geryne þæt þe of roderum cwom
Hu þu eacnunge æfre onfenge
Bearnes þurh gebyrde and þone gebed-scipe
Æfter mon-wisan mod ne cuðes·
Ne we soð-lice swylc ne gefrugnan
In ær-dagum æfre gelimpan
Þæt ðu in sundur-giefe swylce befenge
Ne we þære wyrde wenan þurfon   80
Toweard in tide· Huru treow in þe
Weorð-licu wunade nu þu wuldres þrym
Bosme gebære and no gebrosnad wearð
Mægð-had se micla· Swa eal manna bearn
Sorgum sawað swa eft ripað
Cennað to cwealme· Cwæð sio eadge mæg
Symle sigores full Sancta maria·
Hwæt is þeos wundrung þe ge wafiað
And geomrende gehþum mænað
Sunu solimæ somod his dohtor·   90
Fricgað þurh fyrwet hu ic fæmnan-had

II.

'*O sovran Lady of the blissful skies,*
thou noblest maid through all the realm of earth,
that the ocean-dwellers have ever heard tell of,
unfold the mystery that came to thee from heaven,
how thou didst in some wise receive increase
by child-conception, and yet thou knewest not
communion after human fashion.
Truly we have not heard that ever yet,
in days of yore, the like hath come to pass,
such as thou in special grace receivedst,
nor may we hope that it will ever chance
in future time.   Lo, the faith that dwelt in thee
was worshipful, since thou didst in thy bosom bear
the flower of glory, and thy great maidenhood
was not destroyed.   All the children of men
as they sow in sorrow, so afterwards they reap,
they bring forth for death.'   *Spake the blessed maiden,*
ever full of triumph, the holy Mary :—

   '*What is this wonder which ye wonder at,*
and grievously bemoan 'mid lamentations,
thou son and thou daughter of Salem ?
Ye ask full anxiously how I preserved

Mund minne geheold and eac modor gewearð
Mære meotudes suna· Forþan þæt monnum nis
Cuð geryne ac crist onwrah
In dauides dyrre mægan
Þæt is euan scyld eal for-pynded .
Wærgða áworpen and gewuldrad is
Se heanra hád· Hyht is onfangen
Þæt nu bletsung mot bæm gemæne
Werum and wifum á to worulde forð   100
In þam up-lican engla dreame
Mid soð-fæder symle wunian·
Eala earendel engla beorhtast
Ofer middan-geard monnum sended
And soð-fæsta sunnan leoma
Torht ofer tunglas· Þu tida gehwane
Of sylfum þe symle inlihtes·
Swa þu god of gode gearo acenned
Sunu soþan fæder swegles in wuldre
Butan anginne æfre wære   110
Swa þec nu for þearfum þin agen geweorc
Bideð þurh byldo þæt þu þa beorhtan us
Súnnan onsende and þe sylf cyme
Þæt ðu inleohte þa þe longe ǽr
Þrosme beþeahte and in þeostrum her
Sæton sin-neahtes synnum bifealdne·

my maidenhood, my troth, and yet became
great mother of the Creator's Son.   Verily to men
the mystery is not known ; but Christ revealed
in David's kinswoman, beloved of Him,
that the guilt of Eve is all concluded now,
the curses overthrown, and the lowlier sex
is now made glorious.   Hope is vouchsafed
that now for men and women equally
blessing may for evermore abide,
amid the harmony of angels high above,
with the Father of truth, to all eternity.'

   Hail, heavenly beam, brightest of angels thou,
sent unto men upon this middle-earth !
Thou art the true refulgence of the sun,
radiant above the stars, and from thyself
illuminest for ever all the tides of time.
And as thou, God indeed begotten of God,
thou Son of the true Father, wast from aye,
without beginning, in the heaven's glory,
so now thy handiwork in its sore need
prayeth thee boldly that thou send to us
the radiant sun, and that thou come thyself
to enlighten those who for so long a time
were wrapt around with darkness, and here in gloom
have sat the livelong night, shrouded in sin ;

Deorc deaþes sceadu dreogan sceoldan·
Nu we hyht-fulle hælo gelyfaðˇ
Þurh þæt word godes weorodum brungen
Þe on frymðe wæs fæder ælmihtigum   120
Efen-ece mid god and nu eft gewearðˇ
Flæsc firena leas þæt seo fæmne gebær
Geomrum to geoce·   God wæs mid us
Gesewen butan synnum somod eardedon
Mihtig meotudes bearn and se monnes sunu
Geþwære on þeode·   We þæs þonc magon
Secgan sige-dryhtne symle bi gewyrhtum
Þæs þe he hine sylfne us sendan wolde·
Eala gæsta god hu þu gleawlice
Mid noman ryhte nemned wære   130
Emmanuhel swa hit engel gecwæðˇ
Ærest on ebresc þæt is eft gereht
Rume bi gerynum nu is rodera weard
God sylfa mid us·   Swa þæt gomele gefyrn
Ealra cyninga cyning and þone clænan eac
Sacerd soðˇ-lice sægdon toweard·
Swa se mære iu melchisedech
Gleaw in gæste god-þrym on-wrah
Eces alwaldan·   Se wæs ǽ bringend
Lara lædend þam longe his   140
Hyhtan hider-cyme swa him gehaten wæs

12

death's dark shadow had they to endure.

Hopeful now, we trust in the salvation
brought to the hosts of men through God's own word,
which was in the beginning co-eternal
with God, the Almighty Father, and is now .
flesh void of blemish, that the maiden bare
to help the wretched.   God was seen 'mong us
in all His sinlessness ; together they dwelt,
the Creator's mighty Son and the son of man,
in peace on earth.   Wherefore, as it is meet,
we may well thank the Lord of triumph aye,
that He vouchsafed to send to us Himself.

O thou God of spirits ! how wisely thou
wast named, with name aright, Emmanuel !
as the angel spake the word in Hebrew first,
which in its secret meaning fully now
is thus interpreted :—' The Guardian of the skies,
God's Self, is now with us'; e'en as of yore
old men said truly that the King of kings,
and eke the cleanly Priest, would come anon.
Thus long ago the great Melchizedek,
so wise of soul, revealed the majesty
of the eternal Ruler ; he was the law-bringer ;
he gave them precepts, who had awaited long
His advent hither, for it was promised them,

Þætte sunu meotudes sylfa
Wolde gefælsian foldan mægðe
Swylce grundas eac gæstes mægne
Siþe gesecan· Nu hie softe þæs
Bidon in bendum hwonne bearn godes
Cwome to cearigum· Forþon cwædon swa
Suslum geslæhte· Nu þu sylfa cum
Heofones heah-cyning bring us hælo-lif
Werigum wite-þeowum wope forcymenum 150
Bitrum bryne-tearum· Is seo bot gelong
Eal æt þe anum . . . . ofer-þearfum·
Hæftas hyge-geomre hider [gesece
Ne læt] þe behindan þonne þu heonan cyrre·
Mænigo þus micle ac þu miltse on us
Gecyð cyne-lice crist nergende·
Wuldres æþeling ne læt awyrgde ofer us
Onwald agan· Læf us ecne gefean
Wuldres þines þæt þec weorðien
Weoroda wuldor-cyning þa þu geworhtes ær 160
Hondum þinum· Þu in hean-nissum
Wunast wide ferh mid waldend fæder.

that the Son Himself of the all-ruling Lord
would purify the nations of the earth,
and in His course would seek too the abyss,
by the might of His spirit.   Patiently
have they waited in their fetters, till God's Child
should come to the afflicted ; wherefore spake thus
those cast in torments :—' Come thou now thyself,
Sovran of heaven ! bring us salvation,
weary thralls oppressed, worn out with weeping,
with bitter burning tears.   With thee alone
resteth their cure for those in direst need.
Visit us here, captives so sad of mood,
nor leave behind thee, when thou turn'st from hence,
so great a throng ! but royally show forth
thy mercy unto us, O Saviour Christ !
O Prince of glory ! let not the accursed
hold sway o'er us ; thy glory's endless joy
vouchsafe to us, that those may worship thee,
great Lord of hosts, whom thou createdst erst
with thine own hands.   Thou in the heights above
dwellest for ever with the all-ruling Father.'

III.

EALA ioseph min iacobes bearn
    Mæg dauides mæran cyninges
Nu þu freode scealt fæste gedælan
Álætan lufan mine· Ic lungre eam
Deope gedrefed dome bereafod
Forðon ic worn for þe worde hæbbe
Sidra sorga and sár-cwida
Hearmes gehyred and me hosp sprecað   170
Torn-worda fela· Ic tearas sceal
Geotan geomor-mod· God eaþe mæg
Gehælan hyge-sorge heortan minre
Afrefran fea-sceaftne· Eala fæmne geong
Mægð maria· Hwæt bemurnest ðu
Cleopast cearigende ne ic culpan in þe
Incan ænigne æfre onfunde
Womma geworhtra and þu þa word spricest
Swa þu sylfa sie synna gehwylcre
Firena gefylled· Ic to fela hæbbe   180
Þæs byrd-scypes bealwa onfongen·
Hu mæg ic ladigan laþan spræce
Oþþe andsware ænige findan
Wraþum to-wiþere· Is þæt wide cuð

16

III.

[MARY.] '*Alas! now, Joseph mine, thou child of Jacob,*
scion of David's stock, the glorious King,
must thou forthwith renounce thy plighted troth,
and leave my love?' [JOSEPH.] '*Too soon am I o'erwhelmed*
with grievous care; too soon bereft of honour.
Forsooth through thee have I heard many a word,
many an agonising bitter taunt,
many an insult, and they revile me now
with words of bitter wrath. My soul is sad;
I must shed tears. God may easily
heal the grievous sorrow of my heart,
and comfort me, forlorn. Alas, young damsel,
Mary maiden!' [MARY.] '*Why bemoanest thou,*
and criest aloud lamenting? Ne'er found I
a fault in thee, or any cause of blame
for evil done, and yet thou speak'st such words,
as thou thyself wert filled with every sin
and all transgression.' [JOSEPH.] '*Too much misery*
have I received from this conception.
How can I escape the hateful words,
or how can I find any answer now
against mine angry foes? 'Tis widely known,

Þæt ic of þam torhtan temple dryhtnes
Onfeng freo-lice fæmnan clæne
Womma lease and nu gehwyrfed is
Þurh nat-hwylces· Me nawþer deag
Secge ne swige· Gif ic soð sprece
Þonne sceal dauides dohtor sweltan   190
Stanum astyrfed· Gen strengre is
Þæt ic morþor hele scyle man-swara
Laþ leoda gehwam lifgan siþþan
Fracoð in folcum· Þa seo fæmne onwrah
Ryht-geryno and þus reordade·
Soð ic secge þurh sunu meotudes
Gæsta geocend þæt ic gen ne conn
Þurh gemæc-scipe monnes ower
Ænges on eorðan· Ac me eaden wearð
Geongre in geardum þæt me gabrihel   200
Heofones heag-engel hælo gebodade·
Sægde soð-lice þæt me swegles gæst
Leoman onlyhte sceolde ic lifes þrym
Geberan beorhtne sunu bearn eacen godes
Torhtes tir-fruma[n]· Nu ic his tempel eam
Gefremed butan facne in me frofre gæst
Ge-eardode· Nu þu ealle forlæt
Sare sorg-ceare saga ecne þonc
Mærum meotodes sunu þæt ic his modor wearð
18

that from the glorious temple of the Lord
I joyfully received a maiden pure,
immaculate ; and now all this is changed,
through whom I know not.   Neither availeth me,
to speak or to be silent ; speak I the truth,
then must David's daughter suffer death,
slain with stones ; yet 'tis a harder lot
to conceal the crime, and to be doomed to live
a perjurer, henceforth loathed by all the folk,
accursed 'mong men.'   Then did the maid unravel
the mystery so true, and thus she spake :—

' Truly I say, by the Son of the Creator,
the Saviour of souls, that yet I know not
in conjugal communion any man
anywhere on earth ; but it was granted me,
while still a damsel young and in my home,
that Gabriel, heaven's archangel, bade me hail,
and said in very truth, that heaven's Spirit
should with His ray illume me, that I should bear
life's Glory, an illustrious Son, the mighty Child
of God, the bright Creator.   Now, without guilt,
am I become His temple ; the Spirit of comfort
hath dwelt within me.   Wherefore dismiss thou now
all sorry care, and say eternal thanks
to the Lord's great Son, that I became His mother,

Fæmne forð se-þeah and þu fæder cweden 210
Woruld-cund bi wene sceolde witedom
In him sylfum beon soðe gefylled·
Eala þu soða and þu sib-suma
Ealra cyninga cyning crist æl-mihtig
Hu þu ær wære eallum geworden
Worulde þrymmum mid þinne wuldor-fæder
Cild acenned þurh his cræft and meaht·
Nis ænig nú eorl under lyfte
Secg searo-þoncol to þæs swiðe gleaw
Þe þæt asecgan mæge sund buendum 220
Areccan mid ryhte hu þe rodera weard
Æt frymðe genom him to treo-bearne·
Þæt wæs þara þinga þe her þeoda cynn
Gefrugnen mid folcum æt fruman ærest
Geworden under wolcnum þæt witig god
Lifes ord-fruma leoht and þystro
Gedælde dryhtlice and him wæs domes geweald
And þa wisan abead weoroda ealdor·
Nu sie geworden forþ a to widan feore
Leoht lixende gefea lifgendra gehwam 230
Þe in cneorissum cende weorðen·
And þa sona gelomp þa hit swa sceolde
Leoma leohtade leoda mægþum
Torht mid tunglum æfter þon tida bigong·

20

nathless a maiden still, and thou, I ween,
art named His earthly father, should the prophecy
become fulfilled aright in Him Himself.'

O thou true Sovran, and thou peaceful King,
thou King of all Kings, Christ Omnipotent!
how wast thou, with thy glorious Father, aye
existent before all the world's estates,
a child begotten by His skill and might.
There liveth not a mortal under heaven,
no man however wise, who is so wise,
that he can tell unto the ocean-dwellers
and expound aright, how the Warden of the skies
took thee in the beginning for His noble child.
Of all the things that mankind hath e'er heard
here upon earth, this thing first came to pass
beneath the clouds, that God Omniscient,
the Source of life, parted in sovran will
the light from darkness, wielding His decree;
and thus He, Lord of hosts, commanded then:—

'Let there be light for ever and for ever,
a radiant joy for each of living men
who in their generations shall be born.'

And so it came to pass, when 'twas ordained;
a splendour shining bright amidst the stars
lighted, through the course of time, the tribes of men.

Sylfa sette þæt þu sunu wære
Efen-eardigende mid þinne engan frean
Ær þon oht þisses æfre gewurde·
Þu eart seo snyttro þe þas sidan gesceaft
Mid þi waldende worhtes ealle·
Forþon nis ænig þæs horsc ne þæs hyge-cræftig   240
Þe þin from-cyn mæge fira bearnum
Sweotule geseþan·   Cum nu sigores weard
Meotod mon-cynnes and þine miltse her
Arfæst ywe us is eallum neod
Þæt we þin medren-cynn motan cunnan
Ryht-geryno nu we areccan ne mægon
Þæt fædren-cynn fier owihte·
Þu þisne middan-geard milde geblissa
Þurh ðinne her-cyme hælende crist·
And þa gyldnan geatu þe in gear-dagum   250
Ful longe ær bilocen stodan
Heofona heah frea hat ontynan
And usic þonne gesece þurh þin sylfes gong
Eað-mod to eorþan·   Us is þinra arna þearf·
Hafað se awyrgda wulf tostenced
Deor dæd-scua dryhten þin eowde
Wide towrecene þæt ðu waldend ær
Blode gebohtes þæt se bealo-fulla
Hyneð heard-lice and him on hæft nimeð

He had Himself ordained that thou, His Son,
shouldst be co-dwelling with thy only Lord,
ere aught of this had ever come to pass.
Lo, thou art Wisdom ; with the Omnipotent
thou wroughtest all this wide creation ;
wherefore is none so wise or so profound
that he can tell thy origin aright
to the sons of men.   Come now, Lord of triumph,
Creator of mankind, and graciously
show forth thy mercy here ; we all desire
that we may know aright thy mother-kin,
a mystery indeed ; we cannot understand
further in anywise thy kin paternal.
Bless thou benignly all this middle-earth
by thy coming hither, O thou Saviour Christ,
and the golden gates that in the days of old,
through the long ages, stood so firmly locked,
do thou, high Lord of heaven, bid open now,
and visit us, coming thy very Self
humbly to earth! we need thy gracious help ;
the accursed wolf, the beast of darkest deed,
hath scattered, Lord, thy flock, and far and wide
dispersed it ; what thou, Omnipotent, of old
didst with thy blood redeem, the baleful one
oppresseth cruelly, and taketh it in bondage,

Ofer usse nioda lust· Forþon we nergend þe   260
Biddað georn-lice breost-gehygdum
Þæt þu hræd-lice helpe gefremme
Wergum wreccan þæt se wites bona
In helle grund hean gedreose
And þin hond-geweorc hæleþa scyppend
Mote arisan and on ryht cuman
To þam up-cundan æþelan rice
Þonan us ær þurh syn-lust se swearta gæst
Forteah and fortylde þæt we tires wone
A butan ende sculon ermþu dreogan   270
Butan þu usic þon ofost-licor ece dryhten
Æt þam leod-sceaþan lifgende god
Helm alwihta hreddan wille·

IV.

Ɛ ALA þu mæra middan-geardes
        Seo clæneste cwen ofer eorþan
Þara [þ]e gewurde to widan feore
Hu þec mid ryhte ealle reord-berend
Hatað and secgað hæleð geond foldan
Bliþe mode þæt þu bryd sie
Þæs selestan swegles bryttan·   280
Swylce þa hyhstan on heofonum eac
Cristes þegnas cweþað and singað

despite our anxious longing.   Wherefore, Saviour,
we pray thee earnestly, with all our thoughts,
that speedily thou grant help unto us,
poor weary wretches, that the soul's destroyer
may fall precipitate to hell's abyss,
and that thy handiwork, Creator of all men,
may then arise and come, as it is meet,
unto that noble realm in heaven above,
whence the swart spirit, through our love of sin,
beguiled us erst; wherefore inglorious
for aye must we this wretchedness endure,
unless thou, Lord eternal, living God,
Helm of all created things, e'en now
will free us speedily from mankind's bane.

IV.

Hail, thou glory of this middle-world,
thou purest woman throughout all the earth,
of those that were from immemorial time,
how rightly art thou named by all endowed
with gift of speech !   All mortals throughout earth
declare, full blithe of heart, that thou art bride
of Him that ruleth the empyreal sphere.
So too the highest in the heavens above,
the thanes of Christ, proclaim aloud and sing,

Þæt þu sie hlæfdige halgum meahtum
Wuldor-weorudes and worl[d]-cundra
Hada under heofonum and hel-wara
Forþon þu þæt ana ealra monna
Geþohtest þrymlice þrist-hycgende
Þæt þu þinne mægð-had meotude brohtes
Sealdes butan synnum·   Nan swylc ne cwom
Ænig oþer ofer ealle men   290
Bryd beaga hroden þe þa beorhtan lac
To heofon-hame hlutre mode
Siþþan sende·   Forðon heht sigores fruma
His heah-bodan hider gefleogan
Of his mægen-þrymme and þe meahta sped
Snude cyðan þæt þu sunu dryhtnes
Þurh clæne gebyrd cennan sceolde
Monnum to miltse and þe maria forð
Efne unwemme a gehealden·
Eac we þæt gefrugnon þæt gefyrn bi þe   300
Soð-fæst sægde sum woð-bora
In eald-dagum esaias
Þæt he wære gelæded þæt he lifes gesteald
In þam ecan ham eal sceawode·
Wlat þa swa wis-fæst witga geond þeod-land
Oþþæt he gestarode þær gestaþelad wæs
Æþelic ingong·   Eal wæs gebunden

that thou by might of holiness art queen
of the hosts of glory, of the ranks of men
on earth 'neath heaven, and of hell's habitants,
for thou alone of all the race of men
with noble aspiration didst resolve
to bring thy maidenhood unto the Lord,
to offer it in all thy sinlessness.
No ring-adorned bride like unto thee
hath ever come again 'mong humankind,
to send with spirit pure the glorious gift
unto the heavenly home.   Wherefore the Lord triumphant
bade His chief messenger fly hitherward
from His great glory, and anon to thee
reveal His might's avail, that thou shouldst bear
in purity the Son of the Supreme,
in mercy to mankind, and nathless, Mary,
thou shouldst be held immaculate for aye.

Eke have we heard the words that long ago
the prophet truly spake concerning thee,
in distant days of old, to wit, Isaiah,
that he was led where he beheld aright
life's dwelling-place in the eternal home ;
looked then the wise soothsayer o'er all the land,
till that he saw where stood immovable
a glorious portal ; bound all about

Deoran since duru ormæte
Wundur-clommum bewriþen· Wende swiðe
Þæt ænig elda æfre meahte   310
Swa fæstlice fore-scyttelsas
On ecnesse o in-hebba
Oþþe ðæs ceaster-hlides clustor onlucan
Ær him godes engel þurh glædne geþonc
Þa wisan onwrah and þæt word acwæð·
Ic þe mæg secgan þæt soð gewearð
Þæt ðas gyldnan gatu giet sume siþe
God sylf wile gæstes mægne
Gefælsian fæder æl-mihtig
And þurh þa fæstan locu foldan neosan   320
And hio þonne æfter him ece stondeð
Simle singales swa beclysed
Þæt nænig oþer nymþe nergend god
Hy æfre ma eft onluceð·
Nu þæt is gefylled þæt se froda þa
Mid eagum þær on-wlatade·
Þu eart þæt weall-dor þurh þe waldend frea
Æne on þas eorðan ut-siðade
And efne swa þec gemette meahtum gehrodene
Clæne and gecorene crist æl-mihtig   330
Swa ðe æfter him engla þeoden
Eft unmæle ælces þinges

with precious metal was the door immense,
begirt with wondrous bands ; he pondered much
how any mortal man might e'er avail
to lift the bolts and bars so firmly fixed,
yea, ever unto all eternity,
or ope the fastening of that city-gate,
until God's angel joyfully to him
disclosed how it would be, and spake these words :—

   ' I may tell thee,'—truly it came to pass,
' that God Himself, Father Omnipotent,
in future time, yea, by His Spirit's might,
will glorify these golden gates withal,
and through these firm-set bolts will visit earth,
and after Him shall they remain for aye,
to all eternity, so firmly closed,
that no one else but He, the Saviour God,
shall e'er avail to open them again.'

   Now is the thing fulfilled that at that time
the sage there with his eyes contemplated.
Thou art the wall-door ; through thee the Omnipotent,
the Ruler, once proceeded to this earth ;
and as He, Christ Almighty, found thee then
adorned with all thy virtues, pure and choice,
so He, the Prince of Angels, Lord of life,
closed thee, immaculate e'en as of yore,

29

Lioþu-cægan bileac lifes brytta·
Iowa us nu þa are þe se engel þe
Godes spel-boda gabriel brohte·
Huru þæs biddað burg-sittende
Þæt ðu þa frofre folcum cyðe
Þinre sylfre sunu·   Siþþan we motan
An-modlice ealle hyhtan
Nu we on þæt bearn foran breostum stariað·   340
Geþinga us nu þristum wordum
Þæt he us ne læte leng owihte
In þisse deað-dene gedwolan hyran
Ac þæt he usic geferge in fæder-rice
Þær we sorg-lease siþþan motan
Wunigan in wuldre mid weoroda god·
Eala þu halga heofona dryhten
Þu mid fæder þinne gefyrn wære
Efen-wesende in þam æþelan ham·
Næs ænig þa giet engel geworden   350
Ne þæs miclan mægen-þrymmes nán
Ðe in roderum up rice biwitigað
Þeodnes þryð-gesteald and his þegnunga
Þa þu ærest wære mid þone ecan frean
Sylf settende þas sidan gesceaft
Brade bryten-grundas·   Bæm inc is gemæne
Heah-gæst hleofæst·   We þe hælend crist

after Him again, as with a wondrous key.
Show us now the grace that God's own messenger,
the angel Gabriel, brought unto thee !
Forsooth we dwellers in earth's cities pray,
that thou reveal their comfort unto men,
thy very son.   Hereafter we may all,
with one accord, look forward hopefully,
if now we see the Child upon thy breast.
Plead thou our cause for us with earnest words,
that He may suffer us no longer here
to list to Error in this vale of death,
but that He lead us to the Father's realm,
where sorrowless we may for evermore
abide in glory with the Lord of hosts.

Hail, thou holy One, thou Lord of heaven,
thou with thy Father wast from ancient time,
co-eval in that noble home on high.
As yet there was not any angel formed,
nor any of the mighty hierarchies,
that guard the kingdom in the skies above,
the palace of the Prince and of His thanes,
when thou together with the Lord eterne
wast first ordaining all this wide creation,
this broad expanse of earth.   Ye twain have fellowship
with the protecting Spirit.   Saviour Christ,

Þurh eað-medu ealle biddað
Þæt þu gehyre hæfta stefne
Þinra nied-þiowa nergende god· 360
Hu we sind geswencte þurh ure sylfra gewill·
Habbað wræc-mæcgas wergan gæstas
Hetlen hel-sceaþa hearde genyrwad
Gebunden bealo-rapum· Is seo bot gelong
Eall æt þe anum ece dryhten·
Hreow-cearigum help þæt þin hider-cyme
Afrefre fea-sceafte þeah we fæhþo wið þec
Þurh firena lust gefremed hæbben·
Ara nu onbehtum and usse yrmþa geþenc
Hu we tealtrigað tydran mode 370
Hwearfiað heanlice· Cym nu hæleþa cyning
Ne lata to lange· Us is lissa þearf
Þæt þu us ahredde and us hælo-giefe
Soð-fæst sylle þæt we siþþan forð
Þa sellan þing symle moten .
Geþeon on þeode þinne willan·

V.

EALA seo wlitige weorð-mynda full
Heah and halig heofon-cund þrynes
Brade geblissad geond bryten-wongas

in lowliness we all beseech thee now,
that thou mayest hear the voice of these thy thralls,
thy captive bondmen here.   O Saviour God,
how are we harassed through our own desires !
Us wretched exiles have the accursed sprites,
the hateful hell-fiends, cruelly constrained,
and bound with baleful bonds.   With thee alone
resteth redemption, O eternal Lord !
Help thou the wretched, and let thine advent hither
comfort the forlorn, though through our lust of sin
we have engaged in feud e'en against Thee.
Pity thy servants !   Bethink thee of our woes,
how in our feebleness we stumble here,
and wander abjectly.   Come now, O King of men,
tarry not too long ; we need thy gentle grace !
Deliver thou us and grant us verily
thy healing gift, so that from now henceforth
we may for evermore, while in this world,
attempt the better things, and work thy will.

V.

Hail, thou Glory, beauteous and worshipful,
high and holy, heavenly Trinity !
blessed far and wide throughout the spacious world.

Þa mid ryhte sculon reord-berende
Earme eorð-ware ealle mægene
Hergan healice nu us hælend god
Wærfæst onwrah þæt we hine witan motan·
Forþon hy dæd-hwæte dome geswiðde
Þæt soð-fæste seraphinnes cýnn
Uppe mid englum a bremende
Unaþreotendum þrymmum singað
Ful healice hludan stefne
Fægre feor and neah·   Habbaþ folgoþa
Cyst mid cyninge·   Him þæt crist forgeaf
Þæt hy motan his æt-wiste eagum brucan
Simle singales swegle gehyrste
Weorðian waldend wide and side·
And mid hyra fiþrum frean æl-mihtges
Onsyne wear[dia]ð ecan dryhtnes
And ymb þeoden-stol þringað georne
Hwylc hyra nehst mæge ussum nergende
Flihte lacan frið-geardum in·
Lofiað leof-licne and in leohte him
Þa word cweþað and wuldriað
Æþelne ord-fruman ealra gesceafta·
Halig eart þu halig heah-engla brego
Soð sigores fréa simle þu bist halig
Dryhtna dryhten a þin dom wunað

Thee rightly must all men endowed with speech,
all earth's poor mortals, praise with might and main,
for now the trusty Saviour hath revealed
God unto us, that we may know Him right.
Wherefore the heavenly race of Seraphim,
so true, so zealous, and with glory crowned,
doth sweetly sing amid the hosts above,
hymning ever with unwearying notes,
with rapture high, and with exalted strain,
afar and near.   Theirs is the noblest office
in the service of the King.   Christ granted them
that with their eyes they may enjoy His being,
and ceaselessly from pole to pole adore
their Sovran Lord, wreathed with celestial light;
and with their wings do they the presence guard
of the Omnipotent, the eternal Lord,
and throng around the Prince's throne, all eager
which one of them may nearest to our Saviour
disport in flight within the courts of peace;
they praise Him, the Beloved, and in His light
these words they speak to Him, and glorify
the noble Source of all created things :—

' Holy art thou, holy, Lord of archangels,
true Lord of triumph, ever art thou holy,
King of all kings, ever thy glory liveth

Eorð-lic mid ældum in ælce tid
Wide geweorþad· Þu eart weoroda god
Forþon þu gefyldest foldan and rodoras
Wigendra hleo wuldres þines·
Helm al-wihta sie þe in heannessum
Ece hælo and in eorþan lof   410
Beorht mid beornum· Þu gebletsad leofa
Þe in dryhtnes noman dugeþum cwome
Heanum to hroþre· Þe in heahþum sie
A butan ende ece herenis·
Eala hwæt þæt is wræc-lic wrixl in wera life
Þætte mon-cynnes milde scyppend
Onfeng æt fæmnan flæsc unwemme
And sio weres friga wiht ne cuþe
Ne þurh sæd ne cwom sigores agend
Monnes ofer moldan ac þæt wæs ma cræft   420
Þonne hit eorð-buend ealle cuþan
Þurh geryne hu he rodera þrim
Heofona heah frea helpe gefremede
Monna cynne þurh his modor hrif·
And swa forð gongende folca nergend
His forgif-nesse gumum to helpe
Dæleð dogra gehwam dryhten weoroda·
Forþon we hine dom-hwate dædum and wordum
Hergen hold-lice· Þæt is healic ræd
        36

on earth 'mong men, to all eternity,
praised far and wide.   Thou art the Lord of hosts,
for with thy glory thou hast filled the earth
and all the skies, thou Shield of warriors!
Helm of äll things! endless Hosanna be thine
in the heights above, and noble praise on earth,
among the hosts of men.   Abide thou blessed,
that in the Lord's name camest unto men
to comfort the dejected! in the high heavens
eternal praise be thine, world without end!'
How wondrous is the change in mortal life,
since the benign Creator of mankind
took from a damsel flesh immaculate,
nor knew she anything of human love,
nor came the Lord of triumph down to earth
through seed of man; but it was greater craft
than earth's inhabitants might understand,
how the Glory of the skies, through mystery,
the Sovran Lord of heaven, effected help
for all mankind, e'en through His mother's womb.
And aye, unceasingly, the Saviour of men
bestoweth His forgiveness unto folk,
each day, to help them, He the Lord of hosts.
For this should we extol Him loyally,
zealous in deed and word. 'Tis a noble rede,

37

Monna gehwylcum þe gemynd hafað

Þæt he symle oftost and inlocast

And georn-licost god weorþige·

He him þære lisse lean forgildeð

Se gehalgoda hælend sylfa

Efne in þam eðle þær he ær ne cwom

In lifgendra londes wynne

Þær he gesælig siþþan eardað

Ealne widan feorh wunað butan ende·   Amen·

Secundus Passus de Ascensione.

I.

U ðu geornlice gæst gerynum

Mon se mæra mod-cræfte sec

Þurh sefan snyttro þæt þu soð wite

Hu þæt geeode þa se æl-mihtiga

Acenned wearð þurh clænne hád

Siþþan he marian mægða weolman

Mærre meowlan mund-heals geceas

Þæt þær in hwitum hræglum gewerede

Englas ne oðeowdun þa se æþeling cwom

Beorn in betlem·   Bodan wæron gearwe

Þa þurh hleoþor-cwide hyrdum cyðdon

for every mortal mindful of the past,

that aye, most often and most inwardly,

and with all eagerness, he worship God.

He will be recompensed for his sweet love,

yea, by the hallowed Saviour Himself,

e'en in that home where he came ne'er before,

the happy land where the immortals are ;

there blessed shall he abide for evermore,

and dwell eternally, world without end.   Amen.

Part Second.   The Ascension.

I.

Seek earnestly, with all thy secret lore,

with all thy faculties, thou mighty man,

with the wisdom of thy soul, that thou may'st know,

how it befell, when the Omnipotent

was born unto the world in purity,

when he had chosen Mary as protector,

glory of maidenhood, damsel renowned,

that there appeared not angels then arrayed

in robes of white, whenas the noble Chief

came into Bethlehem.   Angels were ready,

for they revealed in accents clear and iold

Sægdon soðne gefean þætte sunu wære   450
In middan-geard meotudes acenned
In betleme.   Hwæþre in bocum ne cwið
Þæt hy in hwitum þær hræglum oðywden
In þa æþelan tid swa hie eft dydon
Ða se brega mæra to bethania
Þeoden þrym-fæst his þegna gedrhyt
Gelaðade leof weorud.   Hy þæs lareowes
On þam wil-dæge word ne gehyrwdon
Hyra sinc-giefan.   Sona wæron gearwe
Hæleð mid hlaford to þære halgan byrg   460
Þær him tacna fela tires brytta
Onwrah wuldres helm word-gerynum
Ærþon up-stige án-cenned sunu
Efen-ece bearn agnum fæder
Þæs ymb feowertig þe he of foldan ær
From deaðe aras dagena rimes.
Hæfde þa gefylled swa ær biforan sungon
Witgena word geond woruld innan
Þurh his þrowinga.   Þegnas heredon
Lufedun leof-wendum lifes agend   470
Fæder frum-sceafta.   He him fægre þæs
Leofum gesiþum lean æfter geaf
And þæt word acwæð waldend engla
Gefysed fréa mihtig to fæder rice.

to shepherds the sure joy that there was born
upon this middle-earth, in Bethlehem,
the Son of the Creator.; yet in books it saith not
that they appeared then at that glorious tide
in robes of white, e'en as they did anon
when the great Leader in Bethania,
the Lord majestic, called His band of thanes,
the host belovéd; on that welcome·day
they slighted not the word their Teacher spake,
their bounteous Dispenser.   Soon were they dight,
men with their Master, for the holy burgh;
there Splendour's Lord, the Helm of bliss, revealed
full many a sign to them in mystic words,
ere He ascended, only begotten Son,
the Child with His own Father co-eternal;
then forty numbered days had run their course,
since He had risen first from earth, from death.
Then had He fulfilled the prophets' words,
as they had sung before throughout the world,
yea, by His passion.   His servants lauded Him,
they praised all-lovingly the Source of life,
the Father of creation !   Wherefore in aftertime
He nobly recompensed His comrades dear;
and these words spake the angels' mighty Lord,
whilst hastening onward to His Father's realm :—

Gefeoð ge on ferððe næfre ic from-hweorfe
Ac ic lufan symle læste wið eowic
And eow meaht giefe and mid-wunige
Awo to ealdre þæt eow æfre ne bið
Þurh gife mine godes onsien·
Farað nu geond ealne yrmenne grund   480
Geond wid-wegas weoredum cyðað
Bodiað and bremað beorhtne geleafan
And fulwiað folc under roderum
Hweorfað to heofonum hergas breotaþ
Fyllað and feogað feond-scype dwæscað
Sibbe sawað on sefan manna
Þurh meahta sped·   Ic eow mid-wunige
Forð on frofre and eow friðe healde
Strengðu staþol-fæstre on stowa gehware·
Ða wearð semninga sweg on lyfte   490
Hlud gehyred heofon-engla þreat
Weorud wlite-scyne wuldres aras
Cwomun on corðre·   Cyning ure gewat
Þurh þæs temples hrof þær hy to-segun
Ða þe leofes þa gen last weardedun
On þam þing-stede þegnas gecorene·
Gesegon hi on heahþu hlaford stigan
God-bearn of grundum·   Him wæs geomor sefa
Hat æt heortan hyge murnende

'Rejoice ye in spirit; ne'er will I turn away,
but I will show my love toward you still,
and grant you might, and will abide with you
to all eternity, and through my grace
ne'er shall ye know the want of sustenance.
Go now o'er all the spacious tract of earth,
o'er the wide ways, announce it unto men,
preach and proclaim the glorious belief,
and baptize folk beneath the firmament;
turn then to heaven; shatter heathen idols,
cast them down and spurn them; extinguish enmity,
and sow ye peace within the minds of men,
by virtue of your gifts.   I will abide with you
in solace, and will keep you aye in peace,
with sure unfailing strength in every place.'

Then suddenly a sound was heard on high,
loud in the air; a band of heavenly angels,
a beauteous host, the messengers of glory,
in legion came; our King departed thence,
e'en through the temple's roof, where they beheld,
they who were watching still the Dear One's track,
His chosen thanes, there in that meeting-place;
they saw their Lord, the Child divine, ascend
from earth into the heights; sad were their souls;
their spirit's grief burned hot within their hearts,

43

Þæs þe hi swa leofne leng ne mostun 500
Geseon under swegle·   Song áhofun
Aras ufan-cunde æþeling heredun
Lofedun lif-fruman leohte gefegun
Þe of þæs hælendes heafelan lixte
Gesegon hy æl-beorhte englas twegen
Fægre ymb þæt frum-bearn frætwum blican
Cyninga wuldor·   Cleopedon of heahþu
Wordum wræt-licum ofer wera mengu
Beorhtan reorde·   Hwæt bidaðge
Galilesce guman on hwearfte· 510
Nu ge sweotule geseoð soðne dryhten
On swegl faran sigores ágend·
Wile up heonan eard gestigan
Æþelinga ord mid þas engla gedryht
Ealra folca fruma fæder eþel-stóll·

II.

Ƿ̵E mid þyslice þreate willað
        ofer heofona gehlidu hlaford fergan
To þære beorhtan byrg mid þas bliðan gedryt·
Ealra sige-bearna þæt seleste
And æþeleste þe ge her onstariað 520
And in frofre geseoð frætwum blican

for now they might no longer see 'neath heaven
One so beloved as He.   Then raised a song
the messengers celestial ; praised they the Prince ;
they lauded life's Creator ; joyed they in the light
that gleamed so brightly from the Saviour's head ;
saw they angels twain, resplendent, fair,
shining in splendour 'round that first-born Child,
the Glory of all Kings ; they cried out from on high,
in wondrous words, o'er all the hosts of men,
with voices resonant :—' Why bide ye here,
and stand about, ye Galilean men ?
Now surely do ye see the Sovran true
wending triumphant to the empyreal sphere.
The Chief of princes with these angel-hosts,
the Lord of all mankind, ascendeth hence
unto His native home, His fatherland.'

II.

' Fain would we o'er the vaulted roof of heaven
conduct the Lord with all this company,
this joyous throng, unto the shining burgh.'
    ' He whom ye gaze on here so rapt, the best
and noblest of the sons of victory,
He whom ye see in solace shine so fair,

Wile eft swa-þeah eorðan mægðe
Sylfa gesecan side herge
And þonne gedeman dæda gehwylce
Þara ðe gefremedon folc under roderum·
Ða wæs wuldres weard wolcnum bifongen
Heah-engla cyning ofer hrofas upp
Haligra helm·   Hyht wæs geniwad
Blis in burgum þurh þæs beornes cyme·
Gesæt sige-hremig on þa swiþran hand   530
Ece ead-fruma agnum fæder·
Gewitan him þa gongan to hierusalem
Hæleð hyge-rofe in ða halgan burg
Geomor-mode þonan hy god nyhst
Up-stigende eagum segun
Hyra wil-gifan·   Þær wæs wopes hring
Torne bitolden·   Wæs seo treow lufu
Hat æt heortan hreðer innan weoll
Beorn breost-sefa·   Bidon ealle þær
Þegnas þrym-fulle þeodnes gehata   540
In þære torhtan byrig tyn niht þa-gen
Swa him sylf bibead swegles agend
Ær þon up-stige ealles waldend
On heofona gehyld hwite cwoman
Eorla ead-giefan englas to-geanes·
Ðæt is wel cweden swa gewritu secgað

46

will surely yet again with ample host
revisit all the races of the earth,
and then will He adjudge their every deed,
that mortals have achieved beneath the skies.'

Then was Glory's Guardian, the archangels' King,
the Helm of holy men, bewrapt in clouds,
high o'er the roofs. Joy was renewed and bliss
in heaven's cities at the Prince's coming;
on His own Father's right-hand sat He down
triumphant, the eternal Source of good.

Sad then in spirit, went the valiant men
and journeyed to Jerusalem's holy burgh,
departing from the place where they so late
beheld with their own eyes God rise aloft,
their kind Dispenser. There was unbroken weeping,
their faithful love was overwhelmed with grief,
their hearts were hot, their bosoms surged within,
their thoughts were all a-glow. His glorious thanes
awaited there their Sovran Lord's behests,
within that noble burgh, ten nights withal,
as He Himself, the Lord of heaven, bade,
e'er He ascended in omnipotence
to heaven's keeping, and white angels came
toward the bounteous Prince of warrior-men.

It is well spoken, as the Scripture saith,

47

þæt him al-beorhte englas togeanes
In þa halgan tįd heapum cwoman
Sigan on swegle þa wæs symbla mæst
Geworden in wuldre·   Wel þæt gedafenað   550
Ðæt to þære blisse beorhte gewerede
In þæs þeodnes burg þegnas cwoman
Weorud wlite-scyne gesegon wil-cuman
On heah-setle heofones waldend
Folca feorh-giefan frætwum ealles waldend
Middan-geardes and mægen-þrymmes·
Hafað nu se halga helle bireafod
Ealles þæs gafoles þe hi gear-dagum
In þæt orlege unryhte swealg·
Nu sind forcumene and in cwic-susle   560
Gehynde and gehæfte in helle grund
Duguþum bidæled deofla cempan·
Ne meahtan wiþer-brogan wige spowan
Wæpna wyrpum siþþan wuldres cyning
Heofon-rices helm hilde gefremede
Wiþ his eald-feondum ánes meahtum·
þær he of hæfte áhlód huþa mæste
Of feonda byrig folces unrim
þisne ilcan þreat þe ge her on-stariað·
Wile nu gesecan sawla nergend   570
Gæsta gief-stol godes agen bearn
       48

that radiant angels at that holy tide,
descending in the clouds, in legion came
to meet Him ; then in glorious heaven arose
the greatest jubilee. 'Twas well befitting
that His servants came to the Beatitude,
unto the Prince's city, brightly clad,
a beauteous host ; they saw their welcome Lord
on His exalted throne, Sovran of heaven,
Source of men's life, ruling in splendour all,—
this middle-earth and the majestic host.

'Now hath the Holy One despoiled hell
of all the tribute that in ancient days
it basely gorged within that home of strife.
Now are they quelled, the devil's champions,
in living torture humbled and held bound,
bereft of prowess, down in hell's abyss ;
the gruesome foes might not in battle speed
with weapon-thrusts, when He, the King of Glory,
the Helm of heaven's realm, waged warfare there
against His ancient foes with His sole might.
Then drew He forth from durance the best spoil,
a folk unnumbered, from the burgh of fiends,
this very band which ye here gaze upon.
Now will He seek the Spirit's throne of grace,
the proper Child of God, Saviour of souls,

D   49

Æfter guð-plegan·   Nu ge geare cunnon
Hwæt se hlaford is se þisne here lædeð·
Nu ge from-lice freondum to-geanes
Gongað glæd-mode·   Geatu ontynað·
Wile into eow ealles waldend
Cyning on ceastre corðre ne lytle
Fyrn-weorca fruma folc gelædan
In dreama dream ðe he on deoflum genom
Þurh his sylfes sygor·   Sib sceal gemæne   580
Englum and ældum á forð heonan
Wesan wide-ferh·   Wær is æt-somne
Godes and monna gæst-halig treow
Lufu lifes hyht and ealles leohtes gefea·
Hwæt we nú gehyrdan hu þæt hælu-bearn
Þurh his hyder-cyme hals eft forgeaf
Gefreode and gefreoþade folc under wolcnum
Mære meotudes sunu þaet nu monna gehwylc
Cwic þendan her wunat geceosan mót
Swa helle hienþu swa heofones mærþu·   590
Swa þæt leohte leoht swa ða laþan niht·
Swa þrymmes þræce swa þrystra wræce·
Swa mid dryhten dream swa mid deoflum hream·
Swa wite mid wraþum swa wuldor mid arum·
Swa líf swa deað swa him leofre bið
To gefremmanne þenden flæsc and gæst

after the conflict. Now ye know right well
what Lord is He that leadeth all this host ;
now boldly go ye forward to meet friends,
joyful in spirit. Open, O ye gates !
the Lord of all, the King, creation's Source,
will lead through you unto the citadel,
unto the joy of joys, with host not small,
the folk which from the devils He hath reft
by His own victory. Peace shall be shared
by angels and by men hence evermore
to all eternity ; 'twixt God and man
there is a covenant, a ghostly pledge,—
love, and life's hope, and joy of all the light.'

Lo ! we have heard now how the Saviour-Child
dispensed salvation by His advent hither,
how He, the Lord's great Son, freed and protected
folk 'neath the clouds, so that each mortal now,
while he is dwelling here alive, must choose,—
be it hell's base shame, or heaven's fair fame,
be it the shining light, or the loathsome night,
be it majestic state, or the rash ones' hate,
be it song with the Lord, or with devils discord,
be it pain with the grim, or bliss with cherubim,
be it life or death, as it shall liefer be
for him to act while flesh and spirit dwell

Wuniað in worulde·   Wuldor þæs age
Þrynysse þrym þonc butan ende·

III.

ÆT is þæs wyrðe þætte wer-þeode
     Secgen dryhtne þonc duguða gehwylcre   600
Þe us sið and ær simle gefremede
Þurh monig-fealdra mægna geryno·
He us æt giefeð and æhta sped
Welan ofer wid-lond and weder liþe
Under swegles hleo sunne and mona
Æþelast tungla eallum scinað
Heofon-condelle hæleþum on eorðan·
Dreoseð deaw and ren duguðe weccaþ
To feorh-nere fira cynne
Iecað eorð-welan·   Þæs we ealles sculon   610
Secgan þonc and lof þeodne ussum·
And huru þære hælo þe he us to hyhte forgeaf
Ða he þa yrmðu eft-oncyrde
Æt [h]is up-stige þe we ær drugon
And geþingade þeod-buendum
Wið fæder swæsne fæhþa mæste
Cyning an-boren cwide eft-onhwearf
Saulum to sibbe se þe ær sungen

within the world. Wherefore let glory be,
thanks endless, to the noble Trinity.

III.

'Tis therefore fitting that the tribes of men
give thanks unto the Lord for every good
which late and early He hath rendered us,
through mystery of wonders manifold.
He giveth us food and fulness of possession,
wealth o'er the spacious earth, and gentle weather
'neath the protecting heavens ; the sun and moon,
noblest of constellations, heaven's candles,
shine forth for all mankind on earth alike ;
dew falleth and rain ; they call abundance forth
to nourish life for all the race of man ;
earth's riches they increase. For all these gifts
must we give thanks and praise unto our Lord,
yet first for our salvation, the hope vouchsafed,
when He at His ascension turned away
the miseries which we had suffered long,
when He, the one-born King, on man's behalf,
compounded with His Father, the Beloved,
the greatest feud, averted the decree,
for our soul's peace, which had been uttered erst

53

Þurh yrne hyge ældum to sorge·

Ic þec ofer eorðan geworhte; on þære þu scealt
    yrmþum lifgan   620

Wunian in gewinne and wræce dreogan

Feondum to hroþor fus-leoð galan

And to þære ilcan scealt eft geweorþan

Wyrmum aweallen þonan wites fyr

Of þære eorðan scealt eft gesecan·

Hwæt ús þis se æþeling yðre gefremede

Þa he leómum onfeng and lic-homan

Monnes magu-tudre siþþan meotodes sunu

Engla eþel upgestigan

Wolde weoroda god· Ús se willa bicwom   630

Heanum to helpe on þa halgan tíd·

Bi þon giedd áwræc iob swa he cuðe

Herede helm wera hælend lofede

And mid sib-lufan sunu waldendes

Freo-noman cende and hine fugel nemde

Þone iudeas ongietan ne meahtan·

In ðære god-cundan gæstes strengðu

Wæs þæs fugles flyht feondum on eorþan

Dyrne and degol þam þe deorc gewit

Hæfdon on hreþre heortan stænne·   640

Noldan hi þa torhtan tacen oncnawan

Þe him beforan fremede freo-bearn godes?

in angry mood for mankind's tribulation:

'I wrought thee on earth, on it shalt thou live in
  want,
shalt dwell in toil, and exile shalt endure,
shalt sing the death-song for thy foes' delight,
and shalt be turned again to that same earth
with worms o'ercharged, from whence thou shalt anon,
thereafter, seek the fire of punishment.'

 Lo! this the noble Prince assuaged for us,
when He took limb and fleshly covering
from child of man; when He, the Maker's Son,
the Lord of hosts, willed to ascend on high
unto the home of angels; at that holy tide,
the wish arose to help us, the forlorn.

 Of Him sang Job a song as he well could;
he praised the Helm of men, lauded the Saviour,
and in his love devised a noble name
for the Ruler's Son, and named Him as a bird,
a name which Jews might no wise understand.
By virtue of the Spirit's strength divine,
hidden and secret from His foes on earth
was that bird's flight, from those who in their breasts
had understanding dark, a stony heart;
they would not recognise the glorious signs
which He, God's noble Child, had wrought 'fore them,

Monig mis-líc geond middan-geard·
Swa se fǽle fugel flyges cunnode
Hwilum engla eard up gesohte
Modig meahtum strang þone maran ham
Hwilum he to eorþan eft gestylde
Þurh gæstes giefe grund-sceat sohte
Wende to worulde· Bi þon se witga song·
He wæs upp-hafen engla fæðmum   650
In his þa miclan meahta spede
Heah and halig ofer heofona þrym·
Ne meahtan þa þæs fugles flyht gecnawan
Þe þæs up-stiges and-sæc fremedon
And þæt ne gelyfdon þætte lif-fruma
In monnes hiw ofer mægna þrym
Halig fróm hrusan ahafen wurde·
Ða us geweorðade se þas world gescop
Godes gæst-sunu and us giefe sealde
Uppe mid englum ece staþelas   660
And eac monig-fealde modes snyttru
Seow and sette geond sefan monna·
Sumum word-laþe wise sendeð
On his modes gemynd þurh his muþes gæst
Æþele andgiet· Se mæg eal fela
Singan and secgan þam bið snyttru cræft
Bifolen on ferðe. Sum mæg fingrum wel

various and manifold, on middle-earth.
E'en thus the noble Bird assayed his flight;
whilom He sought on high the angels' land,
the noble home, so proud, so strong in might;
whilom He came adown to earth again;
He sought earth's region in His spirit's grace,
and wended to the world. · Of this the prophet sang:—

' He was borne aloft embraced in angels' arms
unto the spacious glory of His might,
above the heaven's splendour, high and holy.'

Of that Bird's flight they might no knowledge have,
who made denial of the ascension,
and who believed not that the Source of life,
in form of man, all holy from the earth,
was raised aloft above the glorious hosts.

Then He who shaped the world, God's Spirit-Son,
ennobled us, and granted gifts to us,
eternal homes 'mid angels upon high;
and wisdom, too, of soul, full manifold
He sowed and set within the minds of men.
To one He sendeth, unto memory's seat,
through spirit of the mouth, wise eloquence,
and noble understanding; he can sing
and say full many a thing, within whose soul
is hidden wisdom's power. With fingers deft

57

Hlude fore hæleþum hearpan stirgan
Gleo-beam gretan· Sum mæg god-cunde
Reccan ryhte æ· Sum mæg ryne tungla 670
Secgan side gesceaft· Sum mæg searolice
Word-cwide writan· Sumum wiges sped
Giefeð æt guþe þonne gar-getrum
Ofer scild-hreadan sceotend sendað
Flacor flan-geweorc· Sum mæg fromlice
Ofer sealtne sæ sund-wudu drifan
Hreran holm-þræce· Sum mæg heanne beam
Stælgne gestigan· Sum mæg styled sweord
Wæpen gewyrcan· Sum con wonga bigong
Wegas wid-gielle· Swa se waldend us 680
God-bearn on grundum his giefe bryttað·
Nyle he ængum anum ealle gesyllan
Gæstes snyttru þy læs him gielp sceþþe
Þurh his anes cræft ofer oþre forð·

IV.

DUS god meahtig geofum un-hneawum
Cyning al-wihta cræftum weorðaþ
Eorþan tuddor swylce eadgum blæd
Seleð on swegle sibbe ræreþ
Ece to ealdre engla and monna·

'fore warrior-bands one can awake the harp,
the minstrel's joy.   One can interpret well
the law divine, and one the planets' course
and wide creation.   One cunningly can write
the spoken word.   To one He granteth skill,
when in the fight the archers swiftly send
the storm of darts, the wingéd javelin,
over the shield's defence.   Fearlessly another
can o'er the salt sea urge the ocean-bark
and stir the surging depth.   One can ascend
the lofty tree and steep.   One can fashion well
steeled sword and weapon.   One knoweth the plains' direction,
the wide ways.   Thus the Ruler, Child divine,
dispenseth unto us His gifts on earth ;
He will not give to any one man all
the spirit's wisdom, lest pride injure him,
raised far above the rest by his sole might.

IV.

Thus God Almighty, King of created things,
ennobleth by unsparing gifts, by crafts,
the progeny of earth, and giveth joy
unto the blessed in heaven, and setteth peace
for angels and for men to all eternity.

Swa he his weorc weorþað· Bi þon se witga cwæð 690
Þæt á-hæfen wæren halge gimmas
Hædre heofon-tungol healice upp
Sunne and mona· Hwæt sindan þa
Gimmas swa scyne buton god sylfa·
He is se soð-fæsta sunnan leoma
Englum and eorð-warum æþele scima·
Ofer middan-geard mona lixeð
Gæst-lic tungol swa seo godes circe
Þurh gesomninga soðes and ryhtes
Beorhte bliceð swa hit on bocum cwiþ 700
Siþþan of grundum god-bearn á-stag
Cyning clænra gehwæs þa seo circe hér
Æ-fyllendra eaht-nysse bád
Under hæþenra hyrda gewealdum·
Þær ða syn-sceaðan soþes ne giemdon
Gæstes þearfe ac hi godes tempel
Bræcan and bærndon blod-gyte worhtan
Feodan and fyldon· Hwæþre forð bicwom
Þurh gæstes giefe godes þegna blæd
Æfter up-stige ecan dryhtnes· 710
Bi þon salomon song sunu dauiþes
Giedda gearo-snottor gæst-gerynum
Waldend wer-þeoda and þæt word acwæð·
Cuð þæt geweorðeð þætte cyning engla
60

He honoureth His work, e'en as the prophet spake,
that holy gems were raised on high aloft,
the radiant constellations of the sky,
the sun and moon.   Lo now, what are these gems
that shine resplendent, but e'en God Himself?
He is the true refulgence of the sun,
a noble light for angels and for men.
O'er all the middle-earth the moon doth shine,
a ghostly star, e'en as the Church of God
glisteneth bright, whene'er the True and Just
are linked together ; as it saith in books,
that when the Child divine, the King all pure,
had risen from the earth, then the Church here
of the faithful ones endured oppression
beneath the tyranny of heathen rule ;
then did the sinful take no heed of truth,
nor of their spirit's need, but brake and burned
God's temple ; they hated and destroyed,
and bloodshed wrought ; nathless through the Spirit's grace
the welfare of God's servants was maintained,
after the ascension of the eternal Lord.
Thereof sang Solomon, the son of David,
all-wise in song and secrets spiritual,
the ruler of the nations, and these words spake :—
  ' It shall be known once, that the angels' King,

Meotud meahtum swið munt gestylleð
Gehleapeð hea-dune hyllas and cnollas
Bewrið mid his wuldre woruld alyseð
Ealle eorð-buend þurh þone æþelan styll·
Wæs se forma hlyp þa he on fæmnan astag
Mægeð un-mæle and þær mennisc hiw   720
Onfeng butan firenum þæt to frofre gewearð
Eallum eorð-warum·   Wæs se oþer stiell
Bearnes gebyrda þa he in binne wæs
In cildes hiw claþum bewunden
Ealra þrymma þrym.   Wæs se þridda hlyp
Rodor-cyninges ræs þa he on rode astag
Fæder frofre gæst·   Wæs se feorða stiell
In byrgenne þa he þone beam ofgeaf
Fold-ærne fæst.   Wæs se fifta hlyp
Þa he hell-warena heap forbygde   730
In cwic-susle cyning inne gebond
Feonda fore-sprecan fyrnum teagum
Grom-hydigne þær he gen ligeð
In carcerne clommum gefæstnad
Synnum gesæled·   Wæs se siexta hlyp
Haliges hyht-plega þa he to heofonum astag
On his eald-cyððe þa wæs engla þreat
On þa halgan tid hleahtre bliþe
Wynnum geworden·   Gesawan wuldres þrym
        62

the Lord so strong in might, shall mount a hill,
shall leap the lofty downs, and hills and knolls
shall wreathe with glory, and by that noble leap
shall free the world and all that dwell on earth.'

The first leap was, when He came to the damsel,
the spotless maid, and sinlessly took there
a human form, and was anon the solace
of all mankind.   The second leap was this,—
the Infant's birth, when He was in the manger,
the Glory of all Glories swathed in clothes,
in form of child.   The heavenly King's career
was the third leap, when He, the Father's Solace,
ascended on the rood.   Into the sepulchre
was the fourth leap, when He had left the tree
and lay within that cave.   The fifth leap was,
when He bowed down the multitude of hell
in living torment, and bound their king within,
the devils' advocate, so grim of mood,
with fiery fetters, where he lieth yet,
fastened in prison there with manacles,
and shackled with his sins.   The sixth leap was
the revel of the Holy, when He rose
unto His ancient home ; the angelic host
was blithe with sweetest laughter and with joy
on that holy tide ; they saw the Crown of Glory,

Æþelinga ord eþles neosan 740
Beorhtra bolda· þa wearð burg-warum
Eadgum ece gefea æþelinges plega·
Ðus her on grundum godes ece bearn
Ofer heah hleoþu hlypum stylde
Modig æfter muntum swa we men sculon
Heortan gehygdum hlypum styllan
Of mægne in mægen mærþum tilgan
Ðæt we to þam hyhstan hrofe gestigan
Halgum weorcum þær is hyht and blis
Geþungen þegn-weorud· Is us þearf micel 750
Ðæt we mid heortan hælo secen
Ðær we mid gæste georne gelyfað
Ðæt þæt hælo-bearn heonan up-stige
Mid usse lic-homan lifgende god·
Forþon we a sculon idle lustas
Syn-wunde forseon and þæs sellran gefeon·
Habbað we us to frofre fæder on roderum
Ælmeahtigne· He his áras þonan
Halig of heahðu hider onsendeð
Ða us gescildaþ wið sceþþendra 760
Eglum earh-farum þi læs un-holdan
Wunde gewyrcen þonne wroht-bora
In folc godes forð onsendeð
Of his brægd-bogan biterne stræl·

the noble Chief, approach those bright abodes,
His Fatherland. That revel of the Prince
brought endless joy to those blessed denizens.

Thus God's eternal Child, here upon earth,
sprang boldly o'er the lofty hills, by leaps,
from mount to mount ; and e'en so must we men,
with our hearts' inmost thoughts, by such leaps, spring
from virtue unto virtue, and for glory strive,
so that through holy works we may ascend
to the highest height, where there is joy and bliss
and ministering legions. Great is our need
to seek salvation there with all our hearts,
where earnestly in spirit we repose,
so that the Saviour-Child, the living God,
may with our bodies soar aloft from hence.

Wherefore we must contemn all idle lusts
and wounds of sin, and cherish goodlier things ;
we have our solace in the Omnipotent,
our Father in heaven ; He, the Holy One,
will send His angels hither from on high
to shield us from the noxious arrow-shafts
of those that work our bane, lest gruesome fiends
should deal us wounds, whenas the Enemy,
the great Accuser, sendeth the bitter dart
among the folk of God from his drawn bow.

E   65

Forþon we fæste sculon wið þam fær-scyte
Symle wærlice wearde healdan
Þy læs se attres ord in gebuge
Biter bord-gelac under ban-locan
Feonda fær-searo· Þæt bið frecne wund
Blatast benna· Utan us beorgan þa 770
Þenden we on eorðan eard weardigen·
Utan us to fæder freoþa wilnian·
Biddan bearn godes and þone bliðan gæst
Þæt he us gescilde wið sceaþan wæpnum
Laþra lyge-searwum se us lif forgeaf
Leomu lic and gæst· Si him lof symle
Þurh woruld worulda wuldor on heofnum·

V.

NE þearf him ondrædan deofla strælas
Ænig on eorðan ælda cynnes
Gromra gar-fare gif hine god scildeþ 780
Duguða dryhten· Is þam dome neah
Þæt we gelice sceolon leanum hleotan
Swa we wide feorh weorcum hlódun
Geond sidne grund· Us secgað bec
Hú æt ærestan ead mod astag
In middan-geard mægna gold-hord

66

Verily must we keep constant watch,
and must beware, against the sudden shot,
lest the envenomed point, the bitter dart,
the fiends' pernicious artifice, should strike
beneath the bones' enclosure; its wound is grievous,
the ghastliest of gashes.   May we guard us then,
whilst we hold habitation upon earth;
and be we wishful for the Father's peace;
pray we the Son of God, and the kindly Spirit,
that He protect us from the spoilers' weapons,
the wiles of foes; He gave us life and limb,
body and eke soul; ever to Him be praise
and glory in the heavens, world without end!

V.

Not any of the race of men on earth
need ever dread him of the devils' shafts,
the fiends' spear-storm, if God, the Lord of hosts,
protecteth him.   The day of doom is nigh,
when each of us shall gain the recompense
that by our works we have through life amassed
on this wide world.   'Tis told to us in books,
how the Treasury of glory, God's noble Son,
descended humbly to this middle-earth,

In fæmnan fæðm freo bearn godes
Halig of heahþu· Huru ic wene me
And eac ondræde dóm ðy reþran
Ðonne eft cymeð engla þeoden   790
Þe ic ne heold teala þæt me hælend min
On bocum bibead· Ic þæs brogan sceal
Geseon sýn-wræce þæs þe ic soð talge
Þær monig beoð on gemot læded
Fore onsyne eces deman·
Þonne · ᚻ · cwacað gehyreð cyning mæðlan
Rodera ryhtend sprecan reþe word
Þam þe him ær in worulde wace hyrdon
Þendan · ᚻ · and · ᛏ · yþast meahtan
Frofre findan· Þær sceal forht monig   800
On þam wong-stede werig bidan
Hwæt him æfter dædum deman wille
Wraþra wita· Biþ se · ᚹ · scæcen
Eorþan frætwa · ᚼ · wæs longe
ᚱ · flodum bilocen lif-wynna dæl
ᚠ · on foldan þonne frætwe sculon
Byrnan on bæle· Blac rasetteð
Recen reada leg reþe scriþeð
Geond woruld wide wongas hreosað
Burg-stede berstað brond bið on tyhte   810
Æleð eald-gestreon unmurnlice

68

into the Virgin's womb, when He came first,
holy from on high.   Alas! my mind presageth;
I fear that then 'twill be a sterner doom,
when He, the Lord of hosts, cometh again,
for feebly kept I what my Saviour
bade in His books.   Wherefore shall I see
terror and tribulation, I know full well,
when many to the synod shall be led,
into the presence of the eternal Judge.

 The **K**eenest there shall quake, when he heareth the Lord,
the heaven's Ruler, utter words of wrath
to those who in the world obeyed Him ill,
while they might solace find most easily
for their **Y**earning and their **N**eed.   Many afeard
shall wearily await upon that plain
what penalty He will adjudge to them
for their deeds.   The **W**insomeness of earthly gauds
shall then be changed.   In days of yore **U**nknown,
Lake-floods embraced the region of life's joy,
and all earth's **F**ortune; then each precious thing
shall be consumed in fire; bright and swift
the ruddy flame shall rage, and fiercely stride
o'er the wide world; the plains shall waste away;
the citadels shall crash; the fire shall speed;
unpityingly shall he, greediest of guests,

Gæsta gifrast þæt geo guman heoldan
Þenden him on eorþan onmedla wæs·
Forþon ic leofra gehwone læran wille
Þæt he ne agæle gæstes þearfe
Ne on gylp geote þenden god wille
Þæt he her in worulde wunian mote
Somed siþian sawel in lice
In þam gæst-hofe·   Scyle gumena gehwylc
On his gear-dagum georne biþencan   820
Þæt us milde bicwom meahta waldend
Æt ærestan þurh þæs engles word·
Bið nu eorneste þonne eft cymeð
Reðe and ryhtwis·   Rodor bið onhrered
And þas miclan gemetu middan-geardes
Beheofiað þonne beorht cyning leanað
Þæs þe hy on eorþan eargum dædum
Lifdon leahtrum fá.   Þæs hi longe sculon
Ferð-werige onfon in fyr-baðe
Wælmum biwrecene wraþ-lic and-lean·   830
Þonne mægna cyning on gemot cymeð
Þrymma mæste þeod-egsa bið
Hlud gehyred bi heofon-woman
Cwaniendra cirm cerge reotað
Fore onsyne eces deman
Þa þe hyra weorcum wace truwiað·

consume the treasures which men prized of old,
whilst pride abode with them upon this earth.
Wherefore would I instruct each well-beloved,
lest he be careless of his spirit's need,
or pour it forth in boasting, whilst God willeth
that he may here abide within the world,
whilst soul with body, the guest-house it is in,
may journey on together. It behoveth each,
during his life-days, to remember well,
how all-benign was the Omnipotent
when He first came, e'en as the angel spake.
He will be stern then, when He cometh again,
wrathful and rigorous. The heavens shall quail,
and all the great estates of middle-earth
shall quake, when He, bright King, requiteth them,
for that they lived on earth in wickedness,
stained with transgression; wherefore they shall long,
weary of life, beset with flames, endure
dire retribution in a sea of fire,
when the great King in highest majesty
to that tribunal cometh; then men's dismay,
the cry of anguish, shall be heard aloud
amid the noises of the heavens; sadly
shall they bewail before the eternal Judge,
who have but faint reliance in their works.

Ðær biþ oð-ywed egsa mara
Þonne from frum-gesceape gefrægen wurde
Æfre on eorðan.   Ðær bið æghwylcum
Syn-wyrcendra on þa snudan tid   840
Leofra micle þonne eall þeos læne gesceaft
Ðær he hine sylfne on þam sige-þreate
Behydan mæge þonne herga fruma
Æþelinga ord eallum demeð
Leofum ge laðum lean æfter ryhte
Þeoda gehwylcre·   Is us þearf micel
Ðæt we gæstes wlite ær þam gryre-brogan
On þas gæsnan tid georne biþencen·
Nu is þon gelicost swa we on lagu-flode
Ofer cald wæter ceolum liðan   850
Geond sidne sæ sund-hengestum
Flod-wudu fergen·   Is þæt frecne stream
Yða ofermæta þe we her on lacað
Geond þas wacan woruld windge holmas
Ofer deop gelad·   Wæs se drohtað strong
Ær þon we to londe geliden hæfdon
Ofer hreone hrycg þa us help bicwom
Ðæt us to hælo hyþe gelædde
Godes gæst-sunu and us giefe sealde
Ðæt we oncnawan magun ofer ceoles bord   860
Hwær we sælan sceolon sund-hengestas

Then greater terror shall be manifest
than ever hath been heard of upon earth,
yea, from the first beginning; at that sudden time
each evil-doer will have liefer far
than all this transient creation
some place where, in that onward rush of triumph,
he may conceal him, when the Lord of hosts,
the Chief of Princes, shall adjudge to all,
to friends and foes alike, to every man,
a righteous recompense.   Great is our need,
that in this barren time, ere that grim dread,
we should bethink us of our spirit's grace.

Now 'tis most like as if we fare in ships
on the ocean-flood, over the water cold,
driving our vessels through the spacious seas
with horses of the deep.   A perilous way is this
of boundless waves, and these are stormy seas,
on which we toss here in this feeble world,
o'er the deep paths.   Ours was a sorry plight,
until at last we sailed unto the land,
over the troubled main.   Help came to us,
that brought us to the haven of salvation,
God's Spirit-Son, and granted grace to us,
that we might know, e'en from the vessel's deck,
where we must bind with anchorage secure

Ealde yð-mearas ancrum fæste·
Utan us to þære hyðe hyht staþelian
Ða us gerymde rodera waldend
Halge on heahþu þa he heofonum astag·

Tertius Passus de Die Judicii.

I.

ONNE MID FERE fold-buende
Se micla dæg meahtan dryhtnes
Æt midre niht mægne bihlæmeð
Scire gesceafte swa oft sceaða fæcne
Þeof þrist-lice þe on þystre fareð   870
On sweartre niht sorg-lease hæleð
Semninga for-fehð slæpe gebundne
Eorlas ungearwe yfles genægeð·
Swa on syne beorg somod up cymeð
Mægen-folc micel meotude getrywe
Beorht and bliþe·   Him weorþeð blæd gifen·
Þonne from feowerum foldan sceatum
Þam ytemestum eorþan rices
Englas æl-beorhte on efen blawað
Byman on brehtme beofað middan-geard   880
Hruse under hæleþum·   Hlydað tosomne

74

our ocean-steeds, old stallions of the waves.
O let us rest our hope in that same port,
which the Lord Celestial opened for us there,
holy on high, when He to heaven ascended!

Part Third.   The Day of Judgment.

I.

*W*ITH *sudden fear, at midnight, direfully,*
        the great day of the Lord Omnipotent
shall overwhelm the denizens of earth
and bright creation, e'en as some wily robber,
some daring thief that prowleth in the dark,
in the swart night, surpriseth suddenly
careless mortals bound in happy sleep,
and basely challengeth them unprepared.
Then unto Zion's hill a mighty host,
radiant and blissful, shall ascend together,
the faithful of the Lord; glory shall be theirs.
Then, too, from all four corners of the world,
from furthest regions of the realm of earth,
resplendent angels shall with one accord
sound their loud trumpets, and mid-earth shall quake
beneath the feet of men.   Gloriously and long

Trume and torhte wið tungla gong
Singað and swinsiaþ suþan and norþan
Eastan and westan ofer ealle gesceaft
Weccað of deaðe dryht-gumena bearn
Eall monna cynn to meotud-sceafte
Eges-lic of þære ealdan moldan hatað hy upp-astandan
Sneome of slæpe þy fæstan· Ðær mon mæg sorgende
    folc
Gehyran hyge-geomor hearde gefysed
Cearum cwiþende cwicra gewyrhtu   890
Forhte á-færde· Ðæt bið fore-tacna mæst
Ðara þe ær oþþe sið æfre gewurde
Monnum oþ-ywed þar gemengde beoð
Onhælo gelac engla and deofla
Beorhtra and blacra. Weorþeð bega cyme
Hwitra and sweartra swa him is ham sceapen
Ungelice englum and deoflum·
Ðonne semninga on syne beorg
Suþan eastan sunnan leoma
Cymeð of scyppende scynan leohtor   900
Ðonne hit men mægen modum ahycgan
Beorhte blican þonne bearn godes
Ðurh heofona gehleodu hider oð-yweð·
Cymeð wundorlic cristes onsyn
Æþel-cyninges wlite eastan fram roderum

shall they blow together toward the stars' career,
and sing melodiously from south and north,
from east and west, o'er all creation's realm,
and wake from death unto the final doom,
aghast from the old earth, the sons of men
and all mankind, and bid them then arise
forthwith from their deep sleep.   There shall one
     hear
a sorrowing host and dismal, hard bestead,
sorely afeard, bewailing woefully
their deeds when living.   Of all presaging signs,
which aye, erewhile or since, were shown to men,
this shall be greatest; to wit, the hidden hosts
of angels and of devils, the bright and dark,
shall be commingled there ; yea, both shall come,
the white and black, e'en as a home is shaped
for angels and for devils all unlike.

   Then unto Zion's hill, full suddenly,
a sun-beam from south-east shall come anon
from the Creator, shining more brilliantly
than mortals may conceive of in their minds,
gleaming full brightly ; then the Son of God
shall hitherward appear o'er heaven's vaults ;
wondrous from the east of heaven shall come
the aspect of the noble King, Christ's presence,

On sefan swete sinum folce
Biter bealo-fullum gebleod wundrum
Eadgum and earmum ungelice·
He bið þam godum glæd-mod on gesihþe
Wlitig wynsumlic weorude þam halgan 910
On gefean fæger freond and leoftæl·
Lufsum and liþe leofum monnum
To sceawianne þone scynan wlite
Weðne mid willum waldendes cyme
Mægen-cyninges þam þe him on mode ær
Wordum and weorcum wel gecwemdun·
He bið þam yflum eges-lic and grim-lic
To geseonne synnegum monnum
Þam þær mid firenum cumað forð for-worhte·
Þæt mæg wites to wearninga þam þe hafað wisne
    geþoht 920
Þæt se him eallunga owiht ne ondrædeð
Se for ðære onsyne egsan ne weorþeð
Forht on ferðe þonne he frean gesihð
Ealra gesceafta andweardne faran
Mid mægen-wundrum mongum to þinge·
Ond him on healfa gehwone heofon-engla þreat
Ymb-utan farað ælbeorhtra scolu
Hergas haligra heapum geneahhe·
Dyneð deop gesceaft and fore dryhtne færeð

78

benign with sweetest grace for His own folk,
bitter for the baleful, marvellously visaged,
diversely for the blessed and the forlorn.

Unto the good, the host of holy ones,
His presence shall be winsome, beauteous, glad,
loving and gracious, fraught with fair delight.
Sweet shall it be and pleasant for His beloved
to gaze upon that aspect all so fair,
benign of will, the advent of their Lord,
their mighty Sovran, for in former days
their words and works were pleasing unto Him.
Unto the evil, unto sinful men,
grim shall He be and fearful to behold ;
with their sins they come there, damned eternally.

He that is wise of thought may well regard
  it
as a sign that he need be nowise adread,
if he, afore that Presence, becometh not
dismayed with terror in his soul, when he see'th
creation's Lord advance before him there,
with mighty wonders, to the doom of many,
while on each side of Him angelic hosts
fare round about, legions of radiant ones,
armies of saints, with numerous multitudes.
Then shall creation's depth resound ; o'er earth,

79

Wælm-fyra mæst ofer widne grund·   930
Hlemmeð hata leg heofonas berstað
Trume and torhte tungol of-hreosað
Þonne weorþeð sunne sweart gewended
On blodes hiw seo ðe beorhte scán
Ofer ær-woruld ælda bearnum·
Mona þæt sylfe þe ær mon-cynne
Nihtes lyhte niþer gehreoseð
And steorran swa some stredað of heofone
Þurh ða strongan lyft stormum abeatne·
Wile ælmihtig mid his engla gedryht   940
Mægen-cyninga meotod on gemot cuman
Þrym-fæst þeoden·   Bið þær his þegna eac
Hreþ-eadig heap·   Halge sawle
Mid hyra frean farað þonne folca weard
Þurh egsan þrea eorðan mægðe
Sylfa geseceð·   Weorþeð geond sidne grund
Hlud gehyred heofon-byman stefn
And on seofon healfa swogað windas
Blawað brecende bearhtma mæste
Weccað and woniað woruld mid storme·   950
Fyllað mid feore foldan gesceafte·
Ðonne heard gebrec hlud ún-mæte
Swar and swiðlic·   Sweg-dynna mæst
Ældum eges-lic eawed weorþeð

before the Lord, the fiercest fire shall rage;
the burning flames shall roar; the heavens shall burst;
the planets, bright and steadfast, shall fall down,
and the sun itself shall then be changed, all swart,
to the hue of blood,—the sun that shone so bright,
above the former world, for all mankind;
likewise the moon, that erewhile gave forth light
for mortals through the night, shall fall adown,
and the stars shall fall from heaven precipitate,
tempest-driven through the stormy air.

   Then to the judgment, with His angel-host,
will come the Omnipotent, the King of Kings,
the Lord majestic, and eke a glorious band
shall be there of His own thanes; yea, holy souls
shall journey with their Lord, when the Guardian of men
shall visit all the races of the earth
with direful penalty. From pole to pole
the blast of heaven's trumpet shall be heard,
and from all seven sides the winds shall moan,
and with tumultuous roar shall blow and break,
waking and wasting all the world with storm,
o'erthrowing all creation with their breath;
a grievous crash shall then be manifest,
loud and immeasurable; of all fierce dins
this shall be fiercest, a terror unto folk.

Þær mægen werge monna cynnes
Wornum hweorfað on widne leg
Þa þær cwice meteð cwelmende fýr
Sume up sume niþer ældes fulle·
Þonne bið untweo þæt þær adames
Cýn cearena full cwiþeð gesargad   960
Nales fore lytlum leode geomre
Ac fore þam mæstan mægen-earfeþum·
Ðonne eall þreo on efen nimeð
Won fyres wælm wide tosomne
Se swearta lig sæs mid hyra fiscum
Eorþan mid hire beorgum and up-heofon
Torhtne mid his tunglum·   Teon-leg somod
Þryþum bærneð þreo eal on án
Grimme togædre·   Grornað gesargad
Eal middan-geard on þa mæran tid·   970

II.

SWA se gifra gæst grundas geond-seceð
    Hiþende leg heah-getimbro
Fylleð on fold-wong fyres egsan·
Wid-mære blæst woruld mid-ealle
Hat heoro-gifre·   Hreosað geneahhe
To-brocene burg-weallas·   Beorgas gemeltað

82

Then legions of the race of men, accursed,
shall throng unto the all-embracing flame,
and living feel the fire's fatal touch,
some up, some down, with burning all fulfilled.
Small doubt that there the cheerless race of Adam
shall utter lamentations, woebegone,
afflicted with no feeble tribulation,
but with great anguish, direfullest and worst;
the livid surge of fire, the swarthy flame,
shall seize all there alike, at the same time,
afar and wide; to wit, seas with their fish,
earth with her hills, and eke the heaven above
bright with its constellations; the avenging flame
shall forthwith ravage all the regions three,
fiercely, with fearful onset; all middle-earth,
afflicted at that mighty time, shall mourn.

II.

E'en thus the greedy guest shall visit earth,
the ravaging flame shall hurl with fire's terror
the loftiest piles adown unto the plain;
the fierce-devouring, hot, wide-spreading blast
shall overthrow the world withal; shattered
the city-walls shall fall: the hills shall melt

And heah-cleofu þa wið holme ær
Fæste wið flodum foldan scehdun
Stið and stæð-fæst staþelas wið wæge
Wætre windendum·   Þonne wihta gehwylce   980
Deora and fugla deað-leg nimeð
Færeð æfter foldan fyr-swearta leg
Weallende wiga·   Swa ær wæter fleowan
Flodas afysde þonne on fyr-baðe
Swelað sǽ-fiscas sundes getwæfde
Wæg-deora gehwylc werig swelteð·
Byrneþ wæter swa weax·   Þær bið wundra má
Þonne hit ænig on mode mæge aþencan
Hu þæt gestun and se storm and seo stronge lyft
Brecað brade gesceaft·   Beornas gretað   990
Wepað wanende wergum stefnum
Heane hyge geomre hreowum gedreahte·
Seoþeð swearta leg synne on fordonum
And góld-frætwe gleda forswelgað
Eall ær-gestreon eþel-cyninga·
Ðær bið cirm and cearu and cwicra gewin
Gehreow and hlud wop bi heofon-woman
Earmlic ælda gedreag·   Þonan ænig ne mæg
Firen-dædum fah frið gewinnan
Leg-bryne losian londes ower·   1000
Ac þæt fyr nimeð þurh foldan gehwæt

and the high cliffs, that erewhile parted earth
stoutly and steadfastly from ocean, barriers
against the floods, bulwarks against the waves
and circling waters.   Yea, the fatal flash
shall seize each living creature, beast and bird;
the swarthy flame shall then bestride the world
like a raging warrior; where erst the waters flowed,
the rushing floods, a sea of fire shall burn
the fishes of the deep; reft of their craft,
all ocean's monsters shall a-weary die;
water shall burn as wax; more wonders shall be there
than any mortal may conceive in mind,
when the roar and the storm and the raging blast
shall shatter all creation; men shall then wail,
with abject voices shall they weep and moan,
humbled, saddened, with penitence o'erwhelmed.
Those damned by sin shall surge in swarthy fire,
and gledes shall gorge the golden ornaments,
the ancient treasures of the kings of earth.
'Mid heaven's roar a cry of woe shall rise,
the anguish of the living, grief and lament,
the sorry plight of men.   No mortal there,
with sinful deeds o'erstained, may peace achieve,
or anywhere escape the burning flame;
forsooth the fire shall seize each thing on earth,

Græfeð grim-lice georne aseceð
Innan and utan eorðan sceatas
Oþþæt eall hafað ældes leoma
Woruld-widles wom wælme forbærned·
Ðonne mihtig god on þone mæran beorg
Mid þy mæstan mægen-þrymme cymeð
Heofon-engla cyning halig scineð
Wuldorlic ofer weredum waldende god·
Ond hine ymb-utan æþel-duguð betast   1010
Halge here-feðan hlutre blicað
Eadig engla gedryht in-geþoncum
Forhte beofiað fore fæder egsan·
Forþon nis ænig wundor hu him woruld-monna
Seo unclæne gecynd cearum sorgende
Hearde ondrede ðonne sio halge gecynd
Hwit and heofon-beorht heag-engla mægen
For ðære onsyne beoð egsan afyrhte
Bidað beofiende beorhte gesceafte
Dryhtnes domes·   Daga eges-licast   1020
Weorþeð in worulde þonne wuldor-cyning
Þurh þrym þreað þeoda gehwylce
Hateð á-risan reord-berende
Of fold-grafum folc anra gehwylc
Cuman to gemote mon-cynnes gehwone·
Þonne eall hraðe adames cynn
          86

shall fiercely delve, and eagerly shall search,
the tracts of earth within and eke without,
until the fire's glow hath purged with heat
each blemish of the world's pollution.

    Then God Almighty, heavenly angels' King,
with greatest majesty shall thither come
to that noble hill; glorious o'er His hosts,
the Sovran Lord in holiness shall shine;
and, Him around, the goodliest chivalry,
the holy warrior-band, blessed angel-troop,
shall brightly gleam; in terror of the Father,
their inmost thoughts afeared, e'en they shall quake.
Yea, 'tis no wonder that the race unclean
of worldly men should sorely be adread,
should direfully lament, when the holy race,
so white and heavenly bright, the archangels' host,
before that Presence is with fear aghast;
trembling the radiant beings shall abide
their Sovran's doom. Most terrible of days
that day shall be, whenas the glorious King
shall mightily o'erwhelm the nations all,
and bid each folk, creatures with speech endowed,
arise from out their earthly sepulchres,
and come each man to that assemblage there.
Full quickly then shall Adam's kin take flesh;

Onfehð flæsce weorþeð fold-ræste
Eardes æt ende sceal þonne anra gehwylc
Fore cristes cyme cwic árisan
Leoðum onfon and lic-homan   1030
Ed-geong wesan hafað eall on him
Þæs þe he on foldan in fyrn-dagum
Godes oþþe gales on his gæste gehlód
Geara gongum·   Hafað æt-gædre bú
Líc and sawle·   Sceal on leoht cuman
Sinra weorca wlite and worda gemynd
And heortan gehygd fore heofona cyning·
Ðonne biþ geyced and geedniwad
Mon-cyn þurh meotud micel ariseð
Dryht-folc to dome siþþan deaþes bend   1040
To-leseð lif-fruma·   Lyft bið onbærned
Hreosað heofon-steorran hyþað wide
Gifre glede gæstas hweorfað
On ecne eard opene weorþað·
Ofer middan-geard·   Monna dæde
Ne magun hord wera heortan geþohtas
Fore waldende wihte bemiþan·
Ne sindon him dæda dyrne ac þær bið dryhtne cuð
On þam miclan dæge hu monna gehwylc
Ær earnode eces lifes   1050
And eall andweard þæt hi ær oþþe sið

their earthly rest and sojourning shall then
have end, for at Christ's advent thitherward
each mortal quickened shall arise again,
and shall take limb and fleshly covering,
and shall be young again, possessed of all,
that he, while here on earth, in former days,
in the course of years, did heap upon his soul,
of good or ill; both shall be joined again,
body and soul; the image of his works,
the memory of his words, the thoughts of his heart,
shall come to light before the heavenly King.
Mankind shall be increased then and renewed
by its Creator; a mighty multitude
shall rise to judgment, when the Source of life
shall loose the bonds of death; the sky shall glow,
the stars of heaven shall fall, the greedy flame
shall ravage far and wide; spirits shall wend
to their eternal home; the deeds of men
shall then be manifest throughout mid-earth.
The treasure-hoard of men, their hearts' deep thoughts,
nowise before the Sovran may be hid;
deeds are not dark to Him; on that great day
it shall be known unto the Lord how each
hath erewhile merited eternal life,
and all shall be revealed that each hath wrought,

Worhtun in worulde· Ne bi 㞋 þær wiht for-holen
Monna gehygda ac se mæra dæg
Hreþer-locena hord heortan geþohtas
Ealle ætywe 㞋· Ær sceal geþencan
Gæstes þearfe seþe gode mynte 㞋
Bringan beorhtne wlite þonne bryne costa 㞋
Hat heoru gifre hu gehealdne sind
Sawle wi 㞋 synnum fore sige-deman·
Ðonne sie byman stefen and se beorhta segn   1060
And þæt hate fýr and seo héa dugu 㞋
And se engla þrym and se egsan þrea
And se hearda dæg and seo hea ród
Ryht aræred rices to beacne
Folc-dryht wera biforan bonna 㞋
Sawla gehwylce þara þe si 㞋 oþþe ær
On lic-homan leoþum onfengen·
Ðonne weoroda mæst fore waldende
Ece and ed-geong andweard gæ 㞋
Neode and nyde bi noman gehatne   1070
Bera 㞋 breosta hord fore bearn godes
Feores frætwe wile fæder eahtan
Hu gesunde suna sawle bringen
Of þam e 㞋le þe hi on lifdon·
Ðonne beo 㞋 bealde þa þe beorhtne wlite
Meotude bringa 㞋 bi 㞋 hyra meaht and gefea

early or late, on earth ; nought shall be hid
of mortals' inmost thoughts, but that great day
shall there disclose the locked mind's treasury,
the meditations of men's hearts.   Erewhile
must he bethink him of his spirit's need,
who fain would bring to God an aspect fair,
when that devouring fire before the Judge
assayeth how souls have been restrained from sin.
Lo, then the trumpet's voice, the standard bright,
the glowing fire, the glorious chivalry,
the noble throng of angels, the pang of terror,
the day so stern, and the exalted rood,
rightwise raised up in sign of mastery,
shall summon forward all the hosts of men,
the souls of all that from eternal time
took limb within the body's covering.
A mighty host, deathless, with youth renewed,
shall pass before the Sovran's presence there
by dire compulsion forced, yea, called by name,
bearing before God's Child their bosom's hoard,
their spirit's treasures ; then will the Father see
how all unmarred His sons may bring their souls
e'en from that land wherein they lived erewhile.
They shall be bold that bring unto the Lord
an aspect fair ; blissful indeed shall be

Swiðe gesælig-lic sawlum to gielde
Wuldor-lean weorca· Wel is þam þe motun
On þa grimman tid gode lician·

III.

ÞÆR him sylfe geseoð sorga mæste
    Syn-fá men sarig-ferðe·
Ne bið him to are þæt þær fore ell-þeodum
Usses dryhtnes ród andweard stondeð
Beacna beorhtast blode bestemed
Heofon-cyninges hlutran dreore
Biseon mid swate þæt ofer side gesceaft
Scire scineð· Sceadu beoð bidyrned
Þær se leohta beam leodum byrhteð
Þæt þeah to teonum weorþeð
Þeodum to þrea þam þe þonc gode
Wom-wyrcende wita ne cuþun
Þæs he on þone halgan beam áhongen wæs
Fore mon-cynnes man-forwyrhtu·
Þær he leof-lice lifes ceapode
Þeoden mon-cynne on þam dæge
Mid þy weorðe þe nó wom dyde
His lic-homa leahtra firena
Mid þy usic alysde· Þæs he eft-lean wile

1080

1090

their might and joy, their souls' great recompence,
the glorious guerdon of their works.   Happy they,
who at that awful time are dear to God !

III.

But sin-stained mortals, sad in soul, shall see
their direfullest affliction there in this,—
not for their glory shall our Sovran's rood,
the brightest of all beacons, stand forth there
'fore all the tribes of earth, wet with the blood
of heaven's King, bedewed with His pure gore,
o'erflowing with His sweat, gleaming effulgent
o'er wide creation.   Shadow shall be scattered,
where'er the bright beam shineth forth for men ;
nathless shall it discomfort and torment
all those who, erewhile working wickedness,
knew not the thanks that due were unto God,
for that He hung upon the holy tree,
all for the base misdeeds of human kind.
There He, the Prince, whose body wrought no sin,
nor guilty was of any wicked deed,
sold His life lovingly upon that day,
for mankind's sake, e'en for the self-same price
wherewith He ransomed us.   For all this grace

Þurh eorneste ealles genomian

Ðonne sio reade ród ofer ealle 1100

Swegle scineð on þære sunnan gyld·

On þa forhtlice firenum fordone

Swearte syn-wyrcend sorgum wlitað.

Geseoð him to bealwe þæt him betst bicwom

Þær hy hit to gode ongietan woldan·

And eac þa ealdan wunde and þa openan dolg

On hyra dryhtne geseoð dreorig-ferðe

Swa him mid næglum þurh-drifan nið-hycgende

Þa hwitan honda and þa halgan fet

And of his sidan swa some swat forletan 1110

Þær blod and wæter butu æt-somne

Ut bicwoman fore eagna gesyhð

Rinnan fore rincum þa he on rode wæs·

Eall þis magon him sylfe geseon þonne

Open orgete þæt he for ælda lufan

Firen-fremmendra fela þrowade·

Magun leoda bearn leohte oncnawan

Hu hine lygnedon lease on geþoncum

Hysptun hearm-cwidum and on his hleor somod

Hyra spatl speowdon spræcon him edwit 1120

And on þone eadgan andwlitan swa some

Hel-fuse men hondum slogun

Folmum areahtum and fystum eac

94

sternly will He exact His payment then,
when the blood-red rood in the ethereal sky
shall brightly shine, where once the sun was wont.
Fearful and sorrowful shall they look thereon,
dark sinners damned by base iniquity;
the best thing in the world shall seem their bane,
when they would fain regard it as their bliss.
With souls a-weary shall they see withal
the ancient wounds and gashes on the Lord,
e'en as the base contrivers pierced with nails
the hands so white and eke the holy feet,
and from His side, too, let the gore pour forth,
and blood and water both at once, commingled,
came gushing forth before the people there,
before their eyes, while He was on the rood.
All this may they themselves there contemplate
open and manifest, how much He bore
for love of men, for wicked sinners' sake;
the sons of men may easily perceive
how they, false in their thoughts, belied Him then,
mocked Him with insult, and upon His face
e'en spat their spittle, spake to Him with taunt,
and on His blessed countenance withal
the hell-prone miscreants struck Him with their hands,
with their outstretched palms, and with their fists,

95

And ymb his heafod heardne gebigdon
Beag þyrnenne blinde on geþoncum
Dysge and gedwealde· Gesegun þa dumban gesceaft
Eorðan eal-grene and up-rodor
Forhte gefelan frean þrowinga
And mid cearum cwiðdun þeah hi cwice næron
Þa hyra scyppend sceaþan onfengon 1130
Syngum hondum· Sunne wearð adwæsced
Þream aþrysmed þa sio þeod geseah
In hierusalem godwebba cyst
Þæt ær ðam halgan huse sceolde
To weorþunga weorud sceawian
Ufan eall forbærst þæt hit on eorþan læg
On twam styccum þæs temples segl
Wundor-bleom geworht to wlite þæs huses
Sylf slat on tu swylce hit seaxes ecg
Scearp þurh-wode· Scire burstan 1140
Muras and stanas monge æfter foldan
And seo eorðe eac egsan myrde
Beofode on bearhtme and se brada sæ
Cyðde cræftes meaht and of clomme bræc
Up yrringa on eorþan fæðm·
Ge on stede scynum steorran forleton
Hyra swæsne wlite· On þa sylfan tid
Heofon hluttre ongeat hwa hine healice

and round about His head a cruel crown,
a crown of thorns they wreathed, blind in their thoughts,
foolish and erring.   They saw how dumb creation,
the earth all green, and the ethereal sky,
affrighted, felt the sufferings of the Lord;
how sorely mourned they, though they were not quick,
when impious men with sinful hands did seize
their very Maker!   The sun became obscured,
darkened with misery; and in Jerusalem
the people saw the choicest of all webs,
that multitudes were wont to marvel at,
the glory of the holy house of God,
they saw it rent, so that in pieces twain
it lay upon the earth; the temple's veil,
with wondrous colours wrought to deck that house,
was riven asunder, as a falchion's edge,
full sharp, had passed there-through.   Stone walls a-many,
throughout earth's tract, with headlong ruin fell;
and all the earth was troubled sore with fear,
and quaked with sudden shock; the spacious sea
showed forth its mighty power, and burst its bonds,
and o'er earth's bosom dashed in angry mood;
yea, in their radiant homes the stars then lost
their winsome beauty; at that self-same time
the heaven serene discerned who erst had made it

Torhtne getremede tungol-gimmum·

Forþon he his bodan sende þa wæs geboren ærest 1150

Gesceafta scir-cyning·   Hwæt eac scyldge men

Gesegon to soðe þy sylfan dæge

Þe on þrowade þeod-wundor micel

Þætte eorðe ageaf þa hyre on lægun·

Eft lifgende up ástodan

Þa þe heo ær fæste bifen hæfde

Deade bibyrgde þe dryhtnes bibod

Heoldon on hreþre·   Hell eac ongeat

Scyld-wreccende þæt se scyppend cwom

Waldende god þa heo þæt weorud ageaf 1160

Hloþe of þam hatan hreþre hyge wearð mongum blissad

Sawlum sorge to-glidene·   Hwæt eac sǽ cyðde

Hwa hine gesette on sidne grúnd

Tir-meahtig cyning forþon he hine tredne him

Ongean gyrede þonne god wolde

Ofer sine yðe gan eah-stream ne dorste

His frean fet flode bisencan·

Ge eac beamas onbudon hwa hy mid bledum sceop

Monge nales feá ða mihtig god

On hira anne gestag þær he earfeþu 1170

Geþolade fore þearfe þeod-buendra

Laðlicne deað leodum to helpe·

Ða wearð beam monig blodigum tearum

resplendent upon high with starry gems ;
forsooth it sent its heralds when was born
creation's noble King. E'en guilty men
beheld in very sooth on that same day,
whereon He suffered, a marvel passing great,—
to wit, earth yielded those who in her lay ;
then rose they up and living stood again,
whom she had erewhile held with firmest grip,
the dead and buried, who had kept in mind
their Lord's commands. Eke sin-avenging hell
knew that the Maker and the ruling God
was come, when it surrendered up that host
from her hot bosom ; blissful were many hearts,
grief vanished from their souls. Lo ! too, the sea
declared who set it on its spacious bed,—
the glorious King ; certes, it made a path
for Him to tread, when God desired to fare
o'er the ocean-waves ; the water durst not then
submerge its Master's feet with flowing tide.
Yea, many a tree, not few, likewise proclaimed
who shaped them with their blossoms, when mighty God
ascended one of them, where for the need
of earth's inhabitants He suffered pain,
a loathsome death, to succour human kind.
Beneath its bark full many a tree was then

Birunnen under rindum reade and þicce
Sæp wearð to swate· Þæt asecgan ne magun
Fold-buende þurh frod gewit
Hu fela þa onfundun þa gefelan ne magun
Dryhtnes þrowinga deade gesceafte·
Þa þe æþelast sind eorðan gecynda
And heofones eac heah-getimbro   1180
Eall fore þam anum unrot gewearð
Forht afongen· Þeah hi ferð-gewit
Of hyra æþelum ænig ne cuþen
Wendon swa þeah wundrum þa hyra waldend fór
Of lic-homan· Leode ne cuþan
Mod-blinde men meotud oncnawan
Flintum heardran þæt hi frea nerede
Fram hell-cwale halgum meahtum
Alwalda god þæt æt ærestan
Fore-þoncle men from fruman worulde   1190
Þurh wis gewit witgan dryhtnes
Halge hige-gleawe hæleþum sægdon
Oft nales æne ymb þæt æþele bearn
Ðæt se earcnan stan eallum sceolde
To hleo and to hroþer hæleþa cynne
Weorðan in worulde wuldres agend
Eades ord-fruma þurh þa æþelan cwenn·

suffused with tears of blood, all red and thick ;
their sap was turned to gore.   Earth's denizens,
however wise they be, cannot declare
how many things which feel not, insensate things,
experienced then the sufferings of their Lord.
The noblest of the species of the earth,
and eke the lofty structures upon high,
for that alone were seized with sudden fear,
and sad became ; in their inherent nature,
though they no mental understanding had,
yet wondrously they knew it, when their Lord
forth from His body fared.   Benighted men,
harder than flints, would not acknowledge then
their Maker, that the Lord, Almighty God,
had saved them from the agonies of hell,
e'en by His holy might, nor that of yore,
in the world's beginning, the prophets of the Lord,
far-seeing men, holy and wise of mind,
had told to folk anent the noble Child,
oft-times, not once, by wisdom of their souls,
that through the noble woman He should be
a precious Rock here in this world below,
the Refuge and the Help of all mankind,
the Lord of glory, the first Cause of bliss.

HWÆS weneð se þe mid gewitte nyle
    Gemunan þa mildan meotudes lare
And eal ða earfeðu þe he fore ældum adreag   1200
Forþon þe he wolde þæt we wuldres eard
In ecnesse agan mosten·
Swa þam bið grorne on þam grimman dæge
Domes þæs miclan þam þe dryhtnes sceal
Deað-firenum forden dolg sceawian
Wunde and wite on werigum sefan·
Geseoð sorga mæste hu se sylfa cyning
Mid sine lic-homan lysde of firenum
Þurh milde mod þæt hy mostun mán-weorca
Tome lifgan and tires blæd   1210
Ecne agan·   Hy þæs eðles þonc
Hyra waldende wita ne cuþon·
Forþon þær to teonum þa tacen geseoð
Orgeatu on gode ungesælge
Þonne crist siteð on his cyne-stole
On heah-setle heofon-mægna god
Fæder ælmihtig folca gehwylcum
Scyppend scinende scrifeð bi gewyrhtum
Eall æfter ryhte rodera waldend·

IV.

What hope hath he who wittingly disdaineth
to bear in mind his Master's gentle lore,
and all the miseries He endured for men,
wishful that we might possess on high,
to all eternity, the home of bliss?
Grievous indeed shall be their lot, who damned
by deadly sins must on that awful day
of mighty doom behold with souls a-weary
the gashes, wounds, and torments of the Lord;
greatest their woe to see how that the King
with His own body ransomed them from sin,
in meekness, so that they might live, devoid
of their ill-deeds, and have the endless bliss
of heavenly glory.   They did not know the thanks
due to their Sovran for this heritage;
wherefore, to their affliction, shall they see
signs unpropitious manifest in God,
when Christ shall sit there on His kingly throne,
on His high seat, while the Almighty Father,
the radiant Creator, Lord of the hosts
of heaven, prescribeth righteously withal
for every man according to his deeds.

Þónne beoð gesomnad on þa swiþran hond   1220
Þa clænan folc criste sylfum
Gecorene bi cystum þa ær sinne cwide georne
Lustum læstun on hyra lif-dagum·
Ond þær wom-sceaþan on þone wyrsan dæl
Fore scyppende scyrede weorþað·
Hateð him gewitan on þa winstran hond
Sigora soð-cyning synfulra weorud·
Þær hy arasade reotað and beofiað
Fore frean forhte·   Swa fule swa gæt
Unsyfre folc arna ne wenað·   1230
Ðonne bið gæsta dóm fore gode sceaden
Wera cneorissum swa hi geworhtun ær
Þær bið on eadgum eð gesyne
Þreo tacen somod þæs þe hi hyra þeodnes wel
Wordum and weorcum willan heoldon·
An is ærest orgeate þær
Þæt hy fore leodum leohte blicaþ
Blæde and byrhte ofer burga gesetu·
Him onscinað ær-gewyrhtu
On sylfra gehwam sunnan beorhtran·   1240
Oþer is to-eacan andgete swa some
Þæt hy him in wuldre witon waldendes giefe
And ónseoð eagum to wynne
Þæt hi on heofon-rice hlutru dreamas

Then shall be gathered on the right-hand side
of Christ Himself the cleanly multitude,
chosen for their virtues ; in their life-days
joyfully had they performed His word.
Workers of wickedness shall be disposed
before their Maker on the worser side ;
victory's true King shall bid the throng
of sinful mortals wend unto His left ;
discovered, shall they there bewail and quake,
afeard before the Lord ; as foul as goats,
an unpure folk, they may not hope for grace.
When the spirits' doom shall be decreed 'fore God
unto all generations as they wrought,
three signs shall then be plainly visible
at once upon the blessed, for they kept well
their Lord's behest, both by their words and works.
The first sign manifest shall be, to wit,
that they shall shine with light before the folk,
with bliss and brightness, throughout the homes on high ;
their former deeds shall shine upon them there,
upon each of them, e'en brighter than the sun.
Likewise a second sign shall be revealed,—
in glory shall they know their Sovran's grace,
and they shall see their eyes' delight therein,
that they, as saints, 'mid angels, are to own

Eadge mid englum agan motun·
Ðonne bi𝛿 þridde hu on þystra bealo
Þæt gesælige weorud gesih𝛿 þæt fordone
Sar þrowian synna to wite
Weallendne lig and wyrma wlite
Bitrum ceaflum byrnendra scole·

Of þam him áweaxe𝛿 wynsum geféa
Ðonne hi þæt yfel geseo𝛿 o𝛿re dreogan
Þæt hy þurh miltse meotudes genæson·
Ðónne hi þy geornor gode þoncia𝛿
Blædes and blissa þe hy bu geseo𝛿
Þæt he hy generede from ni𝛿-cwale
And eac forgeaf ece dreamas·
Bi𝛿 him hel bilocen heofon-rice agiefen·
Swa sceal gewrixled þam þe ær wel heoldon
Þurh mod-lufan meotudes willan·

Ðonne bi𝛿 þam oþrum ungelice
Willa geworden·   Magon weana to fela
Geseon on him selfum synne genoge
Atol earfo𝛿a ær gedenra·
Þær him sorgendum sar o𝛿clife𝛿
Þroht þeod-bealu on þreo healfa·
An is þara þæt hy him yrmþa to fela
Grim helle fýr gearo to wite
Andweard seo𝛿 on þam hi awo sculon

pure ecstasies in heaven's realm on high.
The third shall be, that in the baleful gloom
the blissful throng shall contemplate the damned
suffering in penance for their sins sore pain,
the surging flame and the bitter-biting jaws
of luring serpents,—a shoal of burning things;
thence winsome joy shall rise within their souls,
beholding other men endure the ills
that they escaped, through mercy of the Lord.
Then the more eagerly shall they thank God
for all their glory and delight, seeing
that He both saved them from these grievous pangs,
and granted unto them eternal joys;
hell shall be locked for them, heaven's realm vouchsafed.
This shall be their lot who erst kept well,
through their souls' love, the will of the Creator.

But all unlike, forsooth, shall be the plight
of the others; they shall see there in themselves
too many woes, a multitude of sins,
direst affliction for their former deeds;
sorrowing there, sore pain shall cleave to them,
anguish and bale, rising from sources three.
The first shall be, that 'fore them they shall see,
all ready for their torment, hell's grim fire,—
too base an ignominy; outcast there,

Wræc-winnende wærgðu dreogan·   1270

Þonne is him oþer earfeþu swa some

Scyldgum to sconde þæt hi þær scoma mæste

Dreogað fordone·   On him dryhten gesihð

Nales feara sum firen-bealu laðlic

And þæt æll-beorhte eac sceawiað

Heofon-engla here and hæleþa bearn

Ealle eorð-buend and atol deofol

Mircne mægen-cræft mán-womma gehwone·

Magon þurh þa lic-homan leahtra firene

Geseon on þam sawlum·   Beoð þa syngan flæsc 1280

Scandum þurh-waden swa þæt scire glæs

Þæt mon yþæst mæg eall þurh-wlitan·

Ðonne bið þæt þridde þearfendum sorg

Cwiþende cearo þæt hy on þa clænan seoð

Hu hi fore gód-dædum glade blissiað

Þa hy unsælge ær forhogdun

To donne þonne him dagas læstun·

And be hyra weorcum wepende sár

Þæt hi ær freolice fremedon unryht

Geseoð hi þa betran blæde scinan·   1290

Ne bið him hyra yrmðu an to wite

Ac þara oþerra ead to sorgum

Þæs þe hy swa fægre gefean on fyrn-dagum

And swa ænlice an-forletun

they shall endure damnation evermore.
Likewise a second woe shall put to shame
the guilty ; they shall endure the greatest contumely,
undone by sin ; the Lord shall see in them
loathsome transgressions, nowise a few,
and the radiant throng, the heavenly angel-host,
shall see the like, and eke the sons of men ;
all earth's inhabitants, and the fell devil,
shall see their darksome craft and every stain ;
through their bodies they shall see upon their souls
their shameful crimes ; abjectly the sinful flesh
shall be transparent, as it were clear glass,
that men most easily may see all through.
A third affliction shall the wretched know,
yea, dire lament, when they behold the pure,
how gladly they rejoice in the good deeds,
that they, unhappy ones, despised to do
erewhile, when still the days of life ran on ;
and weeping sore because of their own works
because they wrought unrighteousness before,
they shall behold their betters shine in glory.
Not merely their own misery shall be their bale ;
the bliss of those others shall increase their grief,
seeing how they in former days forsook
delights so fair and so incomparable

Þurh leaslice lices wynne
Earges flæsc-homan idelne lust·
Þær hi ascamode scondum gedreahte
Swiciaꝺ on swiman syn-byrþenne
Firen-weorc beraꝺ on þæt þa folc seoꝺ·
Wære him þon betre þæt hy bealo-dæde   1300
Ælces unryhtes ær gescomeden
Fore anum men eargra weorca
Godes bodan sægdon þæt hi to gyrne wiston
Firen-dæda on him·   Ne mæg þurh þæt flæsc se scrift
Geseon on þære sawle hwæþer him mon soꝺ þe lyge
Sagaꝺ on hine sylfne þonne he þa synne bigæꝺ·
Mæg mon swa þeah gelacnigan leahtra gehwylcne
Yfel unclæne gif he hit anum gesegꝺ
And nænig bihelan mæg on þam heardan dæge
Wom unbeted ꝺær hit þa weorud geseoꝺ·   1310
Eala þær we nu magon wraþe firene
Geseon on ussum sawlum synna wunde
Mid lic-homan leahtra gehygdu
Eagum unclæne in-geþoncas·
Ne þæt ænig mæg oþrum gesecgan
Mid hu micle elne æghwylc wille
Þurh ealle list lifes tiligan
Feores forhtlice forꝺ aꝺolian
Syn-rust þwean and hine sylfne þrean

for the body's vain and all-delusive joy,
and for the idle lust of the vile flesh.
There they abashed, o'erwhelmed with ignominy,
shall wander giddily, bearing their evil deeds,
the burden of their sins, whilst all folk gaze ;
'twere better for them had they erst felt shame
for each base deed and each transgression,
for all their evil works, before one man,
telling God's servant that too well they knew
ill-deeds within them.   The confessor cannot look
through the flesh unto the soul, whether a man
telleth truth or lie, when he his sins avoweth ;
nathless a wight can heal each noxious ill,
each unclean sin, if he tell it but to one ;
and none may there conceal, on that stern day,
guilt unamended ; multitudes shall see it.
Verily, we shall then, with bodily sight,
behold the wounds of sin upon our souls,
our base iniquities, our inmost thoughts
of wickedness, our unclean cogitations.
Not any man may tell it to another,
with how great zeal, by every artifice,
each mortal striveth to attain life's goal,
anxious to protract existence forth,
to wash sin's rust away, afflicting himself,

And þæt wom ærran wunde hælan   1320
Ðone lytlan fyrst þe her lifes sy
Ðæt he mæge fore eagum eorð-buendra
Unscomiende eðles mid monnum
Brucan bysmerleas þendan bu somod
Lic and sawle lifgan mote.

V.

NV we sceolon georne gleawlice þurh-seon
      Usse hreþer-cofan heortan eagum
Innan uncyste.   We mid þam oðrum ne magun   .
Heafod-gimmum hyge-þonces ferð
Eagum þurh-wlitan ænge þinga   1330
Hwæþer him yfel þe god under wunige
Ðæt he on þa grimman tid gode licie
Ðonne he ofer weoruda gehwylc wuldre scineð
Of his heah-setle hlutran lege·
Ðær he fore englum and fore elþeodum
To þam eadgestum ærest mæðleð
And him swæslice sibbe gehateð
Heofona heah-cyning halgan reorde
Frefreð he fægre and him friþ beodeð
Hateð hy gesunde and gesenade   1340
On eþel faran engla dreames

to heal the blemish of some former wound,
during the little span of life on earth,
so that before the eyes of all the world,
he may enjoy his home in the midst of men,
blameless and unabashed, as long as here
body and soul may both together dwell.

V.

Now, with the mind's eye, it behoveth us,
with wisdom, fain to pierce the bosom's case
unto the sin within,—with our other eyes,
the jewels of the head, we may no whit
survey the hidden home of inmost thought,
whether good or ill abide there in those depths,—
so that at that dread time God may be pleased,
when, from His lofty throne, with flame all-pure,
He shall shine in glory o'er the multitudes ;
and before angels and before all folks
He shall speak first unto the happiest there,
and lovingly shall promise them His grace ;
yea, with His holy voice, the Heaven's high King
shall gently comfort them, and grant them peace,
and He shall bid them then, all safe and blessed,
fare to the home of angels' harmony,

And þæs to widan feore willum neotan·

Onfo∂ nu mid freondum mines fæder rice

Þæt eow wæs ær woruldum wynlice gearo

Blæd mid blissum beorht e∂les wlite

Hwonne ge þa lif-welan mid þam leoſ[s]tum

Swase swegl-dreamas geseon mosten·

Ge þæs earnedon þa ge earme men

Woruld-þearfende willum onfengun

On mildum sefan· Ðonne hy him þurh minne noman 1350

Ea∂mode to eow arna bædun

Þonne ge hyra hulpon and him hleo∂ gefon

Hingrendum hlaf and hrægl nace dum

And þa þe on sare seoce lagun

Æf[n]don únsofte adle gebundne

To þam ge holdlice hyge staþeladon

Mid modes myne.   Eall ge þæt me dydon·

Ðonne ge hy mid sibbum sohtun and hyra sefan try-
   medon

For∂ on frofre·   Þæs ge fægre sceolon

Lean mid leofum lange brucan·   1360

Onginne∂ þonne to þam yflum ungelice

Wordum mæ∂lan þe him bi∂ on þa wynstran hond

Þurh egsan þrea alwalda god·

Ne þurfon hi þonne to.meotude miltse gewenan

Lifes ne lissa ac þær lean cuma∂

114

and joyously possess it evermore :—

' Receive ye now, 'mid friends, My Father's realm,
the blissful glories and the beauteous home,
dight winsomely for you, ere worlds were wrought,—
yours, when ye might behold, with the best beloved,
life's true wealth, the sweet delights of heaven.
This meed ye merited, when gladsomely,
with gentle cheer, ye welcomed needy men,
the wretched of the world ; when in My name
they humbly prayed you for compassion,
then helped ye them, and gave them sheltering,
bread to the hungry, garments to the naked,
and those that lay sick and in sorry pain,
suffering grievously, bound by disease,
their spirits ye sustained in kindly wise,
with loving hearts.   All this ye did for Me,
when ye in friendship sought them, and with comfort
ye stayed their souls ; wherefore ye shall in
     bliss
longtime enjoy reward with My beloved.'

Then will Almighty God, with other words,
with fearful threatening, begin to speak
unto the wicked, those upon His left.
They may not hope for pity from the Lord,
nor life nor grace ; reward for words and deeds

Werum bi gewyrhtum worda and dæda
Reord-berendum sceolon þone ryhtan dóm
Ænne geæfnan egsan fulne·
Bið þær seo miccle milts áfyrred
Þeod-buendum on þam dæge   1370
Þæs ælmihtigan þonne he yrringa
On þæt fræte folc firene stæleð
Laþum wordum hateð hyra lifes riht
Andweard ywan þæt he him ær forgeaf
Syngum to sælum·   Onginneð sylf cweðan
Swa he to anum sprece and hwæþre ealle mæneð
Firen-synnig folc frea ælmihtig·
Hwæt ic þec mon minum hondum
Ærest geworhte and þe andgiet sealde
Of lame ic þe leoþe gesette geaf ic ðe lifgendne gæst 1380
Arode þe ofer ealle gesceafte gedyde ic þæt þu onsyn
         hæfdest
Mæg-wlite me gelicne geaf ic þe eac meahta sped
Welan ofer wíd-londa gehwylc nysses þu wean ænigne
         dæl
Ðystra þæt þu þolian sceolde þu þæs þonc ne wisses·
Þa ic ðe swa scienne gesceapen hæfde
Wynlicne geworht and þe welan forgyfen
Þæt ðu mostes wealdan worulde gesceaftum
Ða ic þe on þa fægran foldan gesette
     116

shall come to all men there, creatures of speech,
according to their works ; they shall endure
the only righteous, though an awful, doom.
On that day then the great compassion
of the Omnipotent shall be afar
from earth's inhabitants, when wrathfully,
in angry words, He chargeth their misdeeds
on impious folk, and biddeth them there present
their life's account before Him, which erst He gave
to them, base sinners, for their bliss. The Sovran Lord
Himself shall speak as if He spake to one,
and nathless shall He mean all sinning folk :—

   'Lo, man ! with Mine own hands I fashioned thee
in the beginning, and wisdom granted thee ;
I formed thy limbs of clay ; I gave thee living soul ;
I honoured thee o'er all created things ; I
        wrought
thine aspect like to Mine ; I gave thee might,
wealth o'er each land ; of woe thou knewest
        nought,
nought of the gloom to come ; yet thankless thou.
When I had shapen thee thus beauteously,
had made thee comely, and had given thee power,
that thou mightst rule the creatures of the world,
when I had set thee in that fair domain,

To neotenne neorxna wonges
Beorhtne blæd-welan bleom scinende 1390
Ða þu lifes word læstan noldes
Ac min bibod bræce be þines bonan worde
Fæcnum feonde furþor hyrdes
Sceþþendum sceaþan þonne þinum scyppende·
Nu ic ða ealdan race anforlæte
Hu þu æt ærestan yfle gehogdes
Firen-weorcum forlure þæt ic ðe to fremum sealde
Ða ic þe goda swa fela forgiefen hæfde
And þe on þam eallum eades to lyt
Mode þuhte gif þu meahte sped 1400
Efen-micle gode agan ne moste·
Ða þu of þan gefean fremde wurde
Feondum to willan feor aworpen
Neorxna wonges wlite nyde sceoldes
Agiefan geomor-mod gæsta eþel
Earg and únrót eallum bidæled
Dugeþum and dreamum and þa bidrifen wurde
On þas þeostran weoruld þær þu þolades siþþan
Mægen-earfeþu micle stunde
Sâr and swar gewin and sweartne deað 1410
And æfter [h]ingonge hreosan sceoldes
Hean in helle helpendra leas·
Ða mec ongon hreowan þæt min hond-geweorc

the bright and blissful riches to enjoy
of Paradise, resplendent with its hues,
then wouldst thou not fulfil the word of Life,
but, at the word of thy Bane, didst break My bidding ;
a treacherous foe, a mischievous destroyer,
didst thou obey, rather than thy Creator.
Now will I let that ancient story pass,
how at the first thou didst so ill devise,
and didst lose by sin the grace I granted thee ;
when I had given thee all these goodly things,
nathless it seemed unto thy mind withal
too little bliss, if thou mightst not possess
fulness of power equally with God ;
then thou becamest, to thy foes' delight,
an alien to that joy, cast out afar ;
perforce then hadst thou sadly to forego
the charm of Paradise, the spirits' home,—
a craven wight and wretched, cut off from all
its blessings and its mirths ; then wast thou driven
into this gloomy world, where thou hast suffered,
from that time forth, so long, dire miseries,
pain and heavy toil and swarthy death,
doomed, after thy going hence, abased to fall
down into hell, with none to lend thee help.
Then did it rue Me that Mine handiwork

On feonda geweald feran sceolde
Mon-cynnes tuddor mán-cwealm seon
Sceolde uncuðne eard cunnian
Sare siþas þa ic sylf gestag
Maga in modor þeah wæs hyre mægden-had
Æghwæs onwalg·   Wearð ic áná geboren
Folcum to frofre mec mon folmum biwond   1420
Biþeahte mid þearfan wædum and mec þa on þeostre
    alegde
Biwundenne mid wonnum claþum hwæt ic þæt for
    worulde geþolade
Lytel þuhte ic leoda bearnum læg ic on heardum stane
Cild geong on crybbe mid þy ic þe wolde cwealm afyr-
    ran
Hat helle bealu þæt þu moste halig scinan
Eadig on þam ecan life forðon ic þæt earfeþe wónn·

VI.

ÆS me for mode ac ic on magu-geoguðe
    Yrmþu geæfnde arleas lic-sár
Þæt ic þurh þa wære þe gelic
And þu meahte minum weorþan   1430
Mæg-wlite gelic mane bidæled·
And fore monna lufan min þrowade

should pass into the power of the fiends,
that mankind's progeny should see dire pangs,
and should experience a loveless home,
sorry vicissitudes; then I descended
as a son unto his mother, yet was her maidenhood
wholly inviolate. I was born alone
for mankind's solace; with their hands they swathed Me,
wrapped Me in a poor man's weeds, laid Me in
  darkness,
swaddled in dusky clothes. Lo! this for the world I
  suffered;
little seemed I to the sons of men; on the hard stone I lay,
a young child in its crib, for that I would remove from
  thee
hell's torture and hot bale; that thou mightst shine as saint,
blessed in the life eternal, therefore I bore that pain.

VI.

'Twas not for pride that in My youth I bore
such wretchedness, such ignominious pain,
but that I might thereby be like to thee,
and that thou, freed from sin, mightst thus become
like to that human form of Mine so fair;
yea, for my love of men my head and face

Heafod hearm-slege hleor geþolade·
Oft and-lata arleasra spatl
Of muðe onfeng mán-fremmendra·
Swylce hi me geblendon bittre tosomne
Unswetne drync ecedes and geallan·
Ðonne ic fore folce onfeng feonda geniðlan
Fylgdon me mid firenum fæhþe ne rohtun
And mid sweopum slogun·   Ic þæt sar for ðe   1440
Þurh eaðmedu eall geþolade
Hosp and heard cwide·   Þa hi hwæsne beag
Ymb min heafod heardne gebygdon
Þream biþrycton se wæs of þornum geworht·
Ða ic wæs ahongen on heanne beam
Rode gefæstnad ða hi ricene
Mid spere of minre sidan swat ut-gotun
Dreor to foldan·   Þæt þu of deofles þurh þæt
Nyd-gewalde genered wurde
Ða ic womma leas wite þolade   1450
Yfel earfeþu oþþæt ic anne forlet
Of minum lic-homan lifgendne gæst·
Geseoð nu þa feorh-dolg þe gefremedun ær
On minum folmum and on fotum swa some
Þurh þa ic hongade hearde gefæstnad
Meaht hér eác geseon orgete nu gen
On minre sidan swatge wunde·

endured the suffering of their baleful strokes ;
oft on My visage spittle fell from mouths
of impious workers of iniquity ;
they mingled, too, for Me full bitterly
an unsweet drink of vinegar and gall ;
for mankind bore I then the wrath of foes ;
they followed Me with torments ; reckless in hate,
they struck Me with their scourges,—all that pain,
their scorn and cruel gibes, in humbleness
I bore for thee,—and round about My head
a bitter-biting crown they bent anon,
fiercely they pressed it on,—'twas wrought of thorns.
Then was I hanged upon a lofty tree,
and fastened to a rood ; with a spear there
from my side they poured out on to earth
My blood and gore.   That thou thereby shouldst be
delivered from the devil's tyranny,
all sinless suffered I this punishment,
this sore affliction, till from my body
the living spirit sent I forth alone.
See now the fatal wounds they made of yore
upon My palms and eke upon My feet,
by which I hung full firmly fastened there ;
here mayest thou see, too, manifest e'en yet,
the gory wound, the gash upon My side.

123

Hu þær wæs únefen racu unc gemæne·

Ic onfeng þin sár þæt þu moste gesælig

Mines eþel-rices eadig neotan   1460

And þe mine deaðe deore gebohte

Þæt longe lif þæt þu on leohte siþþan

Wlitig womma leas wunian mostes·

Læg min flæsc-homa in foldan bigrafen

Niþre gehyded se ðe nængum scód

In byrgenne þæt þu meahte beorhte uppe

On roderum wesan rice mid englum·

Forhwon forlete þú líf þæt scyne

Þæt ic þe for lufan mid mine lic-homan

Heanum to helpe hold gecypte·   1470

Wurde þu þæs gewitleas þæt þu waldende

Þinre alysnesse þonc ne wisses·

Ne ascige ic nú owiht bi þam bitran

Deaðe minum þe ic adreag fore þe·

Ac forgield me þin líf þæs þe ic iú þe mín

Þurh woruld-wite weorð gesealde·

Ðæs lifes ic manige þe þu mid leahtrum hafast

Ofslegen synlice sylfum to sconde·

Forhwan þu þæt sele-gescót þæt ic me swæs on þe

Gehalgode hús to wynne   1480

Þurh firen-lustas fule synne

Unsyfre bismite sylfes willum·

124

How unequal was the reckoning 'twixt us two !
. I there received thy pain that thou in bliss
mightst happily enjoy My native realm ;
and dearly by My death I bought for thee
long life, that thou mightst thenceforth evermore
dwell in the light, beauteous, void of sin.
My body's flesh, the which had harmed no man,
lay buried in the earth, hidden deep beneath,
down in its sepulchre, that thou mightst shine
mighty 'mid angels, in the skies above.
Wherefore didst thou forsake the beauteous life,
which graciously I bought for thee, in love,
with Mine own body, to help thee in thy plight ?
So witless wast thou, that thou didst not show
thanks to thy Lord for thy redemption.
Nought claim I now for that sore death of Mine,
so bitter, which I there endured for thee,
but render Me thy life, for which, in martyrdom,
I gave thee formerly Mine own as price.
I claim of thee the life thou hast so sinfully
destroyed to thine own shame, with base transgression.

Why hast thou wittingly with filth defiled,
through wicked lust and through foul sinfulness,
the tabernacle I sanctified in thee,
to be the cherished home of My delight ?

Ge þu þone lic-homan þe ic alysde me
Feondum of fæðme and þa him firene forbead
Scyld-wyrcende scondum gewemdest·
Forhwon áhenge þu mec hefgor on þinra honda rode
Ðonne íu hongade·   Hwæt me þeos heardra þynceð·
Nu is swærra mid mec þinra synna rod
Þe ic unwillum on beom gefæstnad
Ðonne seo oþer wæs þe ic ær gestag   1490
Willum minum þa mec þin weá swiþast
Æt heortan gehreaw þa ic þec from helle áteah
Ðær þu hit wolde sylfa siþþan gehealdan·
Ic wæs on worulde weadla þæt ðu wurde welig in
    heofonum
Earm ic wæs on eðle þinum þæt þu wurde eadig on
    minum·
Ða ðu þæs ealles ænigne þonc
Ðinum nergende nysses on mode·
Bibead ic eow þæt ge broþor mine
In woruld-rice wel aretten
Of þam æhtum þe ic eow on eorðan geaf   1500
Earmra hulpen earge ge þæt læstun·
Ðearfum forwyrndon þæt hi under eowrum þæce mosten
In-gebugan and him æghwæs oftugon
Ðùrh heardne hyge hrægles nacedum
Moses mete-leasum þeah hy him þurh minne noman

126

Yea, thou didst shamefully pollute with guilt
that body which I ransomed for Myself
from the grasp of foes, and then forbade it sin.
Why hast thou hanged Me worse on thy hands' cross
than when of old I hung ?   Methinks this harder ;
thy sins' cross is now heavier for Me,
on which I am bound fast, unwillingly,
than was that other which I erst ascended,
with Mine own will, whenas thy misery
rued Me so much at heart, when I drew thee from hell,
where thou thyself wouldst afterwards abide.
I in the world was poor, that thou in heaven mightst be
    rich,
wretched was I in thy world, that thou in Mine mightst
    blissful be.
But for all this thou knewest not in thy heart
the gratitude due to thy Saviour.
I bade that ye should cherish tenderly
My brethren throughout all the world's domain ;
with the wealth which I had granted you on earth
that ye should help the poor ; ill have ye done so ;
ye forbade the poor to enter 'neath your roof,
and ye withheld from them full everything,
in your hard hearts,—raiment from the naked,
food from the foodless ; though weary and infirm,

127

Werge wonhale wætan bædan
Drynces gedreahte duguþa lease
Þurste geþegede ge him þriste oftugon·
Sarge ge ne sohton ne him swæslic word
Frofre gespræcon þæt hy þy freoran hyge   1510
Mode gefengen·   Eall ge þæt me dydan
To hynþum heofon-cyninge·   Þæs ge sceolon hearde
    adreogan
Wite to widan ealdre wræc mid deoflum geþolian·
Ðonne þær ofer ealle egeslicne cwide
Sylf sigora weard sares fulne
Ofer þæt fæge folc forð forlæteð·
Cwið to þara synfulra sawla feþan·
Fa012ð nu awyrgde willum biscyrede·
Engla dreames on ece fír
Þæt wæs satane and his gesiþum mid   1520
Deofle gegearwad and þære deorcan scole
Hat and heoro-grim on þæt ge hreosan sceolan·
Ne magon hi þonne gehynan heofon-cyninges bibod
Rædum birofene sceolon raþe feallan
On grimne grund þa ær wiþ gode wunnon·
Bið þonne rices weard reþe and meahtig
Yrre and egesful.   Andweard ne mæg
On þissum fold-wege feond gebidan·

void of all sustenance, yearning for drink,
yea, parched with thirst, for water they entreated
in My name, yet harshly ye denied it them.
The sick ye sought not, nor spake a kindly word
of comfort unto them, that their hearts might win
a cheerful spirit.   All this ye did in scorn
of Me, heaven's King ; wherefore ye shall
      endure
torment for evermore, exile 'mid devils.'

   Then over all of them, over that fated folk,
the Lord of triumph shall Himself send forth
a dreadful edict, full of tribulation,
and to that host of sinful souls shall say :—
' Go now accursed, wilfully cut off
from angels' joy, into eternal fire,
which, hot and fiercely grim, was dight of yore
for the devil, Satan, and his comrades eke,
and all that swarthy shoal ; therein shall ye fall.'

   They may not then deride, bereft of rede,
the King's command ; they who erst warred 'gainst God
shall quickly fall into the grim abyss.
The Lord of empire shall be stern and mighty,
angry and fearful ; upon this track of earth
no foe may then abide before His face.

SWAPEÐ sige-mece mid þære swi[ð]ran hond
  Þæt on þæt deope dæl deofol gefeallað 1530
In sweartne leg synfulra here
Under foldan sceat fæge gæstas
On wraþra wic womfulra scolu
Werge to forwyrde on wite-hus
Deað-sele deofles·   Nales dryhtnes gemynd
Siþþan gesecað synne ne aspringað
Þær hi leahtrum fâ lege gebundne
Swylt þrowiað bið him syn-wracu
Andweard undyrne þæt is ece cwealm·
Ne mæg þæt hate dæl of heoloð-cynne   1540
In sin-nehte synne forbærnan
To widan feore wom of þære sawle·
Ac þær se deopa seað dreorge fedeð
Grundleas giemeð gæsta on þeostre
Æleð hy mid þy ealdan lige and mid þy egsan forste
Wraþum wyrmum and mid wita fela
Frecnum feorh-gomum folcum scendeð·
Þæt we magon eahtan and on ân cweðan
Soðe secgan þæt se sawle weard
Lifes wisdóm forloren hæbbe   1550
Se þe nú ne giemeð hwæþer his gæst sie

VII.

He shall sweep the victor-sword with His right hand,
that the devils shall fall down the deep abyss
into swart flame ; the bands of sinful ones
into earth's realm beneath ; the fated spirits
into the camp of foes ; the guilty shoal,
damned to perdition, into the prison-house,
the devil's death-hall.   Ne'er shall they seek again
remembrance of the Lord, nor 'scape their sins,
but, crime-stained, they shall there, bewrapt with flame
endure destruction ; vengeance for their sins
shall they see revealed ; that is eternal death ;
through all the livelong night the fiery gulf
may ne'er avail to purge their sins away
from that hell-race, the stain from off their soul.
But the deep pit feedeth still the weary ones ;
bottomless it keepeth the spirits in its gloom ;
with its old flame it burneth them ; and with terrors chill,
with hateful serpents, and with torments many,
with sharp and deadly jaws, it scatheth folk.
Wherefore we may believe and aye declare,
soothly affirm, that that soul's guardian
hath wholly lost the wisdom of this life,
who heedeth not now whether his spirit shall be

Earm þe eadig þær he ece sceal
Æfter hin-gonge hamfæst wesan·
Ne bisorgað he synne to fremman
Wonhydig mon ne he wihte hafað
Hreowe on mode þæt him halig gæst
Losige þurh leahtras on þas lænan tid·
Ðonne man-sceaða fore meotude forht
Deorc on þam dome standeð and deaðe fáh
Wommum awyrged bið se wær-loga   1560
Fyres afylled feores únwyrðe
Egsan geþread andweard gode·
Won and wliteleas hafað werges bleo
Facen-tacen feores·   Ðonne firena bearn
Tearum geotað þonne þæs tid ne biþ
Synne cwiþað ac hy to sið doð
Gæstum helpe ðonne þæs giman nele
Weoruda waldend hu þa wom-sceaþan
Hyra eald-gestreon on þa openan tíd
Sare greten·   Ne biþ þæt sorga tíd   1570
Leodum alyfed þæt þær læcedóm
Findan mote se þe nu his feore nyle
Hælo strynan þenden her leofað·
Ne bið þær ængum godum gnorn ætywed
Ne nængum yflum wel ac þær æghwæþer
Anfealde gewyrht andweard wigeð·

wretched or happy, where, after its going hence,
it shall be resident eternally.
He dreadeth nowise sin to perpetrate,
thoughtless man! nor hath he aught of ruth
within his heart, e'en though his holy spirit
perish, in this fading time, through guilt.
When the evil-doer, afeared before his Maker,
at the judgment standeth, black and foul with death,
accursed with crime, then shall the treacherous wight
of life unworthy, be fulfilled of fire,
and overwhelmed with terror before God;
sightless and swart, he shall have a felon's hue,
the token of a life of perfidy.   The sons of men
shall then shed tears and shall bewail their sins,
when time availeth not; too late shall they devise
help for their spirits, when the Lord of hosts
will not give heed how base transgressors there,
so sorely, at that all-disclosing time,
deplore what erst they cherished; that time of sorrowing
will not avail that he who will not now
gain life's salvation, while he liveth here,
may there find out the healing remedy.
No grief to any good man shall there be known,
nor joy to any evil; but there each one
shall bear before God's sight his own desert.

Forðon sceal onettan se þe ágan wile
Lif æt meotude, þenden him leoht and gæst
Somod-fæst seon· He his sawle wlite
Georne bigonge on godes willan   1580
And þær weorðe worda and dæda
Þeawa and geþonca þenden him þeos woruld
Sceadum scriþende scinan mote
Þæt he ne forleose on þas lænan tid
His dreames blæd and his dagena rim
And his weorces wlite and wuldres lean
Þætte heofones cyning on þa halgan tid
Soðfæst syleð to sigor-leanum
Þam þe him on gæstum georne hyrað·
Þonne heofon and hel hæleþa bearnum   1590
Fira feorum fylde weorþeð
Grundas swelgað godes andsacan
Lacende leg laðwende men
Þreað þeod-sceaþan and no þonan lætað
On gefean faran to feorh-nere·
Ac se bryne bindeð bid-fæstne here
Feoð firena bearn· Frecne me þinceð
Þæt þas gæst-berend giman nellað
Men on mode þonne mán hwæt
Him se waldend to wrace gesette   1600
Laþum leodum· Þonne lif and deað

134

Lo, eager must he be, while light and life
hold fast together, who wisheth to possess
life from his Maker; let him foster zealously
the beauty of his soul, after God's will;
let him be wary in his words and works,
his habits and his thoughts, while this world here,
speeding with mystic shadows, may still shine for him,
so that he lose not in this fading time
the blossom of his joy, the number of his days,
the beauty of his work, and glory's recompense,
which heaven's righteous King dispenseth then,
at that holy time, as the rewards of victory,
to those who fain, with all their soul, obey Him.
All heaven and hell shall then become fulfilled
with the sons of men, with the souls of mortal men;
the abyss shall gorge the adversaries of God;
the flickering flame shall harass erring folk,
workers of injury, and shall not let them thence
depart in joy unto security;
the fire shall keep that host immovable;
it shall vex mankind. Foolhardy me thinketh it,
that men, creatures with soul endowed, will not
be heedful in their minds, since that their Sovran
may put, in vengeance, upon hateful folk
any evil whatsoe'er. When life and death

Sawlum swelgað bið susla hús
Open and oðeawed að-logum ongean
Ðæt sceolon fyllan firen-georne men
Sweartum sawlum· Þonne synna wracu
Scyldigra scolu ascyred weorþeð
Heane from halgum on hearm-cwale·
Ðær sceolan þeofas and þeod-sceaþan
Lease and forlegene lifes ne wenan
And mân-sworan mo[r]þor-lean seon   1610
Heard and heoro-grim þonne hel nimeð
Wærleasra weorud and hi waldend giefeð
Feondum in forwyrd fã þrowiað
Ealdor-bealu egeslic earm bið se þe wile
Firenum gewyrcan þæt he fâh scyle
From his scyppende ascyred weorðan
Æt dóm-dæge to deaðe niþer
Under helle cinn in þæt hate fyr
Under liges locan þær hy leomu ræcað
To bindenne and to bærnenne   1620
And to swingenne synna to wite·
Ðonne halig gæst helle biluceð
Morþer-husa mæst þurh meaht godes
Fyres fulle and feonda here
Cyninges worde· Se bið cwealma mæst
Deofla and monna· Ðæt is dreamleas hús·

shall gain their share of souls, the house of torment
shall be full manifest to perjurers' sight ;
sin-loving men, with swarthy souls, shall fill it.
Then, in retribution for their sins,
the shoal of guilty ones shall be disparted,
the base from the holy, unto pernicious death ;
there thieves, and such as wrought cruel injury,
liars and adulterers, shall have no hope of life ;
and the forsworn shall see their crimes' reward,
grievous and fiercely grim ; then hell shall take
the host of faithless ones ; the Lord shall give them
in perdition to the fiends ; sinners shall endure
dire racking agony ; wretched shall he be
who fain doth wickedly ; as a guilty wretch
upon that judgment-day shall he be severed
from his Creator, doomed to the death below,
among hell's race, adown in the hot fire,
'neath the barriers of flame ; there shall men stretch
their limbs, to be bound and to be burnt anon,
and to be scourged, in punishment for sin.

    Then the Holy Spirit, through the might of God,
at the King's command, shall lock the gates of hell,
the worst of torture-houses, full of fire,
with the host of fiends therein ; for devils and for men
this torment shall be direst.   That is a joyless home ;

Ðær ænig ne mæg ower losian
Caldan clommum hy bræcon cyninges word
Beorht boca bibod forþon hy abidan sceolon
In sin-nehte sar ende-leas   1630
Firen-dædum fâ forð þrowian
Ða þe her [for-]hogdun heofon-rices þrym·
Þonne þa gecorenan fore crist berað
Beorhte frætwe hyra blæd leofað
Æt dom-dæge agan dream mid gode
Liþes lifes þæs þe alyfed biþ
Haligra gehwam on heofon-rice·
Ðæt is se eþel þe no geendad weorþeð
Ac þær symle forð synna lease
Dream weardiað dryhten lofiað   1640
Leofne lifes weard leohte biwundne
Sibbum bisweðede sorgum biwerede
Dreamum gedyrde dryhtne gelyfde
Awa to ealdre engla gemanan
Brucað mid blisse beorhte mid lisse
Freogað folces weard fæder ealra
Geweald hafað and healdeð haligra weorud·
Ðær is engla song eadigra blis
Þær is seo dyre dryhtnes onsien
Eallum þam gesælgum sunnan leohtra   1650
Ðær is leofra lufu líf butan ende-deaðe

no one may evermore escape from thence,
from those cold bonds; they broke their King's command,
the Scriptures' bright behests; they must abide
the livelong night, and, stained with wicked deeds,
thenceforth must they endure pain without end,
who here despised the bliss of heaven's realm.

   Then shall the chosen carry before Christ
resplendent treasures; their happiness shall live;
with God, at doomsday, shall they have the joy
of life serene, for it shall be vouchsafed
to every holy man in heaven's realm.
That is the home that never shall know end,
but there the sinless henceforth evermore
shall hold their joyous mirth, and praise the Lord,
their life's dear Guardian; there, begirt with light,
bewrapt in peace, shielded from sorrowing,
glorified by joy, endeared unto the Lord,
radiant with grace, shall they for evermore
enjoy in bliss the angels' fellowship,
and cherish mankind's Guardian, Father of all,
Sovran Preserver of the holy hosts.

   There is angels' song; the bliss of the happy;
there is the gracious presence of the Lord,
brighter than the sun, for all the blessed ones;
there is the love of the beloved; life without death's end;

Glæd gumena weorud gioguð butan ylde
Heofon-duguða þrym hælu butan sare
Ryht-fremmendum ræst butan gewinne
Dóm-eadigra dæg butan þeostrum
Beorht blædes full blis butan sorgum
Frið freondum bitweon forð butan æfestum
Gesælgum on swegle sib butan niþe
Halgum on gemonge· Nis þær hungor ne þurst
Slæp ne swár leger ne sunnan bryne   1660
Ne cyle ne cearo ac þær cyninges giefe
Awo brucað eadigra gedryht
Weoruda wlite-scynast wuldres mid dryhten·

a gladsome host of men ; youth without age ;
the glory of the heavenly chivalry ; health without pain
for righteous workers ; and for souls sublime
rest without toil ; there is day without dark gloom,
ever gloriously bright ; bliss without bale ;
friendship 'twixt friends for ever without feud ;
peace without enmity for the blest in heaven,
in the communion of saints.   Hunger is not there nor thirst,
sleep, nor grievous sickness ; nor sun's heat,
nor cold, nor care ; but there that blissful band,
the fairest of all hosts, shall aye enjoy
their Sovran's grace, and glory with their King.

APPENDIX

I. SAINT GUTHLAC.

[? Christ, ll. 1664-1692.]

SE BIÐ GEFEANA FÆGRAST þonne hy
æt frymðe gemetað
engel and seo eadge sawl ofgiefeþ hio þas
eorþan wynne
forlæteð þas lænan dreamas and hio wiþ ham lice
gedæleð.
Ðonne cwið se engel hafað yldran hád
greteð gæst oþerne abeodeð him godes ærende·
Nu þu most feran þider þu fundadest
longe and gelome·   Ic þec lædan sceal·
wegas þe sindon weþe and wuldres leoht
torht ontyned·   Eart nu tid-fara
to þam halgan hám þær næfre hreow cymeð   10
eder-gong fore yrmþum ac þær biþ engla dream
sib and gesælignes and sawla ræst
and þær á to feore gefeon motun
dryman mid dryhten þa þe his domas her
æfnað on eorþan·   He him ece lean
healdeð on heofonum þær se hyhsta ealra

144

I. SAINT GUTHLAC.

*That shall be the fairest of joys, when they at first shall
    meet,*
the angel and the happy soul, when it resigneth the joys of earth,
forsaketh these frail delights, and from the body shall depart.
Then shall the angel speak, (his the more exalted state,)
*one spirit shall greet the other, and announce to it God's
    errand :—*
    ' Now thou mayst depart whither thou wast yearning
longtime and often ; I am to lead thee ;
the ways shall be pleasant for thee, and the glory's bright light
shall be revealed ; thou art now a traveller
unto that holy home where sorrow never cometh,
the refuge from affliction ; but there is angels' harmony,
goodwill and happiness and souls' repose ;
and there for evermore may they rejoice
and revel with the Lord, who here, on earth,
fulfil his judgments ; He holdeth for them, in heaven,
eternal recompense ; over the cities there,

K   145

yn i nga cyning ceastrum wealdeð·

Ðæt sind þa getimbru þe no tydriað

ne þam fore yrmþum þe þær in-wuniað

lif aspringeð ac him bið lenge hu sel   20

geoguþe brucað and godes miltsa·

Þider soðfæstra sawla motun

cuman æfter cwealme þa þe ær cristes æ

lærað and læstað and his lof rærað·

oferwinnað þa awyrgdan gæstas bigytað him wuldres
    ræste

hwider sceal þæs monnes mod astigan

ær oþþe æfter þonne he his ænne her

gæst bigonge þæt se gode mote   30

womma clæne in geweald cuman·

the most high, the King of kings, holdeth sway.
These are the structures which do not decay,
nor, through misery, shall life fail those
who dwell therein, but the longer the better it shall be for
    them ;
youth shall they enjoy and the grace of God.
Thither, after death, the souls of righteous men
may come, who erewhile teach and do
the law of Christ and raise on high His praise ;
they shall o'ercome the cursed sprites and gain that glorious
    rest,
whither, sooner or later, the spirit of each man
shall rise, whenas he cherisheth
his one soul here, that it may come
to God's dominion, clean of blemishes.'

II. HOMILIA IN ASCENSIONE DOMINI.

(Cp. passus secundus.)

(§ 9.) Hoc autem nobis primum quærendum est, quidnam fit quod nato Domino apparuerunt Angeli, et tamen non leguntur in albis vestibus apparuisse : ascendente autem Domino missi Angeli in albis leguntur vestibus apparuisse. Sic etenim scriptum est : *Videntibus illis elevatus est, et nubes suscepit eum ab oculis eorum. Cumque intuerentur in cœlum euntem illum, ecce duo viri steterunt juxta illos in vestibus albis.* In albis autem vestibus gaudium et solemnitas mentis ostenditur. Quid est ergo quod nato Domino, non in albis vestibus ; ascendente autem Domino, in albis vestibus Angeli apparent : nisi quod tunc magna solemnitas Angelis facta est, cum cœlum Deus homo penetravit? Quia nascente Domino videbatur divinitas humiliata : ascendente vero Domino, est humanitas exaltata. Albæ etenim vestes exaltationi magis congruunt quam humiliationi. In assumtione ergo ejus Angeli in albis vestibus videri debuerunt : quia qui in nativitate sua apparuit Deus humilis, in Ascensione sua ostensus est homo sublimis.

(§ 10.) Sed hoc nobis magnopere, fratres carissimi, in hac solemnitate pensandum est : quia deletum est hodierna die chirographum damnationis nostræ, mutata est sententia corruptionis nostræ. Illa enim natura cui dictum est : *Terra es, et in terram ibis,* hodie in cœlum ivit. Pro hac ipsa namque carnis nostræ sublevatione per figuram beatus Job Dominum avem vocat. Quia enim Ascensionis ejus mysterium Judæam non intelligere conspexit, de infidelitate ejus sententiam protulit, dicens : *Semitam ignoravit avis.* Avis enim recte appelatus est

148

Dominus; quia corpus carneum ad æthera libravit. Cujus avis semitam ignoravit quisquis eum ad cœlum ascendisse non credidit. De hac solemnitate per Psalmistam dicitur: *Elevata* Psal. vi *est magnificentia tua super cælos.* De hac rursus ait: *Ascendit* Psal. x: *Deus in jubilatione, et Dominus in voce tubæ.* De hac iterum dicit: *Ascendens in altum, captivam duxit captivitatem, dedit dona* Psal. l: *hominibus.* Ascendens quippe in altum, captivam duxit captivitatem: quia corruptionem nostram virtute suæ incorruptionis absorbuit. Dedit vero dona hominibus; quia misso desuper Spiritu, alii sermonem sapientiæ, alii sermonem scientiæ, alii 1 Cor. gratiam virtutum, alii gratiam curationum, alii genera linguarum, alii interpretationem tribuit sermonum. Dedit ergo dona hominibus. De hac Ascensionis ejus gloria etiam Habacuc ait: *Elevatus est sol, luna stetit in ordine suo.* Quis enim solis nomine Habac. nisi Dominus, et quæ lunæ nomine nisi ecclesia designatur? Quousque enim Dominus ascendit ad cælos, sancta ejus Ecclesia adversa mundi omnimodo formidavit: at postquam ejus Ascensione roborata est, aperte prædicavit, quod occulte credidit. Elevatus est ergo sol, et luna stetit in ordine suo: quia cum Dominus cœlum petiit, sancta ejus Ecclesia in auctoritate prædicationis excrevit. Hinc ejusdem Ecclesiæ voce per Salomonem dicitur: *Ecce iste venit saliens in montibus, et tran-* Cant. ii *siliens colles.* Consideravit namque tantorum operum culmina, et ait: *Ecce iste venit saliens in montibus.* Veniendo quippe ad redemtionem nostram, quosdam, ut ita dixerim, saltus dedit. Vultis, fratres carissimi, ipsos ejus saltus agnoscere? De cœlo venit in uterum, de utero venit in præsepe, de præsepe venit in crucem, de cruce venit in sepulcrum, de sepulcro rediit in cœlum. Ecce ut nos post se currere faceret, quosdam pro nobis

149

saltus manifestata per carnem veritas dedit : quia *exultavit ut gigas ad currendam viam suam,* ut nos ei diceremus ex corde :

Trahe nos post te, curremus in odorem unguentorum tuorum.

(§ 11.) Unde, fratres carissimi, oportet ut illuc sequamur corde, ubi eum corpore ascendisse credimus. Desideria terrena fugiamus, nihil nos jam delectet in infimis, qui patrem habemus in cœlis. Et hoc nobis est magnopere perpendendum : quia is qui placidus ascendit, terribilis redibit : et quidquid nobis cum mansuetudine præcepit, hoc a nobis cum districtione exiget. Nemo ergo indulta pœnitentiæ tempora parvipendat : nemo curam sui, dum valet, agere negligat : quia Redemtor noster tanto tunc in judicium districtior veniet, quanto nobis ante judicium magnam patientiam prærogavit. Hæc itaque vobiscum, fratres, agite : hæc in mente sedula cogitatione versate. Quamvis adhuc rerum perturbationibus animus fluctuet : jam tamen spei vestræ anchoram in æternam patriam figite, intentionem mentis in vera luce solidate. Ecce ad cœlum ascendisse Dominum audivimus. Hoc ergo servemus in meditatione, quod credimus. Et si adhuc hic tenemur infirmitate corporis, sequamur tamen eum passibus amoris. Non autem deserit desiderium nostrum ipse qui dedit, Jesus Christus Dominus noster, qui vivit et regnat cum Deo Patre in unitate Spiritus Sancti Deus, per omnia secula seculorum. Amen.

[Sancti Gregorii Magni xl Homiliarum in
Evangelia Lib. ii., Homil. xxix.]

III. HYMNUS DE DIE IUDICII.

(*Cf. Passus Tertius.*)

Apparebit repentina dies magna domini,
Fur obscura velut nocte improvisos occupans.

Brevis totus tum parebit prisci luxus saeculi,
Totum simul cum clarebit praeterisse saeculum.

Clangor tubae per quaternas terrae plagas concinens,
Vivos una mortuosque Christo ciet obviam.

De coelesti iudex arce, maiestate fulgidus
Claris angelorum choris comitatus aderit:

Erubescet orbis lunae, sol et obscurabitur,
Stellae cadent pallescentes, mundi tremet ambitus

Flamma, ignis anteibit iusti vultum iudicis,
Coelos, terras et profundi fluctus ponti decorans.

Gloriosus in sublimi rex sedebit solio,
Angelorum tremebunda circumstabunt agmina.

Huius omnes ad electi colligentur dexteram,
Pravi pavent a sinistris hoedi velut foetidi:

Ite, dixit rex ad dextros, regnum coeli sumite,
Pater vobis quod paravit ante omne saeculum;

Karitate qui fraterna me iuvistis pauperem,
Karitatis nunc mercedem reportate divites.

Laeti dicent : quando, Christe, pauperem te vidimus,
Te, rex magne, vel egentem miserati iuvimus :

Magnus illis dicet iudex : cum iuvistis pauperes,
Panem, domum, vestem dantes, me iuvistis humiles.

Nec tardabit et sinistris loqui iustus arbiter :
In gehennae maledicti flammas hinc discedite ;

Obsecrantem me audire despexistis mendicum,
Nudo vestem non dedistis, neglexistis languidum.

Peccatores dicent : Christe, quando te vel pauperem,
Te, rex magne, vel infirmum contemnentes sprevimus.

Quibus contra iudex altus : mendicanti quamdiu
Opem ferre despexistis, me sprevistis improbi.

Retro ruent tum iniusti ignes in perpetuos,
Vermis quorum non morietur, flamma nec restinguitur,

Satan atro cum ministris quo tenetur carcere,
Fletus ubi mugitusque, strident omnes dentibus.

Tunc fideles ad coelestem sustollentur patriam,
Choros inter angelorum regni petent gaudia,

Urbis summae Hirusalem introibunt gloriam
Vera lucis atque pacis in qua fulget visio.

XPM. regem iam paterna claritate splendidum
Ubi celsa beatorum contemplantur agmina—

Ydri fraudes ergo cave, infirmentes subleva,
Aurum temne, fuge luxus si vis astra petere.

Zona clara castitatis lumbos nunc praecingere,
In occursum magni regis fer ardentes lampades.

IV. HOMILIA IN DIE EPIPHANIÆ.

(*Cf.* ll. 1126—1190.)

(§ 2.) Omnia quippe elementa auctorem suum venisse testata sunt. Ut enim de eis quiddam usu humano loquar : Deum hunc cæli esse cognoverunt, quia sub plantis ejus se calcabile præbuit. Terra cognovit, quia eo moriente contremuit. Sol cognovit, quia lucis suæ radios abscondit. Saxa et parietes cognoverunt, quia tempore mortis ejus scissa sunt. Infernus agnovit, quia hos quos tenebat mortuos, reddidit. Et tamen hunc, quem Dominum omnia insensiblia elementa senserunt, adhuc infidelium Judæorum corda Deum esse minime cognoscunt, et duriora saxis, scindi, ad pœnitendum nolunt : eumque confiteri abnegant, quem elementa, ut diximus, aut signis aut scissionibus Deum clamabant.—(In Evang. Lib. 1. Homilia x.)

CRITICAL NOTES

CRITICAL NOTES.

PART I.

1. It must be borne in mind that the 'Christ' is a fragment; the beginning of the poem is lost; of the missing part a single word still remains, viz., *cyninge* (*i.e.* 'to the king'); this is the first word in the Exeter MS.; I have purposely omitted it, so as to give the appearance of completeness to the poem, but there is no authority for the capital letters. The first words of the MS. run as follows :—

cyninge · ðu eart se weall stan, etc.

1-4. cf. Matthew xxi. 42; Ephes. ii. 20-22; iv. 15, etc.

3. *heafod*, MS. *heafoð*.

6. *b[yri]g*, the *g* is just visible in the MS.; after *b* there is what I take to be the upper part of a curved *y* still traceable, resembling in shape an *o* (certainly not *u*); the letters *ri* are conjectural.

eagna, originally *-nan*; the erased *n* is still visible.

9. *forlæt*, MS. *forlęt*.

11. *cræftga*, MS. *cræstga*.

12-14. cp. Amos ix. 11; Acts xv. 16.

13. *hra* can hardly be read, owing to the action of some liquid, which has almost obliterated a number of words on this and the next page of the MS.

15. cp. Luke i. 71.

17. *þu reccend*, MS. *þa*.

19. *eadga*, after *ga*, which comes at the end of the line in the MS., a small piece of parchment has been cut out; one letter at

157

most could have been written on it; I am inclined to think that *eadga* is what the poet wrote; Grein reads—

> '*eadgað us siges, oðrum forwyrneð,*
> *wlitigan wilsiðes . . .*'

20. *wilsiþes*, the last two letters can scarcely be read, the whole word is barely visible.

22. [*Nu gemærsi*]*giað*, five or six letters are obliterated before *-giað*; the reading in the text is purely conjectural; Gr. suggests [*modgeomre halsi*]*giað*, but the space in the MS. renders the reading impossible.

23. *hete . . . ceose*, two or three letters are obliterated before *ceose*; the first of the missing letters was probably *h*, judging by the alliterative requirements of the line; *her* (*i.e.* 'here,' or 'now') should, perhaps, be supplied. Gr., ignoring the fact that the want of an alliterative word in the second half of the line is due to the obliteration of letters before *ceose*, suggested *héose* for *ceose*, formulating an A. S. *héosan*, 'festinare'; later (Germania, 1865), he withdrew this suggestion in favour of [*heo*]*fe* (*i.e.* 'with lamentation').

I cannot detect, as Schipper seems to have been able to do in 1870, (*v.* Germania, 1874,) any trace of the reading *to hofe* before *ceose*; he adds, 'das MS. ist hier jedoch schwer leserlich.'

25. *wil-sið*, *l-s* almost obliterated in MS. but *ið* quite legible; Grein's suggestion *wyrnde*, (Germania, 1865,) is therefore untenable; it would be best, perhaps, to take *hwonne* as directly dependent on *sorgende*, 'yearning for the time when.'

29. *þe he to wuldre forlet*, 'whom he hath admitted to glory.'

30. *we*, MS. *þe*.   32. *se þe*, hardly legible in MS.

41. *geond-spreot*, so MS.; Gr. *geondspreat*.

46. *ryne gemiclað*, lit. 'enlargeth the course,' *i.e.* 'hasteneth the progress.'   48. *ho*[*r*]*scne*, MS. *hoscne*.

68. *geneðde*, so MS.; Gr. *genedde* (*i.e.* pp. of *genédan*); but the MS. reading is obviously correct; *geneðan* = 'to venture,' 'to strive.' Thorpe was similarly troubled by the line, and suggested that a leaf was wanting after *nearo*.

69. *hu*, so MS.; Gr. *nu*.

76. *mod*, so MS.; Gr. emends to *môt*; but *mod* was often used

in A. S. with special reference to human passions and desires, and might well be rendered by 'desire' in this passage.

90. *solimæ*, MS. *solimę*.

92. *mund minne*, so MS. ; Th. *inne*.

mund; cp. Icel. *mundr*, 'the money paid by the bridegroom to the father of the bride,' also 'the bridegroom's gift to the bride'; this is seemingly the only recorded instance of the word in A. S. literature, here evidently used metaphorically. It must be carefully distinguished from *mund*, 'hand,' 'protection,' which is feminine, though ultimately the words may be connected.

97. *wærgða*, so MS. ; Gr. *wærgðu*.

103. *earendel*, it is difficult to translate the word adequately; some bright star is evidently meant, probably the same as *Örvandels-tá*, 'Orwendel's toe,' mentioned in the Edda. Thor carried Orwendel from Jotunheim in a basket on his back; Orwendel's toe stuck out of the basket, and got frozen; Thor broke it off, and flung it at the sky, and made a star of it, which is called *Örvandels-tá*; (*v.* Grimm's *Deutsche Myth*). That the story of Orwendel was Christianised in mediæval times is attested by the German story of *Orendel* in the *Heldenbuch*, where the hero wins 'the seamless coat' of his master. 'Earendel' does not occur elsewhere in A. S. poetry as a poetical designation of Christ; the word is interpreted in the Epinal glossary by 'jubar.'

The spelling in the Erfurt Gloss ' oerendil ' is noteworthy. It seems probable that ' Earendel '=Orion,' the constellation brightest at winter-time, and Örvandels-tá '=' Rigel,' the chief star of the constellation.

Cp. the opening lines of *Paradise Lost*, Book iii. :—

> ' Hail, holy light, offspring of Heaven first-born !
> Or of the Eternal co-eternal beam,' etc.

Cf. John i. 4, 9.

107. *inlihtes*, so MS. ; Gr. *inlihtest*.

112. *byldo*, corrected in MS. from *hyldo*.

117. *sceadu*, corrected in MS. from *sceaðu*.

118. cf. John i. 1-5, 14.

127. *bi gewyrhtum*, 'accordingly to his deeds,' *i.e.* 'deservedly.'

132. *eft*, MS. *est*.

142. Read '*þætte sunu meotudes sylfa wolde.*'

152. *anum . . . ofer-þearfum*, about five letters obliterated; Gr. *anum oferþearfum*, ignoring the missing word.

153. *Hæftas hyge-geomre hider* [*gesece Ne læt*] *þe behindan þonne þu heonan cyrre.* About ten letters are obliterated after *hider*; the bracketed words are purely conjectural; Gr. '*hider* [*gesohtest*]: [*ne*] *þe behindan nu læt*'; this is obviously untenable, and was, no doubt, due to Thorpe's erroneous reading of the MS., '*hider . . . þe behindan . . . es nu læt.*'

161. *heannissum*, so MS.; Gr. *heahnissum*.

162. *ferh*, so MS.; Gr. *ferð*.

168. *worde*, so MS.; probably a scribal error for *worda*, dependent on *worn*, unless the word must be construed with '*hæbbe gehyred*,' 'I have heard in word,' *i.e.* 'I have heard spoken.'

187. *gehwyrfed*, so MS.; Gr. *gewyrped*.

188. *nat-hwylces*, so MS.; Gr. *nat-hwylces* [*searo*]; *þurh nat-hwylces* may, perhaps, be explained as a confusion of two constructions;—*þurh nát-hwylcne* (the accusative after *þurh*), and *nát hwylces*, (the gen. after *nát*; cp. *nát he þara goda*, Beow. 682.)

189. *sprece*, so MS.; Gr. *spræce*.

201. *heag-engel*, so MS.; Gr. *heah-engel*.

205. *tir-fruma*[*n*], MS. *tir-fruma*.

209. *sunu*, so MS.; Gr. *suna*.

228. *weoroda*, so MS.; Gr. *weroda*.

229. *forþ a*, so MS.; Th. *forþā* (*i.e. forþam*); Gr. *furþum*.

238. Cp. Prov. viii. 22-31.

243. *miltse*, MS. *milstse*.

246. *mægon*, so MS.; Gr. *magon*.

256. *eowde*, *d* corrected from *ð* in MS.

274. *mæra*. Th. suggested that the word was due to an error of the scribe, and should properly be *maria*; there is no evidence for this view, but it is probable that the poet used *mæra* because of its likeness to *maria*,—the sort of popular etymology that the old homilists delighted in.

276. *þara* [*þ*]*e gewurde*, MS. *þara ege wurde*; a letter erased before *ege*.

280. *selesten,* so MS.; Gr. *selestan.*

284. *worl[d]cundra,* MS. *worlcundra.*

299. *gehealden,* this form is either the infinitive (= *gehealdan*), 'and thou shalt hold thyself immaculate,' dependent on *þu sceolde,* or it may, perhaps, be better construed as a past part., dependent on *þu sceolde (wesan);* cp. *sceal gewrixled (wesan),* l. 1259; in this case *þe* must be rendered as an accusative of regard, 'as for thee, Mary, thou shalt be held immaculate for aye.'

302. *Esaias,* an error for *Ezekiel;* cp. Ezek. xliv. 1-3.

309. *Wende swiðe þæt ænig elda æfre meahte;* one would expect *ne* before *meahte, i.e.* 'he felt sure that mortal might not,' etc.; the emendation may be unnecessary, if *wende þæt* = *wende hu þæt, wende* having almost the force of *wundrade.*

312. *in-hebba,* MS. *in hebba;* Gr. *inhebban;* the prefix evidently has the force of O. H. G. *int, ent,* 'to heave up' (O. H. G. *intheffen*); cp. *in-bindan,* 'to unbind,' *e.g. an sceal in-bindan forstes fetre,* 'one shall unbind the fetters of frost,' Gnomic Verses (Exeter Bk.), 75; both forms are hapaxlegomena.

321. *stondeð,* so MS.; Gr. *stondað.*

333. *lioþu-cægan,* lit. 'a limb-key.'

338. *motan,* MS. *motam.*

360. *nied,* MS. *med.*

370. *we,* MS. *þe.*

395. *wear[dia]ð,* MS. *wearð.*

398. *flihte,* so MS.; Gr. *flyhte.*

409. *heannessum,* so MS.; Gr. *heahnessum.*

418. *wiht,* MS. *niht* (= *uiht* = *wiht*).

422. *þrim,* so MS.; Gr. *þrym.*

PART II.

The poet has made very free use of Gregory's 29th Homily, sects. 9-11, in the second part of his poem. For convenience of reference, the text is printed in the appendix. Cynewulf's true poetical talent loses nothing by comparison with his original.

L

445. *mund-heals*, a hapaxlegomenon; (?) = *mund-héals*, (cp. *héals-bóc*), 'salus tutelæ,' *i.e.* 'the safety which comes from the protection (*mund*) afforded by another'; but cp. *mund*, l. 92, and the special use of *heals* in such compounds as *heals-mægeð*, Gen. 2155; *heals-gebedda*, Beow. 63; *mund-heals* may have had a similar meaning, 'beloved maiden.'

455. *brega*, so MS.; Gr. *brego*.

493. *cwomun*, so MS.; Gr. *cwomon*.

495. *weardedun*, MS. *weardedum*.

502. *heredun*, MS. *heredum*.

515. *stóll*, so MS.; Gr. *stól*.

516-518. I take these lines to be the reply of Galileans; another interesting instance of the dramatic bent of Cynewulf's genius. Grein takes ll. 509-525 as one long speech. The MS. is in favour of my view of the passage, as a new section begins with l. 516.

518. *gedryt*, so MS.; Gr. *gedryht*.

526. *bifengun*, a scribal error for *bifangen*, due probably to the Northern *bifen* of the archetype (cp. l. 1156).

536. *wopes hring*, 'a ring of weeping.' This phrase occurs four times in A. S. poetry, an instance occurring in each of the four poems, Elene, Guthlac, Andreas, and Christ; its peculiar force is somewhat doubtful; Grimm explains it 'as *fletus intensissimus quasi circulatim erumpens*; Grein connects *hring* with *hringan*, 'sonare'; I render the phrase by 'unbroken weeping,' taking ' *hring*' in its literal sense of 'ring,' the symbol of continuity.

538. *hreðer*, MS. *hreder*.

539. *beorn*, MS. *bórn*; *bidon*, MS. *bidan*.

547. *al-beorhte*, MS *æl-beorhte*.

557. *bireafod*, so MS.; Gr. *bereafod*.

558. *hi*, fem. sing. referring to *helle* (f.).

559. *orlege*, lit. 'war, strife, hostility,' also 'a place where hostility is shown,' as in this passage; cp. ' *Cwædon ðæt hé on ðam beorge byrnan sceolde . . . gif hé monna dream of ðam orlege eft ne wolde sylfa gesecan*, Guth. 167; also Guth. 426; 'orlege' in both passages = the place which Guthlac had selected for his dwelling, wresting it from the evil spirits.

563. *ne meahtan*, MS. *ne,ᵐᵉahtan*.

585. *gehyrdan*, so MS.; Gr. *gehyrdon*.

589. *wunat*, so MS.; Gr. *wunaþ*.

589-596. Note the rhyme and assonance, used to give special point to the passage.

613. *yrmðu*, so MS.; Gr. *yrmða*.

614. [*h*]*is*, MS. *is*.

618. [*wæs*], evidently omitted by the scribe after *sungen*.

634. *sunu*, so MS.; Gr. *suna*.

653. *flyht*, MS. *flyᵗ*.

658-664. This digression on 'the arts and crafts' is a free paraphrase of the lines in Gregory's Homily, (see Appendix II.,) 'dedit vero dona hominibus; quia misso desuper Spiritu, alii sermonem sapientiæ, alii sermonem scientiæ, alii gratiam virtutum, alii gratiam curationum, alii genera linguarum, alii interpretationem tribuit sermonum. Dedit ergo dona hominibus.' In comparing the Anglo-Saxon and Latin two points are noteworthy; in the first place, the amplification of the theme, so as to include secular as well as spiritual gifts; in the second place, the addition of God's motive in not giving all His gifts to any one man; this is not in the original. It is clear that the poet, when he came to the passage in Gregory's Homily, was reminded of a poem, written, in all probability by himself, at an earlier period, preserved in the Exeter MS. and known as 'Manna Cræftas.' A comparison of the lines under discussion and the poem brings out a large number of parallelisms of expression. I am inclined to think that Gregory's *Commentary on Job*, xxxviii. 4-5, was the original of the poem. Here we have the motive, which is not in the Homily. At the same time I should not be surprised to find a passage in Gregory's works even nearer to the Anglo-Saxon. The original of ll. 682-4 should be words to this effect :—

'Non enim uni dantur omnia, ne in superbiam elatus cadat.'

(Cp. Gregory, Lib. I, Homilia x. sect. 32, on Ezekiel iii. 13, with marginal note, 'cur divisiones gratiarum sint.')

672. *sumum*, MS. *sum²*.

677. *heanne,* so MS.; Gr. *heahne.*

683. *him,* MS. *hī*; Th. Gr. 'MS. *hi.*'

697. *lixeð,* MS. *lixed.*

708. *feodan,* between *o* and *d* a letter erased in MS.

709. *blæd,* MS. *blæð.*

711. *dauiþes,* so MS.; Gr. *dauides.*

718. *ealle,* so MS.; Th. Gr. 'MS. *eall.*'

723. *gebyrda,* so MS., either the nom. plural, or a scribal error for *gebyrdu.*

730. *hell-warena*; MS. *hell-werena*; cp. Juliana, 322, *hell-warena cyning.*

739. *gesawan,* so MS.; Gr. *gesawon.*

742. *eadgum,* so MS.; Th. Gr. 'MS. *eadgu.*'

756. *sellran,* MS. *sell̃an.*

761. *eglum,* MS. *englum.*

765. *fær-scyte,* MS. *fær,scyte.*

776. *si,* MS. *s̓.*

783. *hleotan, h* added by a later hand.

789. *ðy reþran,* MS. *dyreþran*; Th. emended to *ðy reþran.*

795. *læded,* MS. *lædað.*   803. *scæcen,* so MS.

799-806. *v.* 'Excursus on the Runes.'

805. *bilocen,* so MS., (misprinted *bilocan,* Gr.)

807. *blac rasetteð,* MS. *blacra setteð*; Kemble, *blac ræsetteð*; Ettm. *blác rasceteð*; Gr. *blac rasetteð*; cp. *þat fyr meahte réad rásettan,* Boethius, Metre 9, (quoted by Grein with wrong reference, 11, 14;) in this latter passage, too, the editors read *readra settan*; Gr. rightly corrects to *read rasettan.*

808. *recen reada,* Th. *recen-reada,* 'the smoke red'; Gr. *recen reada*; *leg,* so MS.; Th. Gr. *lig.*

810. *on tyhte*; Th. *ontyhte,* 'kindled.'

812. *gæsta,* 'of guests,' so Th.; Gr. *gǽsta,* 'of spirits.'

819. *gæst-hofe,* so MS.; Gr. *gast-hofe.*

820. *on,* so MS.; Gr. *in.*

826. *beheofiað,* so MS.; Gr. *beofiað*; cp. *Heora mædenu ne synt behéofode,* 'virgines eorum ne sunt lamentatæ,' (Lambeth Psalter, 77, 63).

829. *haðe,* MS. *bade.*

164

832. *mæsta*, so MS.; Th. Gr. *mæste*.

834. *cwaniendra*, MS. *cwanendra*. *cerge*, so MS.; 'Ettm. Gr. *cearge*.

841. *leofra*, so MS.; Gr. *leofre*; the change to the neuter is, perhaps, unnecessary, as the word probably anticipated a masculine noun, þær = *sum stede hwær*. *eall*, so MS., Gr. *eal*.

865. *heahþu*, so MS.; Th. *heahþū*; Gr. *heahðum*.

PART III.

The source of the third part of the poem is, undoubtedly, the hymn 'De die Judicii,' (see Appendix III.,) as shown by Professor A. S. Cook, (*Modern Language Notes*, June 1889.) Special interest attaches to this hymn. It is certainly as old as the seventh century, for Bede refers to it in his work, *De Metris*. Daniel says of it: 'Juvat carmen fere totum e Scripturâ sacrâ depromptum comparare cum celebratissimo illo extremi judicii præconio, *Dies iræ, dies illa*, quo majestate et terroribus, non sanctâ simplicitate et fide, superatur.'

873. *genægeð*, 'assaulteth'; *genægan*, with accus. of person, and gen. or instr. of thing; cp. '*we þec níða genægað*, Guth. 261.

874-876. These lines do not paraphrase any words of the Latin hymn; they were, perhaps, vaguely suggested by the second couplet, 'brevis totus . . . sæculum.'

884. *ealle*, MS. *healle*.

894. *onhælo gelac*, 'the hidden hosts'; Gr. renders *onhǽle* = 'entire'; no other instance occurs of '*onhæle*' in the sense of 'whole'; the usual frequent usage is 'secret,' 'hidden'; cp. *wíd is þes wésten, wræcsetla fela, eardas onhæle earmra gæsta*, Guth. 268. Th. renders, 'an unsound assemblage'; Toller, 'the entire hosts.'

907. *gebleod*, cp. *Ða wyrta gréowon mid menigfealdum blostmum mislice gebléode*, 'the plants grew diversely coloured with manifold blossoms,' (the Anglo-Saxon version of the *Hexameron of St. Basil*, ed. Norman, 10, 36.)

920. *þæt mæg wites to wearnunga* (sc. *wesan*), 'that may be for the soul's warning.'

165

923. *þonne*, so MS., not *þon* as Th.

926. *gehwone*, MS. *gehwore*.

933-937; the poet has missed the point of the original:—
'erubescet orbis lunæ sol et obscurabitur.'

959. *untweo*, so Gr.; MS. *untreo*, an obvious scribal error, due, perhaps, to the rare use of *untweo*; no other instance of the word is recorded, but cp. *untweofeald*, '*untwéofealde tréowa*,' (Bœthius, Metre, 11, 95.)

adames, the first and second *a* in this word, as written in the MS., resemble the rounded Celtic *a*, and are different from the ordinary letter employed by the scribe.

960. *gesargad*, MS. *gesargaδ*; cp. *gesargad*, l. 969, where *d* was originally δ, the erased stroke is still visible.

977. *þa*, MS. *þu*.

978. *scehdun*, so MS., probably = *scédun*, past tense of *scéadan*, 'to separate'; Gr. suggests *scéndun*; 'von einem *scénan*, verwandt mit ahd. *scónón*, parcere? oder für *sceldun* = *scildun* schirmten?'

985. *sundes getwæfde*, 'bereft of swimming-craft'; Th., Gr., Toller, render *sund*, 'ocean,' 'cut off from the ocean.' I think the abstract use of the word in the sense of 'natatio' is preferable here; cp. '*he þe æt sunde oferflát*,' Beow. 517.

1025. *adames*, cp. l. 959.

1041. *liffruma*, MS. *liffruman*.

1046. *wera*, so MS.; Th. Gr. read *weras*, making it subj. of *magon*; the change seems unnecessary, if *bemiþan* is construed intransitively.

1078. *motun*, MS. *motum*.

1087. MS. *býdyrned*.

1089. The line is evidently defective; Gr. suggests [*getéod*] *weorþed*.

1091. *wita ne cuþun*, 'they did not know'; *wita* = *witan*; *cuþun* used as auxiliary; Gr. construes *wita* as gen. plur. of *wite*, 'punishment'; cp. l. 1212, *wita ne cuþon*, which Gr. treats similarly; the omission of the infinitive *n* in the phrase is, probably, due to the northern archetype.

1093. *man-forwyrhtu*, so MS. Th. *forwyrhtû* (*i.e. um*).

1099. *genomian*, so MS.; Gr. *gemonian*.

1104. Lit. 'They shall see as their bane that which came to them best.'

1126, etc., cp. Appendix IV.; the same passage was paraphrased by Aelfric, (see *Homilies*, ed. Thorpe, p. 108.)

1129. *cwice*, so MS.; not *cwico*, as Th. Gr.

1130. *þa hyra*; MS. *þa þe hyra*.

1133. The alliteration is wanting; Gr. reads [*hu*] *in hierusalem*, etc.; it is noteworthy that the chief initial letters in the line *h, g, c* approximate to alliterative effect, (? cp. l. 23.)

1156. *bifén*, Northern or Mercian form of p.p. of *bifón*; cp. *gedénra*, 1264.

1157. *bibyrgde*, MS. *bibyrgede* (*i.e. bibyrgde*), not *bibyrgede*, as Th., Gr.

1167. *frean*, MS. *fream*; Gr. by a curious error has misread Th.'s note '*sream*,' and taken it to refer to *eah-stream*.

1174. *rindum*, so MS.; Th. Gr. *roderum*, (a remarkable error.)

1175. *magun*, MS. *magum*.

1207. *hu*, so MS.; Gr. suggests *hy*.

1212. Cp. note, l. 1091.

1230. *wenað*, MS. *wenęað*, (*i.e. wenað*.)

1245. *motun*, MS. *motum*.

1249. *wlite*, so MS.; Th. Gr. *slite*.

1264. *atol*, neut. subst., or, perhaps, one should read *atol-earfoða*.

1269. *þa*, so MS.; Th. Gr. *þam* (*þā*).

1282. *ypæst*, so MS.; Gr. *ypast*.

1293. *gefean*, MS. *gefeon*.

1300. *þon*, so MS.; Th. Gr. *þonne*.

1301. *gescomeden*, so MS.; Gr. *gescomedon*.

1306. *bigæð*, I feel sure that here we have an instance of *bigán* in the sense of 'to confess,' (cp. M. H. G. *bigehan*,) though no instance is recorded in Anglo-Saxon lexicons. The more usual usage of the word is 'to commit'; Th. 'when they commit sins'; similarly, Gr. Toller.

1310. *unbeted*, MS. *ð*, corrected to *d*.

1317. *lifes tiligan*, 'to strive for life'; cp. '*ðonne he æt hilde sceall wið láð werud lifes tiligan*,' (Salomon and Saturn, l. 159).

167

1318. *ðƍolian*, 'to endure.' I can see nothing against this straightforward way of rendering the word; Grein's view that it is O. H. G. *adaljan*, M. H. G. *edelen*, nobilitare, is untenable; the sense of the whole passage has, I think, escaped both Th. and Gr. The rendering of the former is quite meaningless. Gr. takes *wille* as equivalent to *scyle*, so that the lines, according to him, imply man's duty ' *lifes tiligan syn-rust þwean*,' etc.

1319. *syn-rust þwean*, so. MS.; Gr. *þrean*.

1328. *innan*, M.S. *mnan*; *magun*, MS. *magum*.

1336. *mæðleð*, MS. *mædleð*.

1346. *hwonne*, so MS.; Gr. *þonne*; the former reading is altogether preferable, *hwonne* depending on *gearo*, 'ready for the day when'; *leofstum*, MS. *leoftum*.

1349. *onfengun*, MS. *onfengum*.

1355. *æfndon*, MS. *æfdon*; the insertion of the *n* is, perhaps, unnecessary, as *n* is occasionally lost in consonantal-*nan* verbs, *e.g. nemde*, past tense of *nemnan*; but cp. *geæfnde*, l. 1428.

1369. MS. *miccle*.

1374. *ywan*, 'to show,' MS. *yðan*, 'to flow,' (probably due to an earlier error *yþan*.)

1380. *leoþe*, so MS.; Gr. *leoðo* (for *leoþe*).

1389. *neorxnawang*, the etymology of this Old English equivalent of the Latin *paradisus* has been satisfactorily solved by Mr. Henry Bradley (*Acad.* No. 911, p. 254); its Gothic representative would be *nawi-rohsnē waggs*, and its full form in Anglo-Saxon *nēo-rohsna wang*, 'field of the palaces of the dead.' There is, as yet, no evidence as to whether the word was of pagan or Christian origin; probably the former, being perhaps the Saxon equivalent of the Scandinavian *bðainsakr*.

1397. *fremum*, so MS.; not *firenum*, as Th. Gr.

    sealde, MS. *sálde*.

1411. [*h*]*ingonge*, MS. *ingonge*.

1421. *biþeahte mid*, so MS.; Gr. *beþeahte mec mid*.

1429. *wære þe gelic*; MS. *wære wege lic*.

1434. *oft and-lata*, Th. *oft and lata*; Gr. '*andlata* (?) man erwartet die Bedeutung Backenstreiche oder Beschimpfung'; he punctuates accordingly :—

168

'and fore monna lufan min þrowade
heafod hearmslege; hleor geþolade
oft and-lata.' . . .

1445. *heanne*, MS. *hean*ᵘᵉ; Gr. *heahne*.

1447. *utgotun*, so MS.; Gr. *ut-guton*.

1450. *wite*, corrected in MS. from *wita*.

1453. *geseoð*, Gr. suggests that this word may be from *geséon*, 'percolare,' comparing *biséon*, l. 1087, but *éac geseon*, l. 1456, makes it clear that this view is untenable.

gefremedun, so MS.; Gr. *gefremedon*.

1486. *mec*, so MS.; Th. Gr. *me*.

1487. *heardra*, Gr. *heardre*.

1488. *swærra*, Gr. *swærre*.

1489. *gefæstnad*, corrected in the MS. from *gefæstnað*.

1494. *in heofonum*, Th. Gr. *on heofonum*.

1495. *wurde*, MS. *worde*, an evident scribal error; cp. the previous line.

1508. *geþegede*, I take this word to be the weak past participle of *geþicgan*, 'to take'; hence 'taken by thirst'; similarly, *æþelinga bearn ecgum ofþegde*, Gen. 2002; Th. suggests *geþregede*, '*oppressed*'; Gr. derives it from *ge-þecgan*, 'consumere,' suggesting, too, a possible connection with *geþéwan* (*geþéon*), *i.e. geþegde = geþewde*; Toller follows Grein. It does not seem to have occurred to lexicographers to bring the word in connection with *þicgan*, the past participle of which verb seems to be singularly rare.

1511. *dydan*, so MS.; Gr. *dydon*.

1525. *grimne*, originally *grimme*, corrected in MS.

1529 *swi[ð]ran*, MS. *swiran*.

1532. *sceat*, MS. *sc̩at*.

1535. *deofles*, Th. Gr. *deofoles*; but MS. *deofo̧les* (*i.e. deofles*).

1541. *sinnehte*, so MS.; Gr. *sin-nihte*.

1575. *nængum*, so MS.; Gr. *ængum*.

1578. *leoht and gæst*, so MS.; Gr. *lic and gæst*; but cp. *leoht and lif*, (Widsith, 142.)

1594. *lætað*, so MS.; Gr. *læteð*.

1596. *bid*, MS. *bið*.

169

1599. Gr. *þonne mán* [*fremmað*]
    Hwæt him se waldend to wrace gesette.

1610. *mo*[*r*]*þor*, MS. *moþor*.

1620. *bindenne*, over the first *n* there is a badly-formed *m*, or three strokes resembling *m*.

1627. *ower*, MS. *oþer*; Th. *oþerne* (?); Gr. *ower*.

1630. *sin-nehte*, so MS.; Gr. *sin-nihte*.

1632. [*for-*]*hogdun*, MS. *hogdun*, evidently an error for *for-hogdun*, or *ne hogdun*.

1633. *berað beorhte frætwe*, these words evidently render the Latin 'regni petent gaudia'; perhaps the poet read 'regni *ferent* gaudia.'

1645. *beorhte*, so MS.; Th. Gr. *beorht*.

1646. Gr. *freogað folces weard : fæder ealra geweald*
    hafað and healdeð haligra weorud.

I take l. 1647 as merely a poetical periphrasis for *þone wealdendne and healdendne haligra weoruda.*

1649. *þær*, MS. *þæs*.

1650. *leohtra*, so MS.; Gr. *leohtre*.

1661. *giefe*, MS. *gief*, after which there is an erasure.

1663. *wlíte scynast*, Gr. *wlíte-scynast*. *dryhten*, in the MS., is followed by : — : 7, and a blank space of some three lines indicates the close of the poem. The next section of the MS. begins on the following page with a long flourish of capital letters.

AN EXCURSUS

ON

THE CYNEWULF RUNES.

'Her mæg findan forebances gleaw
Se ðe hine lysteð leoðgiddunga
Hwa þas fitte segde.'

THE CYNEWULF RUNES.

CHRIST, 796—806.

THE Runes in this passage stand for the letters CYNWULF, and together form the name of the author. A similar artifice is found in three other poems—'Elene,' 'Juliana,' and 'The Fates of the Apostles.' 'Christ' and 'Juliana' are both in the Exeter Codex; 'Elene' and 'The Fates of the Apostles' in the Vercelli Codex; the latter poem consists of little more than 100 lines; it is certainly no very meritorious piece of work, and it seems strange that the poet should have been so anxious to attest his authorship thereof by a long Runic passage. In the MS. the poem immediately follows the 'Legend of Andreas,' and I am more and more inclined to regard it as a mere epilogue to this more ambitious epic, standing in exactly the same relationship therefore to it that the tenth passus of 'Elene' does to the whole poem. Its relationship is, perhaps, even closer, for, whereas the ninth passus of 'Elene' ends with '*finit*,' there is no such indication of the ending of the poem in the case of 'Andreas.' At the present moment I can see nothing that militates against this view of the Cynewulfian authorship of this latter poem, and further investigation will enable us, I think, to claim that Cynewulf inserted his name in his four most important works—the epics on 'Christ,' 'Elene,' 'Juliana,' and 'Andreas.' The discovery of the runic passage at the end of 'The Fates of the Apostles' was made by Professor Napier some three years ago, and a transcript of the half-obliterated text was published by him in the *Zeitschrift für deutsches Alterthum*, vol. XXXIII. The four runic passages may be divided into two divisions; the first, in which the Runes stand merely for the letters of the poet's name; the second, in which the Runes discharge a two-fold function, representing not merely the letters of the poet's name, but also the words that the letters suggest, the names of the letters or homonyms. To the first class belongs the passage in 'Juliana'; to the second, the other three passages. The interpretation of the Runes in these latter passages is one of difficulty; in the first place, the lines in which they occur are by their very nature intended to puzzle the reader or the hearer, being almost riddles; in the second, several of the Runes bore different names at different periods, and we have not as much information on the subject as we need. Our chief sources of knowledge are the Runic alphabets, which, in many cases, have the names of the letters assigned throughout, and in some cases an interpretation of these names, and the 'Rune Poem,' printed by Hickes from a MS. now lost; in this poem each Rune is followed by its name, together with a short poetical interpretation of its meaning. The explanation of a Rune in any one of these passages should, I think, hold good when applied to the corresponding Rune in the other passages. For convenience of reference I print the four passages, substituting Roman letters for the Runes, and numbering each line.

A. CHRIST, [796—806]

1. þonne · **C** · cwacað gehyreð cyning mæðlan
2. rodera ryhtend sprecan reþe word
3. þam þe him ær in worulde wace hyrdon
4. þendan · **Y** · and · **N** · yþast meahtan
5. frofre findan · þær sceal forht monig
6. on þam wong-stede werig bidan
7. hwæt him æfter dædum deman wille
8. wraþra wita. Biþ se · **W** · scæcen
9. eorþan frætwa · **U** · was longe

174

10. · **L** · flodum bilocen lif-wynna dæl
11. · **F** · on foldan þonne frætwe sculon
12. byrnan on bæle.

B. ELENE, [1257—1271]

1.   A wæs sæcc oð ðæt
2. cynnessed cearwelmum · **C** · drusende
3. þeah he in medohealle maðmas þege
4. æplede gold · **Y** · gnornode
5. · **N** · gefera nearusorge dreah
6. enge rune þær him · **E** · fore
7. milpaðas mæt modig þrægde
8. wirum gewlenced · **W** · is geswiðrad
9. gomen æfter gearum geogoð is gecyrred
10. ald onmedla · **U** · wæs geara
11. geogoðhades glæm nu synt geardagas
12. æfter fyrstmearce forð gewitene
13. lifwynne geliden swa · **L** · toglideð
14. flodas gefysde · **F** · æghwam bið
15. læne under lyfte landes frætwe
16. gewitaþ under wolcnum winde geliccost.

C. FATA APOSTOLORUM, [96—106]

1. Her mæg findan foreþances gleaw
2. se ðe hine lysleð leoðgiddunga
3. hwa þas fitte fegde · **F** · þær on ende standeð
4. eorlas þæs on eorðan br[u]caþ ne moton hie awa [1] ætsomne
5. woruldwunigende · **W** · sceal gedreosan
6. · **U** · on eðle æfter to-h[reosan] [2]
7. læne lices frætewa efne swa · **L** · toglideð

---

[1] Napier reads *awa eardian*, but there is no space in MS.; I follow Sievers' arrangement; v. *Anglia*, xiii. pp. 1-25.
[2] Napier, *to-hreosaþ*.

8. [þonne]¹ · **C** · [and · **Y** ·] cræftes neosað²
9. nihtes nearowe on him [· **N** · ligeð]³
10. [cy]ninges þeodom . nu ðu cunnan miht
11. hwa on þæm wordum wæs werum oncyðig.

D. JULIANA, [704—711].

1.   Geomor hweorfeð
2. · **C** · **Y** · and · **N** · cyning biþ reþe
3. sigora syllend þonne synnum fah
4. · **E** · **W** · and · **U** · acle bidað
5. hwæt him æfter dædum deman wille
6. lifes to leane · **L** · **F** · beofað
7. seomað sorgcearig sar eal genom
8. synna wunde þe ic sið oððe ær
9. geworhte in worulde.

1. *C*-Rune; the name of the rune in all the Runic alphabets
is *cén*, *i.e.* 'a torch,' literally 'a pine'; the word is rare in A. S.;
its sole use seems to have been as the runic-name; no other
instance is recorded. In passage A, B, C, the poet is evidently
using the rune to suggest to his hearers the adjective *cén(e)*, *i.e.*
'keen,' 'bold,' 'active.' In passage B the temptation is strong
to regard *C-drusende* as equivalent to 'a drooping torch,' but in
order to obtain this meaning, it is necessary to emend the MS.,
changing *sæcc*, 'discontent,' into *secg*, 'man'; moreover *drusian*
is specially used in the sense of 'to become inactive' (by reason
of old age); cp. Phœnix, 368, *he drusende deaþ ne bisorgað*.
Cene drusende, *i.e.* 'the ageing warrior,' is, to my mind, the subject of the whole passage, and is added as explanatory of the
words *á wæs sæcc oð ðæt*. I much doubt whether the words con-
veyed any other meaning to Cynewulf's hearers. I differ, too,
from previous commentators in constructing *þeah* in direct connection with the first half-line, regarding *cnyssed* . . . *drusende* as
a parenthesis.

¹ Napier, *swa*; Sievers, *þonne* (?).   ² MS. *neotað*; Sievers, *neosað*.
³ N · *ligeð*, Sievers' suggestion.

The *C*-Rune in passage C is, as will be seen below, capable of similar interpretation.

2. *Y*-Rune. Its name in the A. S. alphabets is *ýr*; in the 'Rune Poem' *ýr* is described in words that lead one to render it as 'a bow':—

> 'yr biþ æþelinga and eorla gehwæs
> wyn and wyrþmynd, byþ on wicge fæger,
> fæstlic on færelde fyrdgeatewa sum.'

Yet, in spite of the Rune poem, *ýr* cannot have meant 'a bow' in A. S.; *ýr* is the old Norse equivalent of the A. S. *éow*, 'yew,' which latter word is actually the name of another rune in the Rune-Poem; it is therefore a fair inference that the interpretation of the *Y*-Rune as a 'bow' in this one place is due to Scandinavian influence on the writer of the passage in question, seeing also that in the Scandinavian Runic alphabet the letter bears the same name *ýr*, constantly glossed '*arcus*'; probably the whole idea of the Rune-Poem was suggested by similar Scandinavian poems, and the writer did not recognise that the Norse *ýr*, in the sense of 'bow,' was identical with the A. S. *éow*, 'yew-tree'; as a modern poet has it:—

> 'Dark down the windy vale I grow,
> The father of the fateful Bow.'[1]

In my opinion, no ordinary Anglo-Saxon would have been able to give any meaning at all to *ýr* as the name of the *Y*-rune, and if told by a scholar that it meant 'a bow,' he would have failed to see any reason for the name; the shape of the rune in A. S. ᚩ certainly does not suggest 'a bow,' though the name applies excellently to the Scandinavian ᚯ. The *Y*-Rune must have been a fairly late creation in A. S., and its symbol is rightly nothing but a modification of the *U*-Rune, ᚾ; similarly the name of the rune, *i.e. ýr*, is, I take it, merely due to the umlauted form of the name of the *U*-Rune, *i.e. úr*; the rune and its name probably passed from England to Scandinavia, and there it was naturally interpreted to mean *ýr*, 'a bow.'

How then is the rune to be interpreted, as used by Cynewulf?

---

[1] W. Morris: *Poems by the Way: Tapestry Trees; The Yew.*

In passage A, it seemingly might stand for *yrmðo*, 'misery'; and this view has been held by most scholars—Thorpe, Kemble, Grein; several points might be urged against the interpretation, and however plausible the suggestion seems, it is, I now think, quite untenable. Apart from other tests, the interpretation will not hold good for passage B. Grimm, Grein, Zupitza, etc., construe the rune in this latter passage as 'bow'; Leo suggests that it is equivalent to the A. S. rune *éa*, and =*edr*, *i.e.* 'earth,' 'the grave,' here = 'verfall der kräfte'; Reiger would substitute the rune *æ*, and read *æðil* (=A. S. *éðel*); similarly in passage A he would substitute Northumbrian *ædil* =A. S. *vædl*, 'mendicitas.'

In passage C, the words represented by the *C*-Rune and *Y*-Rune, which are co-ordinated, must evidently be the same part of speech; if *C*=*céne*, 'the bold warrior,' in the same sense as in the other passages, one would expect *Y* to stand for an adjective or substantive, in any case of masculine gender; but in passage A the *Y*-Rune is co-ordinated with the *N*-Rune; concerning the meaning of this latter rune there is no doubt; it represents the abstract noun *nýd*, 'necessity'; therefore the *Y*-Rune in this latter passage must, I think, stand for some similar abstract noun. Judging by A and C, the *Y*-Rune represents a *y*-word that can discharge the two-fold functions of a masculine adjective (or noun) and of an abstract noun. The only Anglo-Saxon word that satisfies these requirements is *yfel*=(1) wretched; (2) affliction; and there is, I venture to think, strong reasons for favouring this interpretation of the *Y*-Rune in the three passages. In passage A, *yfel and nýd* = 'affliction and distress'; in passage B, *yfel gnornode nydgefera* = 'afflicted, mourned the companion of sorrow'; in passage C, *cene and yfel*= 'the bold warrior and the afflicted wretch.'

May not the name *yfel* have been suggested by the name of the *W*-Rune, *i.e. wynn*, 'joy,' being a sort of antithesis to it? The letter *y* would probably at first have followed *w* immediately in Runic alphabets arranged in the order of the Roman letters, before a special symbol was found for the double letter *x*. In Scandinavian alphabets no separate sign occurs for this latter sound, which is represented by the runes for *hs*.

178

3. *N*-Rune. The interpretation of this rune is simple. As regards passage A, N = *nýd* = 'necessity, hardship,' *Y* and *N* being the subject of *meahtan*. As regards B, the authorities vary on the question of the continuation of *nýd* and *gefera* ; Grimm reads *N gefera nearu sorge dreah*; Ettmüller, *N gefera, nearusorge dreah*; Kemble, *N gefere, nearu sorge dreah*; Grein, Zupitza, etc., *nydgefera*, etc. The point of the expression *nyd-gefera* is, I think, that it serves the purpose of a *double entendre* ; the poet uses it not merely to express its literal meaning 'the companion of sorrow ;' '*yfel*' (*i.e.* the *Y*-Rune) may well be described as *nyd-gefera*, *i.e.* 'the companion of the *N*-Rune' in the poet's name, (cp. *gefera* as a technical word in Ælfric's Grammar, *wordes gefera* = an adverb.)

A similar *double entendre* occurs, I think, in the next line ; *enge rune* = (1) *nearu-sorge*, 'a constraining sorrow '; (2) a description of the *N*-Rune, 'the narrow rune,' ✝ ; in 'Cynewulf' this 'narrow rune' comes between two especially wide ones ; hence, perhaps, the special point of the words.

In C, '*N ligeð*' is the excellent reading suggested by Sievers ; the letters are obliterated in the MS.

4. *E*-Rune. In A and C this rune does not occur, and it would seem that the poet styled himself in these passages 'Cynwulf,' and not 'Cynewulf' (on the philological aspect of the form 'Cynwulf,' see Sievers' remarks, *Anglia* xiii.). Thorpe noted concerning A that the absence of the rune *E*, and the want of connection in the sense, proved the loss of a couplet between *wraþra wita* and *biþse*; Grein similarly suggested the insertion of a line containing an *E*-Rune,

> ' *hwæt him æfter dædum deman wille*
> [*on þam E-fullan dæge engla dryhten*]
> *wraþra wita*,'

interpreting ' E. full ' = *eh-full*, = *egefull*, 'terribilis,' (usually *E* = *eh*, 'equus '). But the passage makes perfect sense without any interpolation, and the discovery of passage C corroborates this view ; the space between *nearowe* and [*cy*]*ninges þeodom* would not suffice for more than the words containing the

N-Rune, as Sievers has pointed out in the article referred to above. Professor Napier was originally of opinion that the obliterated passage might have contained the *Æ*-Rune as well as the *N*-Rune.[1]

In A, *wraþra wita* is, of course, the partitive genitive after *hwæt*; the subject of *wille* is clear in both A and D; the identity of expression in the two passages is remarkable.

The *E*-Rune in B = *eh*, 'horse'; the word *fore* that follows the rune has been variously interpreted—(1) as an adverb formerly; (2) as a preposition governing *him*; (3) = *fóre*, 'on the journey.' I prefer (2) 'before him'; the poet, I take it, was filled with grief when he watched the hunt, but could not join in it; otherwise the passage must mean, 'where once he had joined in the delights of the hunt, he now wandered sorrow-laden.'

5. *W*-Rune. The proper name of this rune = *wyn*, *i.e.* 'joy'; this name of the letter is given in the Salzburg Runic Alphabet, and an interesting piece of additional evidence exists, in the fact that *jubilitate* is glossed þ *sumiaþ*, *i.e.* *wynsumiaþ* in the Ninety-ninth Psalm of the Oxford Interlinear Version, MS. Junius 27, (as pointed out by Professor Logeman;) *uuinne* is also the name of the Gothic letter in the Salzburg MS. A dialectical variety of *wyn* = *wenn*, which was probably identified with *wén*, *i.e.* 'hope'; hence the latter interpretation of the name of the rune. In the Runic poem the lines on *W* run as follows :—

> ' *w (wen) ne bruceþ, ðe can weana lyt,*
> *sares and sorge,*' etc.

If the rune is interpreted as *wén* = 'hope' in this passage, it is impossible to understand the lines; but *wen ne = wenne = wynne*, genitive of *wyn*, after *bruceþ*. Similarly in the Rhyme Poem, l. 76 :—

---

[1] I may as well point out that I had printed the lines in *Christ* without the interpretation of the *E*-Rune, interpreting it as it stands in my text, before the discovery of the Fata Apost. fragment; I had noted, too, the value of the discovery as corroboration of the form 'Cynwulf,' before the appearance of Sievers' notable article; the same is true of my interpretation of the *W*-Rune as *wyn* (not *wen*, as previous editors).

> '*þonne lichoma ligeð · lima wyrm friteþ*
> *ac him wen ne gewigeð,*' etc.

there, too, *wen ne = wenne = wynne.*

In passage A, B, C, the rune is clearly to be interpreted *wynn*; Grein renders it *wén* in A, *wen = wynn* in B, Napier interpreted the rune in C as *wén*, Sievers as *wynn* (see *Anglia* xiii.). The letters of the alphabet in Anglo-Saxon are masculine; hence *se* W., although *wynn* is feminine.

U-Rune. The name of the rune in the Runic Alphabets = *úr*, interpreted to mean 'a bull,' cp. Runic Poem, l. 4 :—

> *U* (*ur*) *biþ anmod and ofer-hyrned,*
> '*the bull is fierce with horns above his head.*'

The rune in A, B, and C, has baffled the ingenuity of commentators. As regards A, Kemble, Thorpe, and Grein, take the letter to represent *úr*, formerly; but the adverb does not occur in Anglo-Saxon; its equivalent, *or*, is used only as a prefix; and although at first sight it seems that some adverb must be understood in this place, the objections against *úr* are insurmountable; I had thought it possible that perhaps *iu*, 'formerly,' might have stood, but I retract this view now. As regards the rune in B, Grimm takes it merely as the letter *U*, and makes it represent the whole name of the poet—'Cynewulf war ehemals die wonne der jugend'; Kemble, '*U* (I was of old) a gleam of youth'; Leo, *úr=ór*, 'sonst war gold der jugendzeit wonneglanz'; Grein interprets B in the same way as A, 'olim'; Zupitza, *úr=* 'auerochse'; the scholars that interpret the rune as equivalent to *úr*, 'bull,' take it to mean 'property' in general, comparing the use of *feoh*, but there is absolutely no evidence in favour of this view, and Sievers' interpretation of *U on éðle* in C, 'das gut im erbsitze,' seems to me untenable. The only Anglo-Saxon word that will satisfy the three passages seems to be the possessive pronoun *úr*, 'our'; Dr. Cosijn (in 'Verslagen en mededeelingen der koninklijke Akademie van Wetenschappen, Afdeeling Letterkunde,' pp. 54-64) suggested the possibility of this interpretation, noting that *úr* is a frequent form of the pronoun in the Vespasian Psalter; but more important evidence in favour of the view exists in the fact that *in a Runic Alphabet (Domitian,*

A, 9) *the rune is actually glossed 'noster.'* It is strange that this point has not been noticed; it confirms the probability. The alphabet in question is printed in Hicke's, p. 136. Finally, therefore, A=*úr . . . lifwynna dæl*; B=*úr . . . geogoðhades glæm*; C=*úr wynn on éðle.* In A '*longe*'='long ago'; cp. Ex. 557, '*wile nu gelæstan, þæt he lange gehet.*' I take it that the words in A refer to the Deluge. With the phrase *wynn on éðle* in C, cp. Rune Poem. l. 38—

eoh byþ . . . wyn on eþle.

7, 8. L and F call for no special comment; the name of the former, *lagu*, and of the latter, *féoh*, fit the passages in which they occur.

In the following rendering of the passages in question I have attempted to bring out the peculiar force of the original. In A, B, C, the Runic letters (*i.e.* their Roman equivalents) CYNE WULF stand respectively for the following words:—Cén(e), yfel, nyd, eh, wynn, úr, lagu, féoh; their English equivalents are printed in italics.

A.

C· Then the *Keen* shall quake; he shall hear the Lord,
the heaven's Ruler, utter words of wrath
to those who in the world obeyed Him ill,

Y·N· while *affliction* and *distress* most easily
might find solace. There many afeared
shall wearily await upon that plain
what dire penalty He will adjudge to them,

W· according to their deeds. The *winsomeness* of earthy
gauds

U· shall then be changed. Long time ago *our* portion of
life's joys

L· was all encompassed by *water*-floods,

F· yea, all our *possessions* upon earth; then each precious
thing
shall be consumed in fire.

182

Till then was nought but discontent,—

C· a *bold* warrior, drooping with age, buffeted by waves of care,—

yea, though in the mead-hall he received precious gifts,

Y·N· apple-shaped gold. *In his affliction, sorrow's* comrade murmured ; grief, the narrowing rune,

E· constrained him, when he beheld *the horse* measuring the mile-paths, rushing proudly on,

W· decked with adornments. *Joy* is now lessened, and delight, after many a year ; youth is gone,

U· the pride of old. *Ours* was once youth's glorious radiance ; now, at appointed time, those days of yore have passed away,

L· life's joy hath departed, as *the waters* ebb, the rushing floods. Transitory 'neath heaven

F· is *the wealth* of every man.

C.

A man of cunning thought may here discover, if he taketh pleasure in song,

F · who wrought this lay. *Wealth* cometh last, the friend of man on earth, while he dwelleth in the world,

but they cannot keep together always.

U·W·*Our* earthly *joy* shall fade, and the frail gauds of the flesh

L · shall afterwards decay, even as *water* glideth away.

C·Y· *Bold warrior* and *afflicted wretch* shall then crave help,

N · in the anxious watches of the night ; but *Destiny* o'errules, the King exacts their service. Now thou canst know, who was revealed to men in these words.

183

D.

Sad shall depart
C · Y · and **N ·** ; the King will be stern,
the Bestower of victory, when, sin-stained,
E · W · and **U ·** trembling shall await
what He will adjudge to them, according to their deeds,
as life's reward ; **L · F ·** shall quake,
and linger sorrowful. All the pain I shall remember,
the wounds of the sins, which I, early or late,
wrought in the world.

GLOSSARY

N

GLOSSARY

Á, *ever*, 386.
ábéatan, *to beat*, 939.
ábéodan, *to command*, 228.
ábídan, *to abide*, 1629.
ábúgan, *to withdraw, retire*, 55.
ácennan, *to beget*, 217, 443, 451.
ácweðan, *to speak*, 315, 473, 713.
ádl, *disease*, 1355.
ádréogan, *to suffer*, 1200, 1474, 1512.
ádwæscan, *to quench*, 1131.
æfest, *enmity*, 1657.
æfnan, *to perform, to endure*, 1355, 1368.
æfre, *ever*, 324.
æfyllende, *following the law, faithful*, 703.
æghwæs, *altogether, entirely*, 1419.
æht, *possession*, 603, 1500.
ælan, *to set on fire*, 811, 1545.
æl-beorht, *resplendent*, 505, 547, 927, 1275.
ælc, *each*, 332, 1301.
ælde, *men*, 581, 619, 998, 1115, 1200.

æled, *fire, conflagration*, 958, 1004.
ælmihtig, *almighty*, 120, 214, 319, 330, 394, 442, 758, 1217, 1371, 1377.
æne, *once*, 328, 1193.
ænig, *any*, 310, 350, 1183, 1315, 1330, 1383, 1496, 1574, 1627.
ænlíc, *excellent, noble*, 1294.
ær, *before, (conj.)*, 314; *(prep.)*, 215, 847, 1344; *(adv.)* 62, 251, 1050, 1051, 1066, 1134, 1156, 1264, 1374.
ær-dagas, *former days*, 78.
ærest *(adv.)*, *first*, 354.
ærest *(adj.)*, *first*, 785, 822, 1189, 1396.
ær-gestréon, *ancient treasure*, 995.
ær-gewyrht, *former work*, 1239.
ærra, *former*, 1320.
ær-woruld, *former world*, 935.
æt, *at*, 499, 614; *against*, 272.

æt, *food*, 603.
ætgædre, *together*, 1034.
ætsomne, *together*, 1111.
æt-wist, *existence, presence*, 391.
ætýwan, *to reveal*, 1055, 1574.
æþel-duguð, *a noble attendance*, 1010.
æþele, *nature*, 1183.
æþele, *noble*, 267, 349, 401, 454, 520, 665, 696, 718, 1179, 1193, 1197.
æþelíc, *noble*, 307.
æþeling, *noble, prince*, 157, 447, 502, 514, 626, 740, 742, 844.
áfǽran, *to terrify*, 891.
áfón, *to seize*, 1182.
áfréfran, *to console*, 367.
áfyllan, *to fill*, 1561.
áfyrhtan, *to frighten*, 1018.
áfyrran, *to remove*, 1369, 1424.
áfýsan, *to hasten*, 984.
ágǽlan, *to be careless*,

187

to hinder, neglect, 815.

ágan, *to possess*, 158, 1202, 1211, 1245, 1401, 1577, 1635.

ágend, *Lord*, 419, 470, 512, 542, 1196.

ágiefan, *to restore, give up*, 1154, 1160, 1258, 1405.

áhebban, *to raise*, 501, 657, 691.

áhladan, *to draw out*, 567.

áhón, *to hang*, 1092, 1445, 1486.

áhreddan, *to deliver, rescue*, 15, 33, 373.

áhycgan, *to conceive*, 901.

álǽtan, *to renounce*, 166.

álecgan, *to lay down*, 1421.

alwealda (alwalda), *Almighty*, 139, 1189, 1363.

alwihta, *all beings*, 273, 409, 686.

álýfan, *to allow, grant*, 1571, 1636.

álýsan, *to let loose, to ransom*, 717, 1098.

álýsnes, *redemption*, 1472.

án, *one*, 1236, 1302, 1376.

ána, *sole, alone*, 556, 1419, 1451.

án-boren, *one born*, 617.

án-cenned, *only begotten*, 463.

ancor, *an anchor*, 862.

and-gete, *manifest*, 1241.

and-giet, *sense, wisdom*, 665, 1379.

andléan, *retribution*, 830.

andsaca, *adversary*, 1592.

andsæc, *denial*, 654.

andswaru, *answer*, 183.

andweard, *present*, 924, 1051, 1069, 1083, 1269, 1374, 1576.

andwlita, *countenance*, 1121.

ánfeald, *single*, 1576.

án-forlætan, *to forsake, let pass*, 1294, 1395.

án-módlíce, *unanimously*, 339.

ár, *mercy*, 69, 254, 334, 1230, 1351 ; *glory*, 1082.

ár, *a messenger*, 492, 758 ; *angel*, 594.

árǽran, *to raise up*, 1064.

árásian, *to discover*, 1228.

áreccan, *to expound, stretch out*, 73, 221, 246.

árétan, *to cheer*, 1499.

árfæst, *merciful*, 244.

árian, *to honour*, 1381 ; *to pity*, 369.

árísan, *to arise*, 266, 1023, 1029.

árléas, *shameful*, 1428, 1434.

áscamian, *to be ashamed*, 1297.

áscyrian, *to part, sever*, 1606, 1616.

ásécan, *to search out*, 1002.

ásecgan, *to tell, ask*, 220, 1175, 1473.

áspringan, *to escape from*, 1536.

ástandan, *to stand*, 1155.

ástígan, *to proceed, descend, arise*, 701, 719, 726, 736, 785.

ástyrfan, *to slay*, 191.

á-teón, *to draw out*, 1492.

atol, *dire, terrible*, 1277 ; *terror*, 1264.

áþencan, *to think*, 988.

áþolian, *to sustain, protract, draw out*, 1318.

áþrysman, *to stifle*, 1132.

áð-loga, *breaker of oath, perjurer*, 1603.

áttor, *poison*, 767.

áwæcnan, *to awake, to be born*, 66.

áweallan, *to stream forth, swarm*, 624.

áweaxan, *to grow, wax*, 1251.

áwéorpan, *to cast down, overthrow*, 97, 1403.

áwiht, *at all*, 342.

áwrecan, *to relate*, 632.
áwyrgian, *to curse*, 157, 255, 1518, 1560.

BÁ, (*v*. begen).
bǽl, *fire*, 807.
bærnan, *to set on fire, burn up*, 707, 968, 1620.
bana, (*v*. bona).
bánloca, *bone-enclosure*, 768.
be, *by, according to, at*, 1288, 1392.
béacen, *a sign*, 1064, 1084.
béag, *ring, crown*, 291, 1125, 1442.
beald, *bold*, 1075.
bealofull, *baleful*, 258, 907.
bealu, *injury, bale*, 181, 1104 ; bealo, 1246.
bealu-dǽd, *evil-deed*, 1300.
bealu-ráp, *balefulcord*, 364.
béam, *a beam, tree, rood*, 677, 728, 1088, 1092, 1168, 1173, 1445.
bearhtm, *clamour, cry*, 949, 1143.
bearn, *child, son*, (*Christ*), 37, 65, 75, 84, 125, 146, 163, 204, 241, 340, 411, 464, 571, 723.
beclýsan, *to shut in*, 322.

bedǽlan, *to deprive*, 562, (*v*. bidǽlan).
befón, *to receive*, 79.
begen, *both*, 356.
behéofian, *to bewail*, 826.
behindan, *behind*, 154.
behýdan, *to hide*, 843.
bemíðan, *to conceal*, 1047.
bemurnan, *to bemoan*, 175.
bend, *bond, chain*, 67, 146, 1040.
benn, *a wound*, 770.
béodan, *to announce*, 482, 1339.
béofian, *to tremble*, 880, 1013, 1019, 1143, 1228.
beorg, *mount, hill*, 874, 898, 966, 976, 1006.
beorgan, *to defend*, 770.
beorht, *bright, radiant*, 204, 291, 411, 482, 509, 518, 741, 826, 876, 895, 1019, 1629, 1656.
beorhte, *brightly*, 551, 700, 902, 1466.
beorn, *chief*, 448, 529, 990.
beornan (byrnan), *to be on fire*, 537, 807, 987, 1250.
beran, *to bear*, 1071, 1299, 1633.
beréafian, *to bereave, plunder*, 167, 557.

berstan, *to resound, to burst*, 810, 931, 1140.
bescyrian, *to deprive*, 31.
bestéman, *to bedew, make wet*, 1084.
betlíc, *excellent*, 65.
beþeccan, *to cover*, 115, (*v*. biþeccan).
bewindan, *to wind round, to wreathe*, 28, 724, 1420, 1422, 1641.
bewríþan, *to bind round*, 309, 717.
bibéodan, *to bid*, 542, 1498.
bibod, *command*, 1157, 1392, 1523, 1629.
bibyrgan, *to bury*, 1157.
bicuman, *to become, happen*, 1104, 1112.
bidǽlan, *to deprive of, to sever*, 1406, 1431.
bídan, *to await, endure*, 146, 509, 703, 801, 1019.
biddan, *to ask, pray*, 112, 261, 336, 358, 773, 1351, 1506.
bíd-fæst, · *stationary, firm*, 1596.
bidyrnan, *to conceal*, 1087.
bifealdan, *to inwrap, enfold*, 116.
bifeolan, *to commit*, 667.
bifón, *to grasp, sur-*

round, encircle, 526, 1156.

bigán, to avow, 1306.

bigangan, to practise, 1580.

bigong, course, way, 234, 679.

bigrafan, to bury, 1464.

bihelian, to conceal, 44, 1309.

bihlǽman, to overwhelm, 868.

bilúcan, to lock up, 251, 333, 805, 1258, 1622.

bindan, to bind, 307, 364, 872, 1596, 1620.

binn, manger, 723.

biréofan, to bereave, deprive, 1524.

birinnan, to bedew, 1174.

bisceran, to cut off, 1518.

bisencan, to submerge, 1167.

biséon, to percolate, 1086.

bismítan, to defile, 1482.

bisorgian, to care, 1554.

bisweðian, to wind round, bind, inwrap, 1642.

biteldan, to overwhelm, 537.

biter, bitter, 151, 764, 768, 907, 1250, 1436, 1473.

biþeccan, to cover, 1421.

biþencan, to remember, 820, 848.

biþryccan, to press on, 1444.

biwerian, to defend, protect, 1642.

biwitian, to observe, 352.

biwrecan, to surround, 830.

blác, pale, livid, 807, 895.

blǽd, glory, 687, 709, 876, 1210, 1238, 1255, 1290, 1345, 1585, 1634, 1656.

blǽd-wéla, fruitful riches, 1390.

blǽst, blast, 974.

blát, ghastly, 770.

bláwan, to blow, 879, 949.

bléd, flower, fruit, 1168.

bléo, colour, hue, 1563, 1390.

blícan, to shine, 506, 521, 700, 902, 1011, 1237.

blind, blind, 1125.

bliss, bliss, joy, 551, 1255, 1345, 1645, 1648, 1656.

blissian, to gladden, 1161, 1285.

blíþe, blithe, 279, 518, 738, 773, 876.

blód, blood, 258, 1084, 1111.

blód-gýte, bloodshed, 707.

blódig, bloody, 1173.

bóc, book, 452, 700, 784, 792, 1629.

boda, a messenger, 1150, 1303.

bold, house, 741.

bona, slayer, destroyer, devil, 263, 1392.

bonnan, to summon, call together, 1065.

bord - gelác, missile, 768.

bót, remedy, redemption, 151, 364.

brád, broad, 356, 379, 990, 1143.

brægd-boga, a drawn bow, 764.

brecan, to break, 707, 949, 990, 1144, 1392, 1628.

brego, prince, 402, 455.

brehtm, sound, 880.

bréman, to celebrate, to announce, 386, 482.

bréost, breast, 340, 1071.

bréost-gehygd, breast-thoughts, 261.

bréost-sefa, thoughts of the breast, 539.

bréotan, to break, 484.

bringan, to bring, 119.

bróga, terror, 792.

brond, fire, 810.

bróðor, brother, 1498.

brúcan, to enjoy, 391, 1324, 1360, 1645, 1662.

bryne, burning, 1057, 1596, 1660.

bryne-tear, hot tear, 151.

bryten-grund, *spacious earth*, 356.

bryten-wong, *spacious plain, the world*, 379.

brytta, *Lord*, 280, 333, 461.

bryttan, *to dispense*, 681.

burg, *city*, 65, 460, 518, 529, 533, 541, 552, 568, 1238.

burg-lond, *citadel*, 50.

burg-sittende, *city dwellers, citizens*, 336.

burg-stede, *citadel*, 810.

burg-waru, *citizens*, 741.

burg-weall, *city-wall*, 976.

bútan, *without*, (*conj.*), 271, 691 ; (*prep.*), 270, 721.

býme, *a trumpet*, 880, 1060.

byrd, *bride*, 279, 291.

byrd-scipe, *child-bearing*, 181.

byrgen, *tomb*, 728, 1466.

byrhtan, *to shine*, 1088.

byrhtu, *brightness*, 1238.

bysmerléas, *spotless, stainless*, 1324.

CALD, *cold*, 850, 1628.

carcern, *prison*, 24, 734.

ceafl, *bill, jaw*, 1250.

céapian, *to bargain*, 1094.

cearful, *troubled, sad*, 24.

cearian, *to be anxious*, 176.

cearig, *sorrowful*, 147, (*v.* cerg).

cearu, *care*, 890, 996, 1015, 1129, 1284, 1661.

ceaster, *citadel*, 577.

ceaster-hlid, *gate of the city*, 313.

cempa, *a champion*, 562.

cennan, *to bring forth, create*, 80, 231, 297, 635.

céol, *ship*, 850, 860.

céosan, *to choose*, 23, 330.

cerg (=cearge), 834.

cierran, *to turn*, 154.

cild, *child*, 217.

cild-geong, *a young child*, 1424.

cinn, *kind, race*, 1618.

circe, *church*, 698, 702.

cirm, *shout, uproar*, 834, 996.

cláne, *clean, pure*, 135, 186, 275, 297, 330, 443, 702, 1221, 1284.

cláþ, *cloth*, 724, 1422.

cleopian, *to exclaim, call*, 176, 507.

clomm, *a bond, chain*, 734, 1144, 1628.

clústor, *lock*, 313.

cnéorniss, *generation*, 231, 1232.

cnoll, *a knoll*, 716.

corþer, *band, company*, 493, 577.

costian, *to try, prove*, 1057.

cræft, *strength, craft, skill*, 217, 420, 666, 686, 1144.

cræftga, *craftsman*, 11.

crist, *Christ*, 1215, 1221, 1633.

cryb, *a crib*, 1424.

culpa, *a fault*, 176.

cuman, *to come*, 11, 45, 61, 65, 73, 113, 147, 148, 242, 266, 289, 371, 412, 419, 435, 493, 544, 548 552, 790, 823, 1007, 1025, 1035, 1159, 1365.

cunnan, *to know, to have power, to be able*, 68, 76, 94, 184, 197, 245, 572, 714, 1048, 1091, 1185, 1212.

cunnian, *to prove, have experience of*, 1416.

cwánian, *to bewail*, 834.

cwealm, *death, torture*, 86, 1424, 1539, 1625.

cweccan, *to move, shake*, 796.

cwelman, *to destroy*, 957.

cwén, *woman, queen*, 275, 1197.

191

dryhten, *lord*, 40, 185, 271, 296, 347.

dryht-folc, *a multitude*, 1040.

dryht-guma, *man, warrior*, 885.

dryhtlíce, *majestically, in a lordly manner*, 227.

drync, *drink*, 1437, 1507.

dugan, *to be worth, to avail*, 20, 188.

duguð, *manhood, troop, prowess, good*, 412, 562, 600, 608, 781.

dumb, *dumb*, 1126.

dún, *a down*, 716.

durran, *to dare*, 1166.

duru, *door*, 308.

dwæscan, *to extinguish*, 485.

dynnan, *to din*, 929.

dýre, *dear, beloved*, 95, 1649, (*v.* déore).

dyrne, *secret*, 639, 1048.

dysig, *foolish*, 1126.

ÉAC, *also*, 135, 144, 281, 300.

éaca, *an increase, addition;*

—— to eacan, *besides*, 1241.

éacen, *strong, great*, 204 ; *increased*, 37.

éacnung, *increase*, 74.

éad, *prosperity*, 1197, 1292 ; *happiness*, 1399.

éaden, *given, granted*, 199.

éad-fruma, *source of good*, 531.

éad-giefa, *giver of happiness*, 545.

éadig, *blessed*, 86, 687, 908, 1012, 1121, 1233, 1245, 1336, 1426, 1460, 1495, 1552, 1648.

éadgian, *to bless*, 19.

éad-mód, *humble*, 254, 785, 1351.

éage, *eye*, 6, 326, 391, 535, 1112, 1243, 1314, 1322, 1327, 1330.

éah - stréam, *water stream*, 1166.

éahtan, *to observe, judge*, 1072, 1548.

éahtnyss, *persecution*, 703.

éalá, *lo ! alas !* 17, 49, 70, 163.

eald, *old, ancient*, 1106, 1395, 1545.

eald-cýð, *the old country*, 737.

eald - dagas, *days of yore*, 302.

eald-féond, *enemy of old*, 566.

eald-gestréon, *ancient treasure*, 811, 1569.

ealdor, *life*; to ealdre, *for ever*, 478.

ealdor, *prince*, 7, 228.

ealdor-béalu, *deadly bale*, 1614.

eal-gréne, *all green*, 1127.

eall, *all*, 215, 244, 1114,

1181, 1200, 1219, 1277, 1282, 1317, 1357, 1376, 1381.

eallunga, *wholly*, 921.

earcnan-stán, *precious stone, gem*, 1194.

eard, *dwelling, home*, 62, 513, 645, 771, 1028, 1044, 1201, 1416.

eard-geard, *dwelling-place*, 54.

eardian, *to dwell*, 124, 437.

earendel, *ray, beam*, 103. .

earfeðe, *hardship, woe*, 1170, 1200, 1271, 1426, 1451.

—— earfoð, 1264.

earg, *wretched, vile*, 827, 1296, 1302, 1406.

earge, *badly*, 1501.

earh-faru, *a flight of arrows*, 761.

earm, *wretched, poor*, 16, 69, 381, 908, 1348, 1495, 1501, 1552, 1614.

earmlíc, *wretched*, 998.

earnian, *to earn*, 1050,

eastan, *from the east*, 884.

éaþe, *easily*, 172, (*v.* ýþe).

éað-médu, *reverence, humility*, 358, 1441.

éawan, *to manifest*, 54, (*v.* ýwan).

ebreas, *the Hebrews*, 66.

ebreisc, *Hebrew*, 132.

éce, *eternal, endless*,

139, 271, 304, 321, 531, 795, 1044, 1426, 1552.

eced, *vinegar*, 1437.

ecg, *edge*, 1139.

écnis, *eternity*, 312, 1202.

ed - geong, *growing young again*, 1031, 1069.

edwít, *scorn, contumely*, 1120.

efen, *even, alike*, 299, 329, 963.

efen-eardigend, *co-dwelling*, 236.

efen-éce, *co-eternal*, 121, 464.

efenlíc, *equal*, 38.

efen-micel, *equally great*, 1401.

efen-wesende, *co-eval*, 349.

eft, *again, afterwards*, 132, 324, 332, 1155.

eft-léan, *recompense*, 1098.

egesful, *terrible*, 1527.

egeslíc, *fearful*, 917, 954, 1020, 1514, 1614.

egle, *troublesome, hateful*, 761.

egsa, *terror, fear*, 16, 837, 922, 945, 1013, 1363, 1368, 1562.

ellen, *zeal, prowess*, 1316.

ell - þeód, *foreign people*, 1082.

ende, *end*, 1028

ende-deáð, *final death*, 1651.

ende-léas, *endless*, 1630.

énga, *sole*, 236.

enge, *narrow*, 31.

engel, *angel*, 131, 314, 331, 334, 350, 386, 447, 473, 505, 514, 545, 547, 581, 629, 645, 660, 822, 1012, 1062, 1245, 1335, 1341, 1467, 1519, 1644.

eorl, *man, earl*, 218, 545, 873.

eornest, *earnestness*, 1099.

eorneste, *stern*, 823.

eorð-buend, *an earth-dweller*, 421, 718, 1277, 1322.

eorð-burg, *earth*, 6.

eorðe, *earth*, 199, 328, 620, 625, 813, 827, 1127, 1136, 1179.

eorðlic, *terrestrial*, 405.

eorð - waru, *earth-dwellers*, 381, 696, 722.

eórð - wela, *earth's wealth*, 610.

éowod, *flock, herd*, 256.

ermþu, *misery*, 270, (*v.* yrmþu).

éðel, *country, home*, 31, 435, 629, 740, 1074, 1323, 1341, 1345, 1405, 1495, 1638 ; (*heritage*, 1211.)

éþel-cyning, *king of earth*, 995.

éþel-ríce, *native-realm*, 1460.

éðel-stól, *native seat*, 51, 515.

éð-gesýne, *visible*, 1233.

FÁCEN, *guilt, crime*, 206.

fácen-tácen, *sign of crime*, 1564.

fǽcne, *wicked, deceitful*, 869, 1393.

fæder, *father*, 162, 210, 319, 464, 515, 1013, 1217, 1646.

fæder-ríce, *father's realm*, 344.

fædren-cynn, *father-kin*, 247.

fǽge, *doomed to death*, 1516, 1532.

fæger, *fair*, 911, 1293, 1388.

fægre, *beautifully*, 389, 471, 506.

fǽhð, *feud, hostility*, 616, 1439.

fǽla, *good, noble*, 644.

fǽmne, *virgin, maiden*, 34, 71, 122, 174, 186, 194, 210, 417, 719, 787.

fǽmnan-hád, *maidenhood*, 91.

fǽr-scyte, *sudden shot*, 765.

fǽr-searo, *pernicious-artifice*, 769.

fæst, *firm, secure*, 5, 165, 320.

fæste, *securely*, 978, 1156.

fæstlíce, *firm*, 311.

fæðm, *embrace*, 650, 787, 1145, 1484.

fáh, *stained*, 1559; (?*guilty*), 828, 999, 1537, 1631.

fáh, *guilty*, 1613.

faran, *to go*, 480, 512, 870, 924, 927, 944, 982, 1341, 1414.

féa, *few*, 1169, 1274.

feallan, *to fall*, 1524.

féa-sceaft, *destitute, miserable*, 174, 367.

fédan, *to feed*, 1543.

fela, *many, much*, 171, 180, 1116, 1177, 1262, 1267, 1398, 1546.

féogan, *to hate*, 485, 708, 1597.

féond, *enemy*, 568, 622, 638, 732, 769, 1393, 1403, 1414, 1438, 1484, 1528, 1613, 1624.

féond-scipe, *enmity*, 485.

féor, *far*, 389.

feorh, *life, spirit*, 1072, 1318, 1561, 1564, 1572, 1591; to wi-dan feorh, *for ever*, 276.

feorh-dolg, *deadly wound*, 1453.

feorh-gifa, *giver of life*, 555.

feorh-góma, *deadly jaw*, 1547.

feorh-ner, *life's salvation*, 1595.

feorh-naru, *life's nourishment*, 609.

féowertig, *forty*, 465.

fér, *fear, terror*, 866.

ferhð, *heart, spirit*, 475.

ferian, fergan, *to drive*, 852, *to conduct*, 517.

ferð, *soul, spirit*, 667, 1329.

ferð-gewit, *mental wit*, 1182.

ferð-wérig, *weary of life*, 829.

féða, *troop*, 1517.

findan, *to find*, 183, 1572.

finger, *finger*, 667.

firas, *mankind*, 34, 241, 1564, 1597.

firen, *crime, sin*, 55, 122, 180, 368, 721, 1097, 1102, 1208, 1279, 1311, 1372, 1484, 1615.

firen-bealu, *transgression*, 1274.

firen-dǽd, *sinful deed, crime*, 999, 1304, 1631.

firen-fremmende, *committing crimes*, 1116.

firen-georn, *sin-loving*, 1604.

firen-lust, *sinful lust*, 1481.

firen-synnig, *sinful*, 1377.

firen-weorc, *evil deed*, 1299, 1397.

fisc, *fish*, 965.

fiðere, *a wing*, 394.

flacor, *flickering*, 675.

flǽsc, *flesh*, 122, 417, 596, 1027, 1280, 1304.

flǽsc-homa, *flesh-covering, body*, 1296, 1464.

flán-geweorc, *arrow-work*, 675.

flint, *flint, rock*, 1187.

flód, *flood, water, tide*, 805, 978, 984, 1167.

flód-wudu, *vessel*, 852.

flówan, *to flow*, 983.

flyht, *flight*, 398, 638, 653.

folc, *people*, 194, 224, 337, 425, 568, 578.

folc-dryht, *multitude*, 1065.

fold, *earth*, 71, 143, 278, 320, 806, 877, 982, 1001, 1032, 1141, 1388, 1448, 1464, 1532.

fold-ærn, *earth-cave*, 729.

fold-búend, *earth-dwellers*, 866, 1176.

fold-græf, *earth-grave, sepulchre*, 1024.

fold-ræst, *earthly rest*, 1027.

fold-weg, *earth-way, track of earth*, 1528.

fold-wong, *earth-plain*, 973.

folgian, *to follow*, 1439.

folgoð, *office*, 389.

folm, *hand*, 1123, 1420.

fót, *foot*, 1109, 1167, 1454.

forbærnan, *to burn up*, 1005, 1541.

forbéodan, *to forbid*, 1484.

forberstan, *to burst asunder*, 1136.

forbýgan, *to humiliate, bend down*, 730.

forcuman, *to overcome*, 150, 560.

fordón, *to destroy, damn*, 993, 1102, 1205, 1273.

fore-scyttels, *forebolt, bar*, 311.

fore-spreca, *mediator*, 732.

foretácen, *presage, sign*, 891.

fore-þoncol, *prudent*, 1190.

forfón, *to surprise*, 872.

forgiefan, *to grant*, 390, 586, 775, 1257, 1374, 1386, 1398.

forgieldan, *to requite*, 433, 1475.

forhogian, *to despise*, 1286, (?) 1632.

forht, *afraid*, 800, 891, 923, 1013, 1128.

forht-líc, *fearful*, 1102.

forht-líce, *fearfully*, 1318.

forhwyrfan, *to turn aside, to be depraved*, 33.

forlǽtan, *to leave, send forth, let go*, 9, 29, 207, 1110, 1146.

forlegen, *adulterate*, 1609.

forléosan, *to lose*, 1397, 1550, 1584.

forpyndan, *to turn away*, 96.

forséon, *to despise*, 756.

forst, *frost*, 1545.

forswelgan, *to devour*, 994.

forteón, *to betray*, 269.

fortyllan, *to seduce*, 269.

forþon, *wherefore, therefore*, 240.

forwyrcan, *to ruin*, 919.

forwyrd, *destruction*, 1534, 1613.

forwyrnan, *to refuse, prevent*, 19, 1502.

fracod, *bad, accursed*, 194.

fræt, *proud, obstinate*, 1372.

frætwe, *ornament*, 506, 521, 555, 804, 806, 1072, 1634.

fréa, *lord*, 236, 327, 354, 394, 403, 474, 923, 944, 1128, 1167, 1187, 1229, 1377.

frécne, *dangerous, foolhardy*, 769, 852, 1547, 1597.

fréfran, *to comfort*, 1339.

fremde, *alien*, 1402.

fremman, *to do, accomplish*, 368, 642, 654, 1289, 1554.

fremu, *benefit*, 1397.

fréo, *free, joyful*, 1510.

fréo-bearn, *noble child*, 222, 642, 787.

fréod, *affection*, 165.

fréogan, *to honour, love*, 1646.

fréo-líc, *noble*, 71.

fréo-líce, *joyfully*, 186, 1289.

fréond, *friend*, 574, 1343, 1657.

fréo-noma, *surname*, 635.

fréoðu, *peace*, 772.

frícgan, *to ask*, 91.

frigu, *affection, love*, 36, 418.

frið, *peace*, 488, 999, 1339, 1657.

frið-geard, *dwelling of peace*, 398.

fród, *wise*, 325, 1176.

frófor, *consolation*, 64, 206, 337, 488, 521, 721, 727, 757, 800, 1359, 1420, 1510.

from-líce, *boldly, fearlessly*, 574, 675.

fruma, *creator, beginning*, 43, 224, 293, 515, 578, 843, 1190.

frum-bearn, *first-born child*, 506.

frum-cyn, *race*, 34, 241.

196

frum-gesceap, *first creation*, 838.

frum-sceaft, *first creation*, 471.

frymð, *beginning*, 222.

fugol, *a bird*, 635, 638, 644, 653, 981.

fúl, *foul*, 1229, 1481.

full, *full*, 958.

fullian, *to baptize*, 483.

fús-léoð, *death-song*, 622.

fyllan, *to fill*, 1591, 1604.

fyllan, *to fell*, 485, 708, 973.

fýr, *fire*, 957, 964, 973, 1001, 1061, 1561, 1618, 1624, [fír, 1519].

fýr-bað, *bath of fire*, 829, 984.

fyrn-dagas, *days of yore*, 1032, 1293.

fyrn-weorc, *an ancient work, the creation*, 578.

fyrst, *a space of time*, 1321.

fýr-sweart, *fire-swart*, 982.

fyrwet, *curiosity*, 91.

fyst, *fist*, 1123.

GÆSNE, *barren*, 848.

gæst, *spirit, soul*, 129, 202, 268, 318, 362, 596, 637, 648, 706, 776, 815, 847, 1033, 1043, 1452, 1551, 1622.

gæst, *guest*, 812, 971.

gæst-berend, *spirit-endowed*, 1598.

gæst-geryne, *mystery of the mind*, 439, 712.

gæst-hálig, *holy in spirit*, 583.

gæst-hof, *guest dwelling*, 819.

gæstlíc, *ghostly*, 41, 698.

gæst-sunu, *spirit-son*, 659, 859.

gǽt, *goat*, 1229.

gafol, *tribute*, 558.

gál, *light, pleasant*, 1033.

galan, *to sing*, 622.

gán, gangan, *to go*, 425, 1069, 1166.

gár-faru, *armed band*, 780.

gár-getrum, *storm of darts*, 673.

ge, *and also*, 845.

—— ge eac, 1168.

ge-æfnan, *to endure*, 1428.

gealla, *gall*, 1437.

géar, *year*, 1034.

geard, *dwelling*, 200.

géar-dagas, *days of yore*, 250, 558, 820.

gearnung, *desert, meed*, 39.

gearo, *ready*, 448, 459, 1268, 1344.

gearo-snottor, *very wise*, 712.

geat, *gate*, 250, 317, 575.

gebed-scip, *communion*, 75.

gebéodan, *to bid*, 201.

geberan, *to bear, bring forth*, 83, 122, 204, 1150, 1419.

gebétan, *to restore*, 12.

gebídan, *to await, abide*, 69, 1528.

gebígan, *to twist, bend*, 1124, 1443.

gebindan, *to bind*, 731, 1355, 1537.

gebléod, *of different colours*, 907.

geblandan, *to mix*, 1436.

geblétsian, *to bless*, 411.

geblissian, *to bless, make happy*, 248, 379.

gebrosnian, *to lay waste, destroy*, 12, 83.

gebúgan, *to bend*, 1503.

gebycgan, *to buy, redeem*, 258, 1461.

gebyrd, *birth*, 37, 64, 75, 297.

gecéosan, *to choose*, 445, 496, 589.

gecnáwan, *to understand*, 653.

gecweðan, *to speak*, 131.

gecwéman, *to please*, 916.

ge-cynd, *offspring*, 1015, 1016, 1179.

gecýpan, *to buy*, 1470.

gecýðan, *to reveal*, 156.

gedǽlan, *to part, divide*, 165, 227, 427.

gedafenian, *to be becoming*, 550.

gedón, *to do, cause*, 29, 1264, 1381.

gedræg, *tumult*, 998.

gedreccan, *to afflict, oppress*, 992, 1297, 1507.

gedréfan, *to trouble*, 167.

gedréosan, *to fall*, 264.

gedryht, *band, host*, 456, 514, 518, 940, 1012, 1662.

gedwellan, *to lead astray*, 1126.

gedwola, *error*, 343.

gedýran, *to glorify*, 1643.

ge-eardian, *to dwell*, 207.

ge-edniwian, *to renew*, 1038.

ge-endian, *to end*, 1638.

gefǽlsian, *to cleanse, purify*, 143, 319.

ge-fæstnian, *to fasten*, 734, 1446, 1455, 1489.

geféa, *joy, gladness*, 158, 230, 450, 584, 742, 1076, 1251, 1293, 1402, 1595.

gefélan, *to feel*, 1128, 1177.

geféon, *to rejoice*, 475, 503, 756.

geferian, *to lead, carry*, 344.

gefléogan, *to fly*, 294.

gefóg, *a joining, joint*, 5.

gefón, *to give, seize, receive*, 1352, 1511.

gefréon, *to free*, 587.

gefremman, *to finish, accomplish, afford*, 206, 262, 423, 565, 596, 601, 626, 1453.

gefreoðian, *to protect*, 587.

gefrignan, *to ask, learn, hear*, 77, 224, 300.

gefyllan, *to fill, fulfil*, 180, 212, 325, 407, 467.

gefyrn, *long ago, formerly*, 62, 134, 300, 1523.

gefýsan, *to make ready, to cause to hasten*, 474, 889.

gegán, *to go*, 442.

gegearwian, *to prepare*, 1521.

gehæftan, *to take captive*, 561.

gehǽlan, *to heal*, 173.

gehálgian, *to hallow*, 434, 1480.

gehát, *promise*, 540.

gehátan, *to promise, command, call*, 57, 141, 1070, 1337.

gehealdan, *to hold, preserve, guard*, 299, 1058, 1493.

gehladan, *to load*, 1033.

gehléapan, *to leap*, 716.

gehlid, *covering, roof, enclosure, vault*, 517, 903.

gehogian, *to devise*, 1396.

gehréosan, *to fall down*, 937.

gehréoðan, *to adorn*, 329.

gehréow, *a lamenting*, 997.

ge-hréowan, *to rue*, 1492.

gehðo, *care, anxiety*, 89.

gehwá, *each*, 193, 230.

gehwyrfan, *to change*, 187.

gehýdan, *to hide*, 1465.

gehygd, *thought*, 746, 1037, 1053, 1313.

gehyld, *keeping*, 544.

gehýnan, *to scorn, humble, oppress*, 561, 1523.

gehyran, *to hear*, 170, 491, 585, 833.

gehyrstan, *to adorn*, 392.

gehyrwan, *to despise*, 458.

gelác, '*tumultus*,' *assembly*, 894.

gelácnian, *to cure, heal*, 1307.

gelád, *path*, 855.

gelǽdan, *to lead*, 303, 858.

geléafa, *belief*, 482.

gelíc, *like*, 1382, 1429, 1431.

gelíce, *alike*, 782.

gelimpan, *to happen*,

198

come to pass, 78, 232.

gelíðan, *to sail*, 856.

gelong, *belonging, depending*, 151, 364.

gelýfan, *to believe*, 655, 752.

gelýfan, *to make dear*, 1643.

gemæc-scip, *communion*, 198.

gemǽne, *common*, 356, 580, 1458.

gemǽrsian, *to supplicate*, 22.

gemánan, *fellowship*, 1644.

gemeltan, *to melt*, 976.

gemengan, *to mingle*, 893.

gemet, *measure, boundary*, 825.

gemétan, *to meet*, 329.

gemiclian, *to enlarge*, 46.

gemong, *company, throng*, 1659.

gemót, *assembly*, 794, 831, 941, 1025.

gemunan, *to bear in mind*, 1199.

gemynd, *memory*, 664, 1036, 1535.

genǽgan, *to approach, assault*, 873.

genéahhe, *enough, earnestly, suddenly*, 47, 975.

generian, *to save*, 1256.

genesan, *to be preserved, escape from*, 1253.

geneðan, *to venture*, 68.

geniman, *to take from*, 222, 579.

geníðle, *enmity, hate*, 1438.

geniwian, *to renew*, 528.

genóg, *enough*, 1263.

genomian, *to name, point out*, 1099.

genyrwian, *to oppress*, 363.

géoc, *help*, 123.

géocend, *saviour*, 197.

géomor, *sad, mournful*, 123, 498, 961.

géomor-mód, *sad of mind*, 172, 534, 1405.

géomrian, *to bemoan*, 89.

geond, *throughout*, 6, 58, 70, 278, 305, 379, 468, 480, 481, 784, 809, 851, 854.

geond-sécan, *to pervade*, 971.

geond-spréotan, *to pervade*, 41.

geond-wlítan, *to look around*.

geong, *young*, 34, 174, 200.

georn, *eager*, 396.

georne, *eagerly*, 752, 820, 848, 1002, 1222, 1254, 1326, 1580, 1589.

geþrnlíce, *eagerly*, 261, 432, 439.

géotan, *to pour out*, 172, 816, 1447, 1565.

gereccan, *to explain, interpret*, 132.

gerestan, *to rest*, 52.

gerísan, *to befit, beseem*, 2.

gerýman, *to open up*, 864.

geryne, *mystery*, 40, 73, 94, 133, 422, 602.

gesǽlan, *to bind*, 861.

gesǽlig, *blessed, happy*, 437, 1247, 1459, 1650, 1658.

gesǽlig-líc, *blessed*, 1077.

gesárgian, *to afflict*, 960, 969.

gesceaft, *created things, creation*, 58, 238, 401, 671, 869, 990, 1019, 1126, 1381.

gesceppan, *to make, form, create*, 13, 22, 658, 1385.

gescieldan, *to shield*, 760, 774.

gescomian, *to be ashamed*, 1301.

gesécan, *to seek, visit*, 61, 145, 523, 570, 625, 645, 1536.

gesecgan, *to tell*, 1308, 1315.

gesellan, *to give*, 1476.

gesénian, *to sign, bless*, 1340.

geséon, *to see*, 497, 501, 505, 511, 521, 553, 793, 923, 1104, 1114, 1126, 1132,

1280, 1290, 1305, 1310, 1312, 1347, 1453, 1456.

geset, *habitation, home*, 1238.

geséðan, *to declare, prove*, 242.

gesettan, *to set, establish, create*, 1163, 1380, 1388.

gesihð, *sight*, 6, 49, 909, 1112.

gesíþ, *companion, company*, 472, 1520.

gesíttan, *to sit*, 530.

gesléan, *to strike down*, 148.

gesomnian, *to unite, collect*, 4, 1220.

gesprecan, *to speak*, 1510.

gestarian, *to gaze*, 306.

gestaþelian, *to establish*, 306.

gesteald, *a dwelling*, 303.

gestígan, *to ascend, to descend*, 513, 678, 748, 1170, 1417, 1490.

gestun, *noise, whirlwind*, 989.

gestyllan, *to move rapidly*, 647, 715.

gesund, *sound, unhurt*, 1073, 1340.

gesweotolian, *to display*, 8.

geswíðan, *to strengthen*, 384.

gesyllan, *to give*, 682, (*v.* gesellan).

geþencan, *to consider, to think about*, 287, 369, 1055.

geþéon, *to perform*, 376.

geþicgan, *to take*, 1508.

geþingian, *to intercede, make terms*, 341, 615.

geþoht, *thought*, 1046, 1054.

geþolian, *to suffer*, 1171, 1422, 1433, 1441, 1513.

geþonc, *thought, mind*, 314, 1118, 1125, 1582.

geþréan, *to afflict, oppress*, 1562.

geþwǽre, *peaceful*, 126.

getremman, *to establish*, 1149.

getrywe, *honest, faithful*, 875.

getwǽfan, *to separate, deprive*, 985.

geweald, *power*, 227, 704, 1414, 1647.

gewemman, *to defile*, 1485.

gewénan, *to hope, expect*, 1364.

gewendan, *to turn*, 933.

geweorðan, *to become, to come to pass, to be*, 36, 92, 121, 209, 237, 316, 350,

geweorðian, *to honour*, 406, 658.

gewerian, *to array*, 446, 551.

gewill, *will*, 361.

gewin, *strife, anguish, trouble*, 56, 996, 1410, 1654.

gewinnan, *to gain*, 999.

gewítan, *to depart*, 493, 532, 1226.

gewitléas, *witless*, 1471.

gewitt, *understanding*, 28, 639, 1176, 1191, 1198.

gewrit, *scripture*, 546.

gewrixlan, *to give in exchange, grant*, 1259.

gewuldrian, *to glorify*, 97.

gewyrcan, *to make*, 160, 178, 239, 679, 762, 1138, 1232, 1379, 1386, 1444, 1615.

gewyrht, *work, deed, desert*, 127, 890, 1218, 1366, 1576.

ge-ýcan, *to increase*, 1038.

giedd, *a song*, 632, 712.

giefan, *to give*, 472, 603, 1380, 1500, 1612.

gief-stól, *gift-stool, throne*, 571.

giefu, *grace*, 479, 648, 659, 681, 709, 1242, 1661 (*v.* gíofu).

gield, *a recompense*, 1077, (*v.* gyld).

gielp, *pride*, 683.

gíeman, *to care for*, 705, (*v.* gýman.)

giet, *yet*, 317, 350.

gífre, *greedy*, 812, 971, 1043.

gimm, *a gem*, 691, 694.

giofu, *gift, grace*, 41, (*v.* giefu.)

gioguþ, *youth*, 1652.

glæd, *benign, glad*, 314, 1285, 1652.

glæd-mód, *glad of mood*, 575, 909.

glæs, *glass*, 1281.

gléaw, *wise*, 138, 219.

gléawlíce, *wisely, prudently*, 129, 1326.

gléd, *burning coal*, 994, 1043.

gléo-béam, *glee wood*, 669.

gnorn, *anguish*, 1574.

gód, *sustenance*, (*goods*,) 479.

gód, *good*, 1010, 1104, 1331, 1574.

god, *God*, 323.

god-bearn, *divine child*, 498, 701.

god-cunde, *divine*, 669.

gód-dǽd, *good deed*, 1285.

god-þrym, *divine majesty*, 138.

gold-frætwe, *gold ornaments*, 994.

gold-hord, *treasure*, 786.

gold - webb, *golden tapestry*, 1133.

gomel, *old man*, 134.

gong, *going, journey*, 253, 1034.

gongan, *to go, pass*, 575, (*v.* gangan.)

grafan, *to delve*, 1002.

gréotan, *to weep*, 990, 1570.

grétan, *to greet*, 669.

grim, *grim*, 969, 1079, 1203, 1268, 1332, 1525.

grimlíc, *grim*, 917.

grimlíce, *grimly*, 1002.

grom, *grim, angry*, 780.

grom - hydig, *fierce-minded*, 733.

grorn, *grief, sadness*, 1203.

grornian, *to mourn*, 969.

grund, *bottom, abyss, earth*, 144, 480, 561, 681, 784, 971, 1163.

grundléas, *bottomless*, 1544.

grund-scéat, *region of earth*, 41, 648.

gryre-bróga, *terror*, 847.

guma, *a man*, 426, 510, 812, 1652.

gúð, *battle*, 673.

gúð-plega, *war-play, battle*, 572.

gyld, *substitute, stead*, 1101.

gylden, *golden*, 250, 317.

gylp, *pride, arrogance*, 816.

gýman, *to take heed of*, 1544, 1551, 1567, 1598.

gyrnan, *to desire*, 1165.

gyrne, *earnestly*, 1303.

HABBAN, *to have*, 180, 255.

hád, *condition, rank*, 285.

hádor, *resplendent*, 692.

hǽðen, *heathen*, 704.

hæft, *a captive, servant*, 153, 359.

hæft, *bondage, imprisonment*, 259, 567.

hǽlan, *to heal*, 1320.

hǽlend, *Saviour*, 249, 357, 382, 434, 504, 633, 791.

hǽleþ, *man*, 265, 278, 371, 460, 533, 607, 668, 871, 881, 1192, 1195, 1276, 1590.

hǽlo, hǽlu, *salvation, health*, 118, 201, 410, 751, 858, 1573, 1653.

hǽlo-bearn, *saviour-child*, 585, 753.

hǽlo-líf, *salvation*, 149.

hǽlu-giefu, *healing grace*, 373.

hafela, *head*, 504.

hálig, *holy*, 57, 283, 347, 402, 528, 631, 736, 1008, 1109, 1338, 1425, 1587, 1607.

háls, *salvation*, 586.

O

hám, *home*, 304, 349, 646.

hámfæst, *resident*, 1553.

hangian, *to hang, be suspended*, 1455, 1487.

hát, *hot*, 499, 538, 931, 975, 1058, 1161, 1425, 1522, 1540, 1618.

hátan, *to command*, 252, 278, 293, 1023, 1226, 1340, 1373.

héa, *high*, 1061, 1063.

héafod, *head*, 3, 1124, 1433, 1443.

héafod-gim, *head-gem*, 1329.

héag-engel, *archangel*, 201, (*v.* héah-engel.)

héah, *high*, 281, 378, 652, 677.

héah-boda, *chief-messenger*, 294.

héah-clif, *lofty cliff*, 977.

héah-cyning, *high king*, 149, 1338.

héah-engel, *archangel*, 402, 527.

héah-fréa, *high lord, sovran*, 423.

héah-gæst, *great spirit*, 357.

héah-getimbro, *a lofty building*, 972, 1180.

héah-setl, *high seat, throne*, 554, 1216, 1334.

héahþu, *height*, 497, 507, 759, 788, 865.

healdan, *to keep, hold*, 18, 92, 488, 766, 791, 812, 1158, 1235, 1259, 1647.

healf, *side*, 60, 1266.

héalic, *noble*, 429.

héa-líce, *on high, excellently*, 382, 388, 692, 1148.

heall, *hall*, 3.

héan, *abject, poor, mean*, 98, 264, 413, 631, 992, 1412, 1470, 1607.

héanlíce, *ignominiously*, 371.

héanness, *height*, 161, 409.

héap, *band, throng*, 15, 548, 730, 928, 943.

heard, *severe, stern, hard*, 1063, 1124, 1187, 1309, 1423, 1443, 1487, 1504, 1611.

heard-cwide, *reproach*, 1442.

hearde, *cruelly, sorely*, 363, 1016, 1455, 1512.

heard-líce, *hardly, cruelly*, 259.

hearg, *a heathen temple, an idol*, 484.

hearm, *injury*, 170.

hearm-cwalu, *pernicious death*, 1607.

hearm-cwide, *abusive speech, blasphemy*, 1119.

hearm-slege, *a grievous blow*, 1433.

hearpe, *harp*, 668.

hefige, *grievously*, 1486.

helan, *to hide*, 192.

hel-fús, *hell-prone*, 1122.

hell, *hell*, 264, 557, 561, 590, 1158, 1258.

helle-bealu, *the torment of hell*, 1425.

hell-cwalu, *hell-torment*, 1188.

helle-fýr, *hell-fire*, 1268.

helm, *helm, top, covering*, 409, 462, 528, 565, 633.

help, *help*, 262, 631, 857, 1172, 1470, 1567.

helpan, *to help, aid*, 1501.

helpend, *a helper*, 1412.

hel-sceaþa, *hell-fiend*, 363.

hel-waru, *hell-dwellers*, 285, 730.

heofon, *heaven*, 60, 149, 201, 252.

heofon-beorht, *heavenly bright*, 1017.

heofon-býma, *heaven's trumpet*, 947.

heofon-condel, *heaven's candle*, 607.

heofon-cund, *heavenly, celestial*, 378.

heofon-cyning, *king of heaven*, 1085, 1512, 1523.

heofon-duguð, *heavenly host,* 1653.

heofon-engel, *heavenly angel,* 491, 926, 1008, 1276.

heofon-hám, *heavenly home,* 292.

heofon-mægen, *heavenly host,* 1216.

heofon-ríce, *kingdom of heaven,* 565, 1244, 1258, 1632, 1637.

heofon-steorra, *star of heaven,* 1042.

heofon-tungol, *star of heaven,* 692.

heofon-wóma, *heavenly sound,* 833, 997.

heoloð-cyn, *hell race,* 1540.

heonan, *hence,* 154, 513, 581, 753.

heorte, *heart,* 173, 499, 538, 640, ¯746, 751, 1037, 1046, 1054, 1327, 1492. ˌ

heoro-gífre, *eager to destroy, greedy,* 975, 1058.

heoro-grim, *fiercely-grim,* 1522, 1611.

hér, *here,* 1456, 1573.

hér-cyme, *advent,* 249.

here, *multitude, host,* 484, 523, 573, 843, 928, 1276, 1531, 1596, 1624.

here-féða, *a martial band,* 1011.

herenis, *praise,* 414.

hergan, (herian,) *to praise,* 48, 382, 429, 469, 502, 633.

hetol, *malignant,* 363.

hider-cyme, *advent, hither,* 141, 366.

hierusalem, *Jerusalem,* 1133.

hige-gléaw, *prudent, wise,* 1192.

hild, *war,* 565.

hingong, *hence going,* 1411, 1553.

híw, *form, colour,* 656, 720, 724, 934.

hladan, *to load,* 783.

hlǽfdige, *lady, queen,* 283.

hláf, *bread,* 1353.

hláford, *lord, master,* 460, 497, 517, 573.

hleahtor, *laughter,* 738.

hlemman, *to roar, resound, clash,* 931.

hléo, *refuge, protection,* 408, 605, 1195.

hléo-fæst, *protecting,* 357.

hléor, *face, cheek,* 1119, 1433.

hléotan, *to get by lot, to share,* 782.

hléoð, *shelter,* 1352.

hléoþor-cwide, *speech, utterance,* 449.

hliþ, *a hill,* 744.

hlóð, *band, troop,* 1161.

hlúd, *loud,* 388, 491, 668, 833, 997.

hlutor, *pure, bright,* 292, 1011, 1085.

hlutre, *serenely,* 1150.

hlýdan, *to sound,* 881.

hlýp, *leap, jump,* 719, 725, 729, 735, 744, 746.

hold, *gracious,* 1470.

hold-líce, *graciously,* 429, 1356.

holm, *the deep, ocean,* 854, 977.

holm-þracu, *tossing of the waves,* 677.

hond, *hand,* 161, 1109, 1122, 1131, 1220, 1226, 1362, 1378, 1486, 1529.

hond-geweorc, *handiwork,* 265, 1413.

hord, *treasure,* 1046, 1054, 1071.

horsc, *wise, prudent,* 48, 240.

hosp, *insult, contumely,* 170, 1442.

hoðma, *a covering, darkness,* 44.

hrá, *body,* 13.

hrædlíce, *soon, speedily,* 262.

hrægel, *dress, robe,* 446, 453, 1353, 1504.

hraðe, *quickly,* 1026.

hréam, *clamour,* 593.

hreddan, *to rescue,* 273.

hrémig, *exulting,* 53.

hréoh, *rough,* 857.

hréosan, *to fall,* 809, 975, 1042, 1411, 1522.

203

hréoðan, *to adorn*, 291.

hréow, *grief*, 992, 1556.

hréowan, *to repent, rue*, 1413.

hréow-cearig, *afflicted with sad cares*, 366.

hréran, *to stir*, 677.

hréþ-éadig, *glorious, noble*, 943.

hreðer, *heart*, 538, 640, 1158, 1161.

hreþer-cófa, *breast*, 1327.

hreþer-loca, *the breast*, 1054.

hrif, *womb*, 424.

hring, (?) *ring*, 536.

hrof, *roof*, 13, 59, 494, 527, 748.

hróþor, *solace, pleasure*, 413, 622, 1195.

hruse, *earth*, 657, 881.

hrycg, *back, ridge*, 857.

huru, *certainly, forsooth*, 21, 81, 336.

hwæs, *sharp, keen*, 1442.

hwearfian, *to wander*, 371.

hweorfan, *to depart, go*, 30, 475, 484, 956, 1043.

hwít, *white*, 446, 453, 544, 896, 1017, 1109.

hungor, *hunger*, 1659.

hús, *house*, 1134, 1138, 1480, 1602, 1626.

húþ, *spoil*, 567.

hycgan, *to consider*, 1632 (?=forhycgan).

hyder-cyme, *coming hither*, 586.

hyge, *mind, heart*, 499, 1356, 1504, 1510.

hyge-cræftig, *powerful in mind, profound*, 240.

hyge-géomor, *sad at heart*, 153, 889, 992.

hyge-róf, *strong of mind*, 533.

hyge-sorg, *heart's sorrow*, 173.

hyge-þanc, *heart's thought*, 1329.

hyht, *joy, hope*, 57, 98, 528, 584, 863.

hyhtan, *to hope*, 141, 339.

hyht-ful, *hopeful*, 118.

hyht-plega, *joyous play, sport*, 736.

hyll, *a hill*, 716.

hýnan, *to oppress*, 259.

hyngrian, *to hunger*, 1353.

hýnð, (hýnþo, híenþo,) *contempt, disgrace*, 590, 1512.

hýran, *to hear, obey*, 72, 343, 359, 798, 1589.

hyrde, *shepherd*, 449, 704.

hyspan, *to mock, scorn*, 1119.

hýþan, (híþan,) *to lay waste*, 972, 1042.

hyðe, *hythe, haven*, 858, 863.

ÍDEL, *idle, empty*, 1296.

íecan, *to increase*, 610.

inca, *cause of complaint*, 177.

ingeþonc, *thought*, 1012, 1314.

ingong, *entrance, portal*, 307.

in-hebban, *to raise*, 312.

inlíce, *inwardly*, 431.

inlíhtan, *to illumine*, 42, 107, 114.

innan, *within, inside*, 1003, 1328.

iowan, *to show*, 334.

íu, *once, formerly*, 1.

LÁC, *gift*, 291.

lácan, *to play, sport*, 398, 853, 1593.

ládian, (ládigan,) *to clear from blame, to clear one's-self of a charge*, 182.

lǽcedom, *cure, remedy*, 1571.

lǽdan, *to lead, bring*, 140, 573, 794.

lǽfan, *to leave*, 158.

lǽmen, *made of clay*, 14.

lǽne, *transitory*, 841, 1557, 1584.

lǽran, *to instruct*, 814.

lǽstan, *to follow, to do service, to do*, 476, 1223, 1287, 1391.

lǽtan, *leave behind, allow, let go*, 154, 157, 342, 1594.

lagu-flód, *water, flood*, 849.

lám, *clay*, 1380.

lange, *long*, 1360.

lár, *a learning, teaching, lore*, 43, 140, 1199.

láréow, *teacher*, 457.

lást, *track, footprint*, 495.

láð, *hostile, hateful to, loathsome*, 182, 193, 591, 845, 1373, 1601.

láþlíc, *hateful*, 1172, 1274.

láðwende, *evilly disposed*, 1593.

latian, *to delay*, 372.

leahtor, *crime, sin*, 828, 1097, 1279, 1307, 1313, 1477, 1537, 1557.

léan, *reward*, 433, 472, 782, 845, 1360, 1365, 1586.

léanian, *to requite*, 826.

léas, *void of*, 1412, 1450, 1463, 1507, 1639.

léas, *false*, 1118.

léaslíc, *vain, frivolous*, 1295.

lég, *flame*, 808, 956, 972, 982, 993, 1334, 1531, 1537, 1593, (*v.* líg.)

lég-bryne, *burning flame*, 1000.

leger, *sickness*, 1660.

léod, *people*, 1088, 1117, 1172, 1185, 1237, 1423, 1571, 1601.

léod-sceaþa, *injurer of the people, a public enemy, the devil*, 272.

léof, *dear*, 457, 495, 500, 595, 814, 845, 1346, 1360, 1641, 1651.

leofian, *to live*, 441, 1634.

léof-líc, *lovable, dear*, 399.

léof-líce, *lovingly*, 1094.

léof-tǽl, *dear, loving*, 911.

léof-wende, *pleasing, gracious*, 470.

léoht, *light*, 26, 226.

léoht, *bright*, 1088.

léohtan, *to give light*, 233.

léohte, *clearly*, 1117, 1237.

léoma, *light, ray*, 105, 203, 233, 695, 776, 899, 1004, 1619.

libban, lifgan, *to live*, 436, 828, 1155, 1210, 1325, 1452, (cp. leofian).

líc, *body*, 776, 818, 1035, 1295, 1325.

licgan, *to lie*, 44, 733, 1136, 1154, 1423, 1464.

líc-homa, *body*, 627, 754, 1030, 1067, 1097, 1185, 1208, 1279, 1313, 1452, 1469, 1483.

lícian, *to please*, 1079, 1332.

líc-sár, *pain of body*, 1428.

líf, *life*, 226, 333, 1050, 1094.

líf-dæg, *day of life*, 1223.

líf-fréa, *lord of life*, 14, 26.

líf-fruma, *life's Creator, Author of life*, 503, 655, 1041.

líf-wela, *the wealth of this world*, 1346.

líf-wyn, *life's joy*, 805.

líg, *flame*, 1249, 1619, (*v.* lég.)

lim, *joint, limb*, 14.

lioþu-cǽge, *limb-key*, 333.

liss, *favour, love, grace*, 372, 433, 1365, 1645.

list, *artifice*, 1317.

lið, *joint, limb*, 1030, 1067, 1380.

líðan, *to go, sail*, 850.

líðe, *gentle*, 604, 912, 1636.

líxan, *to shine, glitter*, 230, 697.

loca, *key, enclosure*, 18, 320, 1619.

lof, *praise*, 410, 611, 776.

lofian, *to praise*, 503, 399, 1640.

lond, *land*, 1000.

long, *long*, 342.

losian, *to perish, be lost*, 1556; *to stray*,

escape from, 1000, 1627.

lufe, *love*, 476, 1115, 1432.

lufsum, *pleasant*, 912.

lufu, *love*, 584, 1651, (*v.* lufe.)

lungre, *forthwith*, 166.

lust, *desire, lust*, 260, 1296 ; lustum, *joyfully*, 1223.

lyft, *heaven, air*, 218, 490, 989, 1041.

lyge, *a lie*, 1305.

lyge-searu, *artifice*, 775.

lýgnian, *to deny*, 1118.

lýsan, *to release, redeem*, 1208.

lyt, *little*, 1399.

lytel, *little*, 961, 1321.

MÁ, *more, greater*, 420, 987.

mæg, *kinsman, offspring*, 164.

mæg, *maiden*, 86.

mægden-hád, *maidenhood*, 1418.

mæge, *kinswoman*, 95.

mægen, *strength, power, might*, 144, 318, 602, 747, 831 ; *a military force, legion, band*, 955, 1017.

mægen-cræft, *mighty power*, 1278.

mægen-cyning, *mighty king*, 915, 941.

mægen-earfeþe, *great hardship, labour*, 962, 1409.

mægen-folc, *a mighty people*, 875.

mægen-þrym, *great glory, mighty strength*, 295, 351, 556, 1007.

mægen - wundor, *a mighty wonder*, 925.

mægð, (mægeð,) *maid, virgin*, 35, 175, 444, 720.

mægð, *tribe, nation*, 143, 233.

mægð-hád, *maidenhood*, 84, 288.

mæg-wlite, *appearance, form*, 1382, 1431.

mǽnan, *to complain*, 89.

mǽnan, *to tell of, mean*, 1376.

mænigo, *multitude*, 155, (*v.* mengu.)

mǽre, *great, famous, glorious*, 3, 93, 137, 164, 209, 274, 440, 455, 588, 970, 1006.

mǽðlan, *to speak*, 1336, 1362.

mǽrþu, *fame*, 590, 747.

maga, *son*, 1418.

magan, *to be able*, 126, 172, 182, 220, 241.

magu-géoguð, *youth*, 1427.

magu-tudor, *offspring*, 628.

mán, *crime, guilt, evil*, 35, 1431, 1599.

mán-cwealm, *dire torment*, 1415.

mán-fremmende, *doing evil*, 1435.

mán-forwyrht, *sin, crime*, 1093.

manig, monig, *many*, 1141, 1161, 1169, 1173.

manian, *to admonish, to claim what is due*, 1477.

manig-feald, *manifold*, 661 ; monig-feald, 602.

mán-sceaða, *evil-doer*, 1558.

mán-swara, *a perjurer*, 192 ; mán-swora, 1610.

mán - weorc, *crime*, 1209.

mán-womm, *guilty stain*, 1278.

meaht, *might*, 217, 283, 295, 329, 477, 487, 566, 715, 821, 1076, 1144, 1188.

meaht, *mighty*, 867.

meahtig, *mighty*, 1526, (*v.* mihtig.)

mengu, *multitude*, 508, (*v.* mænigo.)

mennisc, *human*, 720.

meotud, *fate, destiny, the Creator, God*, 93, 125, 142, 196, 209, 288.

meotud-sceaft, *decree of fate, doom*, 886.

méowle, *virgin*, 445.

mete-léas, *foodless*, 1505.

micel, *great*, 155, 351, 750, 846.

middan-geard, *middle earth*, 248, 274, 556, 697, 786, 825, 880, 970, 1045.

mihtig, *mighty*, 474, 1169, (*v.* meahtig.)

milde, *merciful, gentle*, 821, 1199, 1209, 1350.

milde, *mercifully*, 248.

milts, *mercy*, 243, 298, 1253, 1364, 1369.

mirce, *dark*, 1278.

mislíc, *various*, 643.

mód, *mind, manner*, 27, 279, 292, 915, 988.

mód-blind, *undiscerning*, 1186.

mód-cræft, *mental power*, 440.

módig, *bold*, 745.

mód-lufe, *soul's love*, 1260.

módor, *mother*, 92, 424, 1418.

molde, *earth*, 420, 887.

mon, *man*, 440.

móna, *moon*, 605, 697, 936.

monig, (*v.* manig.)

monn-cynn, *mankind*, 243, 416, 1025, 1039, 1093, 1095, 1415.

mon-wíse, *human fashion, way*, 76.

morþor, *crime*, 192.

morðor-hús, *house of torment*, 1623.

morþor-léan, *reward of crime*, 1610.

mós, *food*, 1505.

mótan, *to be allowed*, 245, 345, 391, 589.

mund, (?) *troth*, 92.

mund-bora, *protector, guardian-angel*, 27.

mund-héals, (?) *safety*, 445.

munt, *mountain*, 715, 745.

múr, *a wall*, 1141.

murnan, *to mourn*, 499.

múð, *mouth*, 664, 1435.

myntan, *to intend*, 1056.

myrran, *to stumble, err, to be troubled*, 1142.

NACOD, *naked*, 1353, 1504.

nægel, *nail*, 1108.

nǽnig, *none*, 1309.

náles, *not at all*, 961, 1169, 1193, 1274, 1535.

nát-hwylc, '*nescio-quis*,' 188.

náwþer, *neither*, 188.

néah, *near*, 389.

nearo-þearf, *pressing need*, 68.

nemnan, *to name*, 130, 635.

néod, *desire, earnestness*, 244; níod, 260; néode, *earnestly*, 'neode and nyde,' '*by our own desire and by compulsion*,' 1070 (*v.* nýd).

neorxna-wong, *Paradise*, 1389, 1404.

néosan, *to visit*, 320, 740.

néotan, *to enjoy*, 1342, 1389, 1460.

nergend, *Saviour*, 156, 260, 323, 360, 397, 425.

nerian, *to save*, 1187, 1449.

níed-þíow, *slave, thrall*, 360.

niht, *night*, 541, 591, 868, 871.

niman, *to take*, 62, 259, 963, 981, 1001, 1611.

níð, *envy*, 1658.

níð-cwalu, *grievous destruction*, 1256.

niþer, *down*, 958, 1617, 1465.

níð-hycgende, *having malice in heart, malicious one*, 1108.

noma, *name*, 47, 130, 1350, 1505.

norð, *northwards*, 883.

nýd, *necessity*, 1070, 1404 (*v.* néod).

nýd-gewald, *tyranny*, 1449.

nymþe, *unless*, 323.

OFERMǼTE, *immeasurable*, 853.

oferþearf, *extreme need*, 152.

ofgiefan, *to give up, leave*, 728.

ofhréosan, *to fall down*, 932.

207

ofost - lícor, *more quickly*, 271.

ofsléan, *to slay*, 1478.

oftéon, *to withhold*, 1503, 1508.

óht, *aught*, 237 (*v.* áwiht, ówiht).

onbærnan, *to kindle*, 1041.

onbeht, *servant*, 369.

onbéodan, *to proclaim*, 1168.

oncnáwan, *to understand, know*, 641, 860, 1117, 1186.

ondrǽdan, *to fear*, 778, 789, 921, 1016.

onettan, *to hasten, be diligent*, 1577.

onfindan, *to detect, perceive*, 177, 1177.

onfón, *to receive, take*, 74, 98, 181, 417, 627, 1067, 1130.

ongietan, *to see, perceive*, 1105, 1148, 1158.

onginnan, *to begin*, 1361, 1375, 1413.

onhǽle, *hidden*, (? *entire*,) 894.

onhréran, *to stir*, 824.

onhweorfan, *to turn away*, 617.

onlúcan, *to unlock*, 313, 324.

onlýhtan, *to enlighten, illuminate*, 203.

onlýsan, *to loosen*, 67.

onmedla, *pride*, 813.

208

onscínan, *to shine upon*, 1239.

onsendan, *to send*, 113, 759, 763.

onséon, *to look upon*, 1243.

onsíen, *lack*, 479.

onstarian, *to gaze upon*, 520, 569.

onsýn, *presence*, 395, 795, 835, 904, 922, 1018 ; onsíen, 1649.

ontýnan, *to open, reveal*, 18, 26, 252, 575.

onwald, *power*, 158.

onwalg, *uncorrupted*, 1419.

onwlítan, *to look upon*, 326.

onwréon, *uncover, reveal*, 94, 138, 194, 315, 383, 462.

open, *evident, open*, 1044, 1106, 1115, 1569, 1603.

ord, *chief, point*, 740, 767, 844.

ord-fruma, *source, origin*, 226, 401, 1197.

orgete, *manifest*, 1115, 1456; orgeate, 1214, 1236.

orlege, *war, strife*, 559.

ormǽte, *immense*, 308.

óð-clífan, *to cleave to*, 1265.

óðýwan,(éawan,éowan,) *to show, appear*, 447, 453, 837, 893, 1603.

ówer, *anywhere*, 198.

ówihte, *at all*, 247.

PLEGA, *play, sport, revel*, 742.

RACU, *account*, 1395, 1458.

rǽcan, *to reach forth, stretch*, 1619.

rǽd, *advice, counsel*, 429, 1524.

rǽran, *to raise*, 688.

rǽs, *a rush*, 726.

ræst, *rest, repose*, 1654.

rásettan, *to rage*, 807.

raðe, *quickly*, 1524.

réad, *red*, 808, 1100, 1174.

récan, *to care, reck*, 1439.

reccan, *interpret*, 670.

reccend, *ruler*, 17.

recen, *swift*, 808.

rén, *rain*, 608.

reord, *speech, prayer*, 46, 509, 1338.

reord-berend, *endowed with speech*, 277, 380, 1023, 1367.

reordian, *to speak*, 195.

réotan, *to weep*, 834, 1228.

réðe, *fierce*, 797, 808, 824, 1526.

ríce, *power, dominion, empire, kingdom*, 267, 352, 474, 1064, 1343, 1526.

ríce, *mighty*, 1467.

ricene, *forthwith*, 1446.

riht, *account, reckoning*, 1373.

riht, *righteous, true*, 17 (*v.* ryht).

rím, *number*, 466, 1585.

rinc, *a man*, 1113.

rind, *rind*, 1174.

rinnan, *to run*, 1113.

rípan, *to reap*, 85.

ród, *rood, cross*, 726, 1083, 1100, 1113, 1446, 1486, 1488.

ródor, *sky, heavens*, 59, 73, 133, 221, 352, 407.

ródor-cyning, *heavenly king*, 726.

rume, *far and wide, clearly*, 59, 133.

ryht, *right, just*, 1367, —— ered, *erect*, 1064, (*v.* riht).

ryht, *justice*, 699, 1219, (*v.* riht).

ryhte, *rightly*, 130, 670.

ryhtend, *a ruler*, 797.

ryht - fremmend, *a righteous worker*, 1654.

ryht-geryne, *mystery*, 195, 246.

ryhtwis, *righteous*, 824.

ryne, *a course*, 46, 670.

SACERD, *priest*, 136.

sǽ, *sea*, 676, 851, 965, 1143, 1162.

sǽd, *seed*, 419.

sǽ-fisc, *sea fish*, 985.

sǽl, *happiness, bliss*, 1375.

sǽlan, *to bind*, 861.

samod, somod, *together*, 1119, 1234, 1324.

sǽp, *sap*, 1175.

sár, *pain, sorrow*, 1265, 1354, 1440, 1459, 1515, 1630, 1653.

sár, *grievous, sore*, 208, 1417.

sáre, *sorely*, 1570.

sár-cwide, *a bitter speech*, 169.

sárig, *sorrowful*, 1509.

sarig-ferð, *sad in heart*, 1081.

satan, *satan*, 1520.

sáwan, *to sow*, 85, 486, 662.

sáwel, sawl, saul, *soul*, 570, 618, 818, 1035. 1059.

scacan, *to shake*, 803.

scéadan, *to separate*, (?) 978, *to decide*, 1231.

sceadu, *shadow*, 1087, 1583.

scearp, *sharp*, 1140.

scéat, *corner, region*, 71, 877, 1003, 1532.

sceaþa, *spoiler, injurer*, 774, 869, 1130, 1394.

scéawian, *to see, behold*, 304, 913, 1135, 1205, 1275.

scendan, *to injure, scathe*, 1547.

scéotend, *shooter*, 674.

sceþþan, *to injure*, 683, 760, 1394, 1465.

scieldan, *to shield*, 780.

scíene, *beautiful*, 1385; scýne, 1468.

scieppan, *to shape*, 896, 1168.

scild-hréada, *shield-defence*, 674.

scíma, *ray, light*, 696.

scínan, scýnan, *to shine*, 606, 900, 1008, 1290.

scír, *bright*, 869, 1281.

scír-cyning, *bright king*, 1151.

scíre, *brightly*, 1087.

—— *sheer*, 1140.

scirian, *to appoint, assign*, 1225.

scolu, *shoal*, 927, 1250, 1521, 1533, 1606.

scomu, *shame*, 1272.

scond, scand, *disgrace*, 1272, 1281, 1297, 1478, 1485.

scrífan, *to judge*, 1218.

scrift, *confessor*, 1304.

scríðan, *to stride, wander*, 808, 1583.

sculan, *shall, must*, 30, 69, 165, 171, 190, 203, 211, 232, 270, 297, 380, 580, 610, 620, 625, 745, 755, 765, 800, 828.

scyld, *guilt, sin*, 96.

scyldig, *guilty*, 1151, 1272, 1606.

scyld-wreccende, *sin-avenging*, 1159.

scyld-wyrcende, *per-petrating guilt*, 1486.

scyppend, *Creator*, 47, 265, 416, 900, 1130, 1159, 1218, 1225, 1394, 1616.

sealt, *salt*, 676.

searo-þoncol, *cunning of thought, wise*, 219.

searo-cræft, *skill, handiwork*, 8.

searolíce, *cunningly*, 671.

séað, *pit*, 1543.

seax, *sword*, 1139.

sécan, *to seek*, 440, 648, 751, 1358, 1509.

secg, *a man*, 219.

secgan, *to tell, say*, 32, 63, 72, 127, 136, 189, 196, 202, 208, 450, 1192, 1303.

sefa, *heart*, 441, 486, 498, 662, 906, 1206, 1350, 1358.

segel, *veil*, 1137.

segn, *standard*, 1060.

sél, *good*, 280, 519.

sele-gescot, *tabernacle*, 1479.

sellan, *to give*, 289, 374, 659, 688, 1379, 1397, 1588.

semninga, *suddenly*, 490, 872, 898.

sendan, *to send*, 104, 128, 293, 663, 674, 1150.

séoc, *sick*, 1354.

séon, *to see*, 58, 494, 1284, 1299, 1415, 1610.

séoðan, *to seethe*, 993.

settan, *to appoint, set down, place*, 235, 662.

sib, *peace*, 49, 486, 580, 618, 688, 1337.

sib-lufa, *kindly love*, 634.

sibsum, *peaceful*, 213.

síd, *wide*, 4, 58, 238, 784.

síde, *side*, 1110, 1447.

sígan, *to descend*, 549.

sige, *victory*, 19.

sige-bearn, *son of victory*, 519.

sige-déma, *victorious judge*, 1059.

sige-dryhten, *Lord of triumph*, 127.

sige-méce, *victor-sword*, 1529.

sige-þréat, *rush of triumph*, 842.

sige-hrémig, *victorious*, 530.

sigor, sygor, *victory*, 87, 242, 293, 419, 580, 1227, 1515.

sigor-beorht, *beauty, sovran splendour*, 9.

sigor-léan, *reward of victory*, 1588.

simle, *always*, 52, 322, 392, 403, 601, (cp. symle).

sinc, *gold*, 308.

sinc-giefa, *giver of treasure*, 459.

singales, *continually*, 322, 392.

singan, *to sing*, 282, 467, 618, 666, 883.

sin-neaht, *perpetual night*, 116, 1541, 1630.

sittan, *to sit*, 25, 116, 1215.

síð, *journey, course*, 145; *vicissitude*, 1417; *occasion*, 317.

síð, *later*, 892; *late*, 1566.

síðian, *to journey*, 328.

siþþan, *henceforth*, 374.

slǽp, *sleep*, 872, 888, 1660.

sléan, *to strike*, 1122, 1440.

slítan, *to slit*, 1139.

snéome, *quickly*, 888.

snúd, *sudden*, 840.

snúde, *quickly*, 296.

snyttru, *wisdom*, 441, 661, 666, 683.

snyttru-cræft, 666.

sófte, *softly, patiently*, 145.

somod-fæst, *fast together*, 1579.

sóna, *soon, anon*, 9, 232.

song, *song*, 501, 1648.

sorg, *sorrow*, 169, 1080, 1207, 1283, 1570.

sweltan, *to die*, 190, 986.
swencan, *to strike*, 361.
sweord, *sword*, 678.
sweotule, *clearly*, 242, 511.
swéte, *sweet*, 906.
swician, *to wander*, 1298.
swígan, *to be silent*, 189.
swíma, *giddiness*, 1298.
swingan, *to scourge*, 1621.
swinsian, *to sound*, 883.
swip, *a scourge*, 1440.
swíð, *strong*, 715 ; seo swíðre hond, *the right hand*, 1529.
swíðe, *exceedingly*, 219, 309, 1077.
swíðlíc, *excessive*, 953.
swógan, *to roar*, 948.
swylce, *so too*, 281.
swylt, *death*, 1538.
symbel, *revel*, 549.
symle, *ever, always*, 375, 431.
syn, *sin*, 116, 289, 993, 1059, 1248, 1263, 1306, 1312,
syn-byrðen, *burden of sin*, 1298.
syn·fáh, *sin-stained*, 1081.
synful, *sinful*, 1227, 1517, 1531.
synig, (synnig,) *sinful*, 918, 1131, 1280.

synlíce, *sinfully*, 1478.
syn-lust, *love of sin*, 268.
syn-rust, *sin's rust*, 1319.
syn-sceaða, *sinful one*, 705.
syn-wracu, *vengeance for sin*, 1538.
syn-wund, *wound of sin*, 756.
syn-wyrcend, *worker of sin*, 1103.

TÁCEN, *sign*, 53, 461, 641, 1213, 1234.
talian, *to allege*, 793.
téag, *a bond*, 732.
teala, *well*, 791.
tealtrian, *to stumble*, 370.
téar, *a tear*, 151, 171, 1173, 1565.
tempel, *temple*, 185, 205, 1137.
téona, *discomfort*, 1089, 1213.
téon-lég, *avenging flame*, 967.
tíd, *time*, 234, 405, 1079, 1147, 1332, 1557.
tilgan, tiligan, *to strive for*, 747, 1317.
tír, *glory, grace*, 28, 269, 461, 1210.
tír-fruma, *author of glory*, 205.
tír-meahtig, *gloriously powerful*, 1164.
tóbrecan, *to break to pieces*, 976.

tóglídan, *to vanish*, 1162,
tólésan, *to loosen*, 1041.
tóme, *free from, devoid*, 1210.
torht, *bright, beautiful*, 106, 185, 205, 234, 541.
torn, *grief*, 537.
torn-word, *grievous word*, 171.
tó-somne, *together* 1436.
tó-stencan, *to disperse*, 255.
tówiþere, *against*, 184.
tówrecan, *to disperse*, 257.
tredan, *to tread*, 1164.
tréów, *faith*, 81, 583.
tréow-lufu, *true-love*, 537.
trum, *strong*, 882, 932.
trúwian, *to trust*, 836.
trymian, *to encourage*, 1358.
tuddor, *progeny*, 687, 1415.
tungol, *a star*, 106, 234, 606, 670, 698.
tungol-gim, *a star-gem*, 1149.
tydre, *tender, frail*, 28.
tyht, *course*, 810.

ÞÆC, *roof*, 1502.
þearf, *need*, 10, 21, 111, 254, 372.

þearfa, *a poor man*, 1421.

þearfende, *needy*, 1283.

þéaw, *custom, habit*, 1582.

þegn, *thane*, 282, 456.

þegnung, *service*, 353.

þegn-weorud, *host of thanes*, 750.

þéod, *people, nation*, 126, 223, 376, 846, 1022, 1090, 1132.

þéod-bealu, *terrible bale*, 1266.

þéod-buende, *dwellers among the nations, people*, 615, 1171, 1370.

þéod-egesa, *men's dismay*, 832.

þéoden, *prince*, 331, 353, 456, 540.

þéoden-stól, *prince's throne*, 396.

þéod-land, *region*, 305.

þéod-sceaða, *injurer of the people*, 1594, 1608.

þéod-wundor, *marvel exceeding great*, 1153.

þéof, *thief*, 870, 1608.

þéostor (þéostru, þý-stor), *darkness*, 115, 226, 870, 1246.

þéostre, *dark*, 1408.

þicce, *thick*, 1174.

þing, *doom*, 925.

—— *thing*, 223, 1330.

þing-stede, *meeting-place*, 496.

þolian, *to suffer*, 1384, 1408, 1450.

þonc, *thanks*, 126, 208, 598, 600, 611.

þoncian, *to thank*, 1254.

þorn, *a thorn*, 1444.

þracu, *rush*, 592.

þréa, *misery*, 945, 1062, 1090, 1132, 1363.

þrean, *to afflict*, 1319, 1594.

þréat, *a band, troop*, 491, 516, 569, 737, 926.

þringan, *to throng*, 396.

þrist, *bold*, 341, 592.

þriste, *boldly, harshly*, 1508.

þrist-hycgende, *stout-hearted*, 287.

þrist-líce, *boldly*, 870.

þroht, *anguish*, 1226.

þrosm, *vapour, smoke*, 115.

þrowian, *to suffer*, 1116, 1153, 1248, 1432.

þrowing, *suffering*, 469, 1128, 1178.

þrym, þrim, *might, glory*, 70, 82, 203, 387, 422, 592, 725.

þrym-fæst, *majestic*, 456, 942.

þrym-full, *glorious*, 540.

þrymlíce, *gloriously*, 287.

þrýnes, (þrýnyss,) *Trinity*, 378, 598.

þryð, *strength*, 968.

þryð-gesteald, *home of glory, palace*, 353.

þurfan, *to need*, 80.

þurh-drífan, *to pierce through*, 1108.

þurh-séon, *to see through, pierce*, 1326.

þurh-wadan, *to penetrate*, 1140, 1281.

þurh-wlítan, *to look through*, 1282, 1330.

þurst, *thirst*, 1508, 1659.

þwéan, *to wash*, 1319.

þyncan, *to seem, appear*, 1400, 1423, 1487, 1597.

þyrnen, *thorny*, 1125.

þyslíc, *such*, 516.

UFAN-CUND, *celestial*, 502.

unaþréotend, *unwearying*, 387.

unbéted, *unamended*, 1310.

unbræce, *adamantine*, 5.

unclǽne, *unclean*, 1015, 1308, 1314.

uncúð, *unknown, uncouth, evil*, 1416.

uncyst, *vice*, 1328.

undyrne, *clear*, 1539.

unefen, *uneven*, 1458.

ungearu, *unready*, 873.

ungelíce, *unlike*, 897, 908, 1261, 1361.

un-hnéaw, *unsparing*, 685.

un-holda, *monster*, 761.

unmǽle, *immaculate*, 332, 720.

unmǽte, *immeasurable*, 952.

weorð-mynd, *honour, glory*, 377.

weorðung, *honour*, 1135.

wépan, *to weep*, 991, 1288.

wer, *a man, husband*, 36, 415, 418, 508, 633, 1046.

wérig, *weary, hapless, wretched*, 955, 986, 1563.

wer-þéod,*men*,599,713.

wesan, *to be*, 212, 215, 235, 238, 279, 303, 459.

wéðe, *sweet*, 914.

wíc, *camp*, 1533.

wíd, *wide*, 257, 809, 930, 956, 964, 1042.

—— wide ferh, *for ever*, 162.

——to widanfeore,229.

wíde, *widely*, 184, 257.

wíd-gielle, *extensive*, 680.

wíd-lond, *wide earth, spacious land*, 604, 1383.

wíd - mǽre, *far famous*, 974.

wíd-weg, *wide way*, 481.

wíf, *woman*, 39, 70.

wíg, *war*, 672.

wíga, *a warrior*, 983.

wígend, *warrior*, 408.

wiht, *creature, thing*, 418, 980, 1047, 1052, 1555.

wil-cuma, *a welcome person*, 553.

wil-dæg, *day of joy*, 458.

wil-giefa, *giver of good*, 536.

willa, *will, desire, pleasure*, 376, 1260, 1262.

willan, *to wish, desire*, 48, 143, 273, 516, 522.

wilnian, *to desire*, 772.

wil-síð, *propitious course, career*, 20, 25.

windan, *to wind*, 980.

windig, *windy*, 854.

winnan, *to fight, war*, 1525,

winster,*bad, left-hand*, 1226; wynster,1362.

wísdóm, *wisdom*,1550.

wís, *wise*, 920.

wíse, *manner*, 228.

wís-fæst, *very wise*, 63.

wit, *spirit, soul*, 263.

wítan, *to know*, 383, 441, 1303, 1384, 1472.

wíte, *punishment, torment*, 594, 624, 803, 1091.

wítedóm, *prophecy*, 211.

wíte-hús, *house of torment*, 1534.

wíte-þéo, *a tortured thrall*, 150.

wítga, *a prophet*, 63, 690, 1191.

witig, *wise*, 225.

wiðer-broga, *adversary*, 563.

wið-weorpan, *to cast away, reject*, 2.

wlátian, *to behold, gaze at*, 326.

wlítan, *to see, look*, 1103.

wlite, *grace, beauty, glory*, 847, 905, 913, 1036, 1057, 1663.

wliteléas, *ugly, sightless*, 1563.

wlite-scýne, *beauteous*, 492, 553.

wlitig, *beautiful, bright*, 20, 377, 910, 1463.

wolcen, *cloud*, 225, 587.

wom, *blemish, sin*, 53, 178, 187, 1005, 1096, 1310, 1320, 1450.

womful, *malignant*, 1533.

wom - sceaþa, *sin-stained foe*, 1224, 1568.

wom-wyrcende, *working wickedness*, 1091.

won, *lack*, 269.

won, *livid*, 964, 1563, 1422.

wong, *plain*, 679, 809.

wong - stede, *plain*, 801.

wonhál, *infirm*, 1506.

wonhydig,*thoughtless*, 1555.

wonian, *to lay waste*, 950.

wóp, *weeping*, 150, 536, 997.

word, *word*, 178, 341, 428, 458, 468, 473, 508, 1036.

word - cwide, *speech*, 672.

word - gerýne, *mystic word*, 462.

word-laðu, *eloquence*, 663.

worn, *great number*, 168, 956.

woruld, *world*, 597, 649, 777, 798 ; to worulde, *evermore*, 100.

woruld-cund, *worldly, earthly*, 211, 284.

woruld-mann, *worldly man*, 1014.

woruld-ríce, *world's kingdom*, 1499.

woruld-þearfende, *the needy of the world*, 1349.

woruld-widl, *world's pollution*, 1005.

woruld-wíte, *martyrdom*, 1476.

wóð-bora, *prophet*, 301.

wóð-song, *prophetic song*, 45.

wracu, *persecution, exile, misery*, 592, 621, 1513, 1600, 1605.

wræc-mæcg, *exile*, 362.

wræc-líc, *strange, wondrous*, 415.

wræt-líc, *wondrous*, 508.

wráð, *hostile, angry*, 15, 594, 803, 1311, 1533, 1546.

wráðlic, *grievous, severe*, 830.

wrecca, *wretch*, 263.

wrítan, *to write*, 672.

wrixl, *change*, 415.

wróht-bora, *the accuser, the devil*, 762.

wuldor, *glory*, 7, 29, 53, 56, 70, 82, 109.

wuldor-cyning, *King of Glory*, 160, 1021.

wuldor-léan, *glorious reward*, 1078.

wuldorlíc, *glorious*, 1009.

wuldor - weorod, *host of glory*, 284.

wuldrian, *to glorify*, 400.

wulf, *wolf*, 255.

wund, *a wound*, 762, 769, 1106, 1206.

wundor, *a marvel*, 907, 987, 1014, 1184.

wundor - clom, *wondrous bond*, 309.

wundorlíc, *wondrous*, 904.

wundrian, *to wonder*, 7.

wundrung, *marvel*, 88.

wunian, *to dwell*, 82, 102, 162, 346, 404.

wynlíce, *pleasantly, comely*, 1344, 1386.

wynn, *joy*, 70, 436, 739, 1243, 1295, 1480.

wynsum, *pleasant, winsome*, 1251.

wynsumlíc, *winsome*, 910.

wyrcan, *to work*, 707, 1052.

wyrd, *event*, 80.

wyrhta, *worker*, 1.

wyrm, *a worm, serpent*, 624, 1249, 1546.

wyrp, *overthrow, thrust, change*, 66, 564.

wyrðe, *worthy, honoured*, 29, 599.

YFEL, *evil, bad*, 917.

yfel, *an ill*, 873, 1252, 1331.

yld, *age*, 1652.

yrmen, *whole*, 480.

yrmðu, *misery*, 369, 613, 620, 1267, 1291.

yrra, *angry*, 1527.

yrringa, *angrily*, 1145, 1371.

ýtemest, *uttermost*, 879.

ýð, *a wave*, 853, 1166,

ýð-meare, *sea-horse*, 862.

ýwan, *to disclose, present*, 1374.

FINIS

Edinburgh: T. & A. Constable, *Printers to Her Majesty.*